Blood Oath

Felicity Pulman

First published by Random House Australia in 2005
This edition published in 2015 by Momentum
Pan Macmillan Australia Pty Ltd
1 Market Street, Sydney 2000

A CIP record for this book is available at the National Library of Australia

Blood Oath: The Janna Chronicles 1

EPUB format: 9781760082864
Mobi format: 9781760082871
Print on Demand format: 9781760300043

Cover design by Raewyn Brack
Edited by Kylie Mason
Proofread by Laurie Ormond

Macmillan Digital Australia: www.macmillandigital.com.au

To report a typographical error, please visit momentumbooks.com.au/contact/

Visit www.momentumbooks.com.au to read more about all our books and to buy
books online. You will also find features, author interviews and news of any
author events.

Felicity Pulman is the award-winning author of numerous novels for children and teenagers, including A Ring Through Time, the Shalott trilogy, and *Ghost Boy*, which is now in pre-production for a movie. *I, Morgana* was her first novel for adults, inspired by her early research into Arthurian legend and her journey to the UK and France to 'walk in the footsteps of her characters' before writing the Shalott trilogy – something she loves to do. Her interest in crime and history inspired her medieval crime series, The Janna Mysteries, now repackaged as The Janna Chronicles.

Recently awarded the inaugural Di Yerbury writer's fellowship, Felicity will spend several months in the UK in 2015 researching and writing the sequel to *I, Morgana*. She has many years experience talking about researching and writing her novels both in schools and to adults, as well as conducting creative writing workshops in a wide variety of genres. Felicity is married, with two children and five grandchildren, all of whom help to keep her young and technosavvy – sort of! You can find out more about Felicity on her website and blog: www.felicitypulman.com.au or on Facebook.

Also by Felicity Pulman

I, Morgana
Stolen Child: The Janna Chronicles 2
Unholy Murder: The Janna Chronicles 3
Pilgrim of Death: The Janna Chronicles 4
Devil's Brew: The Janna Chronicles 5
Day of Judgment: The Janna Chronicles 6

Chapter 1

The wolf's howl shattered the dark, secretive forest. Startled, Janna spun around, straining to pinpoint the direction of the sound. Her torch flickered and almost died with the sudden movement. Fighting panic, she cupped her fingers around the flame to protect and steady it. The light gave her an illusion of safety and she took courage from it, for she was alone out here, with no protection against the prowling predators of the forest. No protection against wolves.

Janna cursed the quick temper that had sent her fleeing into the night without bringing even a knife to defend herself. She raised the torch higher, watching for movement, listening intently for a telltale rustling.

All was still. Her gaze moved up to the full moon, floating above in a blaze of radiant silver light, brightening the sky almost to daylight. Yet even the moon's brilliance could not penetrate the tree-shadowed darkness that surrounded her. It was heavy with mystery and threat.

The crackle of dry leaves set her heart racing. A deer? A fox? Not loud enough to be a wild boar—but a wolf would move quietly, stealing up on its prey. At once Janna's imagination conjured the beast creeping through the forest toward her. Her first impulse was to run, to put as much distance between her and the wolf as possible, but she remembered her mother's warning: "*Never turn your back on a wild animal.*" She kept still, knowing that she could never outpace a wolf—never.

She swallowed hard, gulping down fear. The thin trail she followed ran deep into the forest, into the wild and tangled places where the wolf was surely lurking. Should she go on, or go back to their cot? The immense forest closed around her, hushed and still. Nothing moved; there was no sound now to break the silence. The wolf's howl wasn't so very loud, she thought. Perhaps it was too far away to be any real threat.

Janna set off once more, leaves crunching, twigs snapping under her boots. If she hurried, she could pick the wild strawberries and leave the forest before the wolf even knew she was there. She couldn't just abandon her mission, for the strawberries were important: her mother needed them for a special potion. They had planned to pick them together.

"It's a foul-tasting mixture. The fruits will add sweetness and strengthen the blood, but we must go tonight for there will be no time to pick them before my visitor comes tomorrow," Eadgyth had fussed, all the while pulling from the shelf the other ingredients she would need. Janna knew, without her mother saying, that it was a mix to bring on a woman's monthly courses and so prevent an unwanted child from developing in the womb. The church forbade the practice and most women remained obedient to both the priest and their husbands. Sometimes, however, worn out with childbirth and with already too many mouths to feed, they were desperate enough to seek Eadgyth's help. Even then, she acted only if she was truly convinced of their need. From Eadgyth's preparations this evening, it was clear she was sympathetic to the woman's cause and was prepared to help her.

"Who is she?" Janna had asked, but her mother hadn't answered, saying only, "I want you out of the cottage by the time she arrives."

"Why won't you let me stay and help you?"

"Not this time."

"You never let me help!"

Eadgyth had sighed impatiently. "You're already responsible for maintaining our herb garden as well as helping me prepare my medicaments. You also have the goats and hens to look after. That's more than enough to keep you busy."

"But I don't want to just keep busy. I want to *learn*."

"I've already taught you everything I know."

"But knowledge isn't enough! I need experience too. How will I ever get that if you never let me help you when you visit the sick, or do anything when they come here?"

"You know enough for now." Eadgyth had turned back to her decoction. Janna knew, from long experience, that the subject was closed. She seethed with resentment. She was seventeen years old. When would her mother stop treating her like a child?

"'Tis well it's a full moon tonight. Picked at night, the strawberries will carry the moon's power," Eadgyth had continued. At that point Janna had stopped listening. If it wasn't the moon, it was the time of day or night, or the alignment of the planets that must be favorable. She'd heard her mother say the same sort of thing a thousand times in the past. Doubtless she'd be saying the same things to Fulk in the future. Once she went into partnership with him. Janna scowled as her mind went back to the scene from which she had fled.

*

The loud knocking had startled both of them. Eadgyth paused in the act of pulling on her boots. "Who could that be?" She'd flashed a sly smile at Janna. "Are you expecting a suitor to come calling? Godric, maybe?"

"No!" Even as Janna issued the denial, Godric's face flashed into her mind. Her cheeks heated at the memory of the sturdy young man who had come to their door late at night some weeks ago, seeking aid for his ailing mother. Somewhat to her disappointment, he hadn't been back. His mother had made a good recovery, so Eadgyth had said.

"I saw the way Godric looked at you. I think you've taken his fancy, Janna." There was a twinkle in Eadgyth's eyes as she teased her daughter.

Janna flushed under her mother's scrutiny, and kept on fastening her cloak.

"He is a fine, well-set fellow, and I know he has a good heart. You could do a lot worse," Eadgyth observed. Another knock came, more urgent this time. "Likely it's some poor soul in trouble. Go to the door, Janna. See who it is." She bent to her boots once more.

Janna opened the door. Her welcoming smile died and her heartbeat slowed to normal. Not Godric but Master Fulk the apothecary. Eadgyth sometimes bought supplies from his shop in Wiltune to make up her own medicaments and creams, although he'd been absent of late. It seemed he'd been summoned to Babestoche Manor to attend Dame Alice during the last few weeks of her pregnancy. Local gossip said that Fulk divided his time between the manor, his shop, and the alehouses in Wiltune, where he boasted of his skill and his noble patronage to any who might listen. What on earth could he want with them?

"Good evening, Johanna. Is your mother home? Might I have a word?" Master Fulk pulled a large square of yellow silk from his scrip and mopped his red, sweating face. Their small cottage was some distance from Babestoche Manor, and the journey had obviously taken its toll on the apothecary's constitution.

Janna bobbed her head and made way for him to enter. His large presence dominated the small, smoke-filled room, lit only by the flickering light of the fire at its center. In unusual deference, the apothecary bowed to Eadgyth.

Janna noted her mother's smile of chilly politeness as she greeted him. She grinned inwardly, knowing her mother's opinion of Fulk both as a man and as an apothecary. "*Wortwyf* I may be called," Janna's mother had declared when news of his presence at the manor became known, "but as a herbwife I know far more of women's troubles than that turnip head! Even Aldith, the midwife, knows more than him. He's a posturing ignoramus. What does he know of the difficulties of carrying and birthing children? What does any man know, or care? In my opinion, Janna, if Fulk was even half so skilled as he claims, he would surely be ministering to King Stephen himself instead of selling his nostrums to any wealthy enough to pay for the privilege of being gulled by him!"

Eadgyth kept her smile firmly in place as Fulk pushed Alfred, their big black cat, off the heavy wooden chair that stood beside the fire. The chair had been crafted by Eadgyth herself, along with the stuffed cushions that provided extra comfort. With a grimace of distaste, the apothecary brushed off black cat hairs then sank down, expelling a sigh of relief.

Janna picked up Alfred and settled onto a stool nearby, waiting eagerly for Fulk's explanation of this unusual visit. His opening was unexpected.

"My dear Eadgyth, I am come here to make you an offer I am sure can work only to your advantage."

Fulk paused, perhaps waiting for Eadgyth's delighted response. When it was not forthcoming, he continued. "You will have heard that I am skilled in the art of healing…" He stopped, frowning at Janna's barely suppressed snort. Eadgyth kept silent, giving him no help at all.

"Of course, my knowledge is far greater than yours for I have taken instruction in *scientia* from scholars in Oxeneford. Small wonder that the infirm and elderly come from far and wide to consult me, knowing that they will benefit from my plasters and poultices, my pills, tonics and mixtures."

And when those fail, they come to my mother! Janna kept her thoughts to herself with difficulty.

Fulk looked expectantly at Eadgyth, searching for an acknowledgment of the honor of his presence here in their cottage. She tilted her head, and waited for him to continue. A heavy silence settled, broken eventually by the apothecary.

"However, there are still many mysteries concerning the human body which are known only to God."

"And perhaps to me. Is that why you're here?" Eadgyth said. "Are you here to ask my advice, Master Fulk?"

"No, no, of course not." With an airy laugh, the apothecary dismissed the thought.

"Then why, pray, do you come knocking at my door so late at night?" Eadgyth settled onto a stool opposite Fulk, and stared at him intently.

"Because…because I have an offer for you to consider. We both practice the healing arts. I thought you might care to share my knowledge."

"You're offering to teach me?" Eadgyth lifted an eyebrow in surprise.

"I expect there are one or two things I might learn from you." Fulk's face flushed a darker shade than before. "For example, some women's troubles may sometimes be beyond my ken…"

"So you're actually asking *me* to teach *you*?" Eadgyth gave him a glacial smile.

Fulk shifted uncomfortably. "You must know there's talk about you in the village," he said, hurriedly changing the subject. "If you come under my tutelage, it would give you a high position in Wiltune." He leaned toward Eadgyth. "It would also help me. I am so busy with customers I have too little time for mixing up those remedies that my patients seek. What I am offering you, my dear Eadgyth, is—"

"A partnership?"

"No! No, not quite that. After all, I have my reputation to consider." At the sight of Eadgyth's ferocious glare, Fulk extracted the yellow kerchief and mopped his brow once more. "I'm offering you a chance to sell your potions through my shop, and I'm asking for your help in the preparation of my own remedies—under my guidance, of course. It would give you a reputable outlet for your medicaments and bring you in a steady income. Of course, I could not put my name to any concoction of yours unless I knew that it was quite sound."

"And how would you be able to tell?"

The contempt behind Eadgyth's question was lost on Fulk. "Why...I would need to know all the ingredients, of course," he blustered.

"And so you would learn my herbal lore under the guise of helping me?"

"You mistake me, mistress. I thought you would be delighted by my offer. It works far more to your advantage than to mine." Janna noted that Fulk's condescending tone didn't quite match the worried expression on his face.

"Delighted by your offer? Delighted to be patronized by a man who knows little but would steal my knowledge while pretending to have my best interests at heart? I think not!" Eadgyth surged to her feet, indicating that Fulk had worn out his welcome. He stayed seated, sweat beading his brow.

"I assure you, Mistress Eadgyth, a business relationship would benefit both of us."

Eadgyth studied him narrowly while she assessed the worth of his offer. "A business relationship, no. A partnership—perhaps."

Aghast, Janna stared at her mother. She could hardly believe what she was hearing. Eadgyth despised Fulk. How could she bear to contemplate a partnership with such a loathsome toad?

Fulk's face, already red, now turned a deep crimson. "You believe yourself to be my equal?" He spat the words as if they were bitter gall in his mouth. And yet, Janna noted, he seemed to be considering the idea. She was sure Fulk wasn't telling them the real reason he'd come knocking on their door so late at night. She wondered what it could be.

"Come with me to see Dame Alice." The invitation seemed more of a command than a suggestion. "Bring with you one of your nostrums. Let us see if you are as good as people say you are." His words were measured, but Janna sensed the urgency behind them, and saw it in the fingers that twisted together in barely concealed impatience. So Dame Alice was the reason he was here.

"What sort of nostrum? Is Dame Alice having difficulty birthing her babe?" Eadgyth asked sharply.

"Not at all," Fulk said proudly. "Thanks to my ministrations, my lady has given birth to a fine son, when it's common knowledge she's lost every other child since the birth of her first little boy. That is why the midwife was put off and why my lord Robert summoned me to see my lady through this pregnancy." He puffed out his chest, swollen with self-importance.

"Why then do you come to see me, Master Fulk?"

Fulk's eyes slid sideways. He would not look at Eadgyth. "Dame Alice needs a mixture for something of which I have limited experience. Something to stop excessive bleeding after childbirth," he mumbled.

"Have you massaged her back with goose grease and given her herbs to help her expel the remains of the afterbirth?" A glance at Fulk's face confirmed that he had no notion what she was talking about.

"I must go to her, and quickly, before an infection sets in. You should have asked for my help at once, Master Fulk, instead of wasting time like this." Eadgyth jumped to her feet and moved to the sprigs of aromatic herbs hanging from the rafters of the thatched roof. Their spicy fragrance scented the air as she picked what she would need. "Tell me, Master Fulk, what have you done to help Dame Alice since the birth of her child?"

"I have purged my lady and placed a triangle of agate on her forehead, but she continues to bleed," Fulk confessed. "She is too weak to take nourishment, and she burns with fever. I have tried all that I may to bring her to good health, but to little avail. Reluctantly, mistress, I have had to come to you for help."

"Hardly the words to make me believe in your offer of a business relationship, Master Fulk, but at least we now have the truth of the matter." Eadgyth pulled a mortar and pestle from the shelf, then carefully lifted down a small pair of scales. While she measured and weighed the herbs, Janna tipped the cat off her lap and moved to hook a pan of water over the fire.

The apothecary watched intently. "What herbs do you use, mistress?" he asked, unable to contain his curiosity any longer.

Eadgyth laughed and shook her head. "You will not learn my secrets, Master Fulk. You may have been trained in Oxeneford, but my knowledge comes from the lore of my ancestors, from the leechcraft of the Saxons, which I have combined with what I have learned of the healing arts practiced by the ancients. I will not share a knowledge so hard won."

"And where did you learn such mysteries?" There was a small measure of respect now in Fulk's tone.

But Eadgyth compressed her lips and answered only: "My herbs will help my lady finish the birthing process and inhibit the bleeding, you have my word on it. I will also brew some bark from a willow tree to reduce her fever, and give her a mite of poppy syrup if she is in pain. I presume you know of them, for they are common enough." As she spoke, she was busy grinding herbs into a fine powder. "I shall add a little honey to sweeten the mixture, and some ale, which will help my lady to relax. I shall encourage her to sneeze, and also massage her back and her stomach to help her expel the remains of the afterbirth. So you may go home now to Wiltune, Master Fulk, and leave Dame Alice to my ministrations."

"She will only see you if you are in my company; I will need to reassure her that you are to be trusted," Fulk protested.

Eadgyth gave a contemptuous snort and continued about her business.

"I'll have to tell Dame Alice that you are in my employ and that I am training you," Fulk persisted.

Eadgyth dropped the bowl of herbs and turned to face him. "Then you may take me to the manor and introduce me as your new partner," she said evenly. "You can also tell Dame Alice that, in the future, I shall be taking care of all the women who come to your shop, no matter what their troubles might be."

Not believing what she was hearing, Janna had spun around from the fire to confront her mother. A level glance from fine gray eyes showed Janna that her mother was in deadly earnest. It seemed she was prepared to abandon Janna, and all those villagers who had come to rely on her help, in order to cut a fine figure at the apothecary's shop in Wiltune. It was too much to bear. Pausing only to snatch up the flaming resin torch brought by the apothecary to light his path to their cottage, Janna had raced out into the moonlit night and plunged into the forest.

Chapter 2

Another high, wild cry shattered the silence. Was the wolf alone? Hunger might make it bold, but she'd have a better chance of survival than if it was hunting as part of a pack. Janna stopped once more to listen. A secretive rustle, the hoot of an owl, then silence. Go on—or turn back? She tilted her head and the moonlight fell on her face like a blessing. "Keep me safe," she whispered, then hurriedly crossed herself, knowing she should more properly be asking God for help, or even St Edith, the patron saint of nearby Wiltune Abbey. Yet she felt comforted as she held the torch a little higher and hurried on.

The trail dwindled to little more than a thin depression of flattened leaves and grass, barely discernible among the shadows. Although Janna knew this part of the forest well, it looked quite different on this dark, shining night. She kept her head bent, looking for the signs that told her she was going the right way. She had walked this path only yesterday, hoping to snare a small something to add to the pot for their dinner, although she would have given the king's forester a different answer if she'd been caught by him so close to the king's hunting lodge. She had seen the wild strawberries growing amid a tangle of bindweed and the beautiful blue flowers whose shape gave deadly monkshood its common name and her mother the ingredients for an ointment to ease stiff and aching joints. Knowing the importance of her find, for it was still early in the season, Janna had told her mother, and Eagyth had vowed to visit the place, to dig up some strawberry plants and repot them in their own herb garden.

"God's bones!" Janna muttered crossly now as she realized that, in her haste to leave the cottage, she'd also left behind a digging trowel and a bag to hold the plants. She would have to make do with picking only the berries. She patted the woven purse that hung from her girdle. There was room enough—if she packed them in carefully she could carry the fruits home without squashing them.

She was moving uphill into a dense grove of beech and oak. Great branches closed over her head, their leafy mantle blocking the moon's light. The flare from the torch was bright as, step by cautious step, she traced her way to the small fruiting plants.

There was a rustle, the crunching of dry leaves and then, sudden and shocking, several sharp explosions of snapping twigs. They sounded alarmingly close. Fighting fear, Janna cast about for signs of the strawberries. With a gasp of relief, she saw the patch of blue flowers. Knowing she was near, for this was the only place she'd noticed monkshood growing wild, she anchored the torch's handle in a patch of soft earth, then fell to her knees to look for the sweet, wild strawberries. They were small, hidden among the leaves, but she was too impatient and too frightened to seek them out and pick them carefully. Instead, she pulled them off in clumps, leaves and strawberries together, and stuffed them into her purse, desperate to be gone.

She seized up the torch once more and sprang to her feet. Now the whole forest seemed loud with sounds: a hooting owl; squeaks; a snuffling grunt; crackling twigs; and a steady thumping that terrified Janna until she recognized it was her own heartbeat reverberating in her chest. Yet there was something else, she realized, as her ears isolated and identified each sound. Something large was blundering through the forest without care or thought of danger. A grunting squeal confirmed Janna's fear. A wild boar was coming her way. Should it find her in its path, it would attack her. She had no knife to defend herself; she had nothing but her wits—and a pair of swift feet. Without stopping to heed her mother's warning about fleeing from a wild animal, she began to run. With each flying step she imagined the huge beast charging behind her, closer, closer, spearing her with its sharp tusks, bringing her down, trampling her. She lost all sense of direction as she ducked and weaved through the trees in a desperate effort to get away.

She found herself in a hazel thicket. The trees grew close together, their thin branches woven into traps that caught and held her. She tried to zigzag around them. Tall weeds and dry leaves covered the ground, shrouding sharp flints and unexpected hollows. She had to slow down; it was too hard to keep her footing. Her cloak snagged on brambles and holly leaves as she blundered on. Her breath came in great sobbing gasps. She knew that she was utterly lost, but she dare not stop. She could hear the boar crashing through the undergrowth. It sounded much closer now; she must be running in circles. Fear surged through her body, urging her to a speed she couldn't sustain. She tripped and fell. At once she staggered to her feet, but the stabbing pain in her side told her she could not go on.

She stood in a small, moonlit clearing. There was nowhere to hide. She would have to face the boar, and fight for her survival. She could hear it coming; she could even smell it now. Sobbing with fear, Janna snatched up a thin branch from the rotting remains of a fallen tree. She held her torch to the leaves and dry twigs at its tip. Her hand was shaking so badly she could hardly connect flame to tinder.

A tinge of red, a thin wisp of smoke, and then the flame caught. As the boar hurtled into the clearing, squealing with rage, Janna leaped aside and thrust the burning brand into its face. Responding to a fear more urgent than its need to attack, the creature skidded to a halt. It began to back away, keeping a wary distance from the source of fire.

Feeling somewhat comforted that her strategy had worked, Janna held aloft the flaming torch and the fiery branch, one in each hand, and considered what to do next. Pointless to go on when every step might take her further from home—yet she couldn't stand here all night. If only she knew which way to go, the branch might burn long enough for her to reach safety. Undecided, she risked a glance upward, wondering if she might tell her direction from the stars. But the moon's radiant aura outshone even the brightest of them, while those few stars visible in the darkness above the trees beyond were too far and too scattered for Janna to make sense of them.

She made a quick rush at the boar and shouted loudly, hoping that the noise and the fire might be enough to scare the beast away so that she could locate a tall tree to climb, to seek safety and also direction. The boar gave an angry squeal and retreated a few steps, but its eyes stayed fixed on her.

"Help!" she called, but without much hope. The royal forest of Gravelinges belonged to King Stephen, but he seldom used his hunting lodge for, in this year of our lord 1140, he was busy defending his kingdom against its rightful heir, his cousin Matilda. Few other than the king were allowed into the forest, and no-one was likely to be around at this time of night, at least not legally. Poachers risked death if they were caught, although hunger sometimes drove them into the forest. Those who sought to escape the king's justice might also hide themselves here. Janna was filled with new fear. A boar, an outlaw, or the king's forester? None would show her mercy.

The boar suddenly charged at Janna.

"Help!" she screamed as she tried to leap out of its way. Its bristles grazed her as it passed; its rank smell filled her nostrils. She whirled to face it, circling the flaming torches in a wide arc in the hope of frightening it.

Was that a faint cry? Janna listened intently. Should she shout again? The boar had turned, ready to charge once more. Its eyes glowed bright in the silvery moonlight.

"*Help!*" Janna didn't care who heard her now, so long as someone did.

"Who goes there?"

"Janna! I'm being attacked by a wild boar." Her voice was shrill with fear.

"Janna! Keep calling so that I may find you."

A man's voice. It sounded familiar. "I'm here, I'm in a clearing," she shouted. "Please, *please* hurry!" The boar hunched up its bulk in front of her. Its form blended into the undergrowth at the edge of the clearing so she could see only its eyes, but she could sense its rage at being thwarted, sense that it was gathering power to launch itself at her once more. "Begone!" she yelled, thrusting the burning brands toward it.

With an enraged squeal, it rushed at her. She tried to leap aside, but its shoulder caught her. Knocked off-balance, Janna staggered and fell. "Help!"

A man burst out from the darkness of the forest. He paused to get his bearings. It seemed to Janna that the moment stretched to an eternity. Why didn't he come after the boar; why didn't he help her? Terrified, she tried to scramble to her feet, all the while expecting the boar to charge at her and gore her to death.

She could hear its angry squeals as it turned, hear the crunch and crackle of leaves and twigs under its feet. It erupted into the moonlit clearing. It was coming at her, coming at speed. She heard a grunting cough. The boar staggered, but its momentum carried it on toward her. Janna shrank back in a last desperate effort to keep out of its way. It kept coming, closer and closer, but she could see now that something was desperately wrong. As it reached her, it skewed sideways then tottered and crashed to the ground. Speechless, Janna's gaze moved from it to the man racing to her. He was coiling a sling as he came. Janna noticed the glint of a blade as he fumbled at his belt.

Realizing at last that she was safe, Janna picked up her fallen torch and scrambled to her feet. The man's voice had sounded familiar. Who was he? She held the torch aloft so that she could see the face of her savior.

"Godric!" A great smile spread over Janna's face as she recognized him. She was so happy to see him, she could have kissed him. But she had no chance to embarrass either herself or him, for he'd made straight for the fallen animal. He kicked it, and the boar shifted and tried to struggle to its feet.

"Don't!" Janna reached out a hand to stop him. Although upset and hurting, she knew that the creature had acted only according to the rules of nature, obeying its instinct for survival. She shuddered as she looked down at the great hairy beast.

"It's a wild pig, not a relative." Godric leaned over the boar. His arm rose and, with a swift movement, he slit its throat. Blood spurted. Janna jerked back with a cry of horror.

Godric wiped his knife clean on a patch of moss, then sheathed it at his waist. "I had no true aim in the dark," he explained. "I had to see if I'd killed it or if it was still conscious. It was lucky I managed to strike it hard enough to stop its charge."

"You didn't have to kill it!"

"Yes, I did. It was ready to get up and go for us again. My knife would have been no defense against it at all."

Speechless with shock, Janna could only nod in understanding.

"Are you all right?" Godric placed a steadying arm around her shoulders.

"It knocked my breath from my body, but it didn't hurt me." She leaned against him briefly, grateful for his warmth, his solid comfort. "Thank you," she said. "You've saved my life tonight."

"What are you doing out in the forest so late?" he asked.

"Gathering strawberries." Janna touched the purse hanging from her belt, grateful that she'd fallen backward. Hopefully the fruit hadn't been crushed when she fell. "What about you? Why are you here?"

"Unlike you, I have permission from both my lord Robert and the abbess to come into the forest." His laughing eyes belied his tone of reproof.

"How so?" Janna asked, intrigued that a common villein like Godric, tied as he was to the lord of Babestoche Manor, should be given the freedom to roam about in a royal hunting forest.

"I've been leading lost souls." Seeing Janna's frown of puzzlement, Godric grinned. "Today I escorted a group of pilgrims who are on their way from the west to Wiltune Abbey and Glastingberie," he explained. "There's an ancient road built by the Romans that crosses the full length of the forest from east to west, but it's visible only to those who know it's there. If the forester is about some other business, I am often asked to lead travelers through the forest to save them from getting lost."

"How do you know about the Roman road?" Janna asked curiously.

"My forefathers were huntsmen here at the time of the Saxons. Their knowledge has been passed down from father to son, through many generations. So shall I pass on the knowledge to my sons, and I'll show them too, when it's time." Godric nodded to himself, confirming his intention.

"So you acted as a guide today. What about tonight?" Janna searched the surrounding forest for signs of the pilgrims, but could see no-one.

Godric laughed. "I'm still on my way home, should ill luck bring the forester my way."

"The knife is for protection, of course." Janna indicated the sheath hanging from his belt.

"Of course." He gestured around the forest. "I might meet outlaws, wolves, or wild boar. I might even need to save a damsel in distress."

"No doubt you'll also have to protect yourself against a savage hare or two," Janna ventured.

Godric's mouth twitched. "That's certainly possible."

He must have abandoned his catch to come to her rescue, Janna thought, feeling sorry that he'd lost his dinner on her account. She stared down at the beast that had so frightened her. Its legs were coated black with mud and dung, and so was its nose, from a lifetime of rooting about for its food. It stank, and yet Janna couldn't help a pang of pity—and then fear as she realized the consequences of their night's work.

"What are we going to do with it?" she asked, pointing at the dead boar.

"I can think of several things." Godric licked his lips in hungry anticipation. "Collops of bacon. Chops. A leg roasted on a spit..."

"Have you taken leave of your wits?" Suddenly becoming conscious of the noise they were making and the need for secrecy, Janna lowered her voice. "Do you want to be caught red-handed and brought before the forest court? You could lose your hands, your eyes, possibly even your life! You know how harsh the laws are. Oh, Godric, I fear that I have put you in far more danger than ever I was."

Godric frowned. "Then we'll leave the body here for the creatures of the forest to pick the flesh off its bones," he said regretfully, after a moment's reflection.

"We can't," Janna contradicted firmly. "The forester knows you've been in Gravelinges today, and if he sees any signs of a dead animal he'll immediately suspect you; he'll make you the scapegoat. We have to bury the boar, Godric. We can't trust the forest to keep our secret safe."

"I'd much rather eat it than bury it," Godric grumbled.

"Eat it, and we could be burying you!" Janna retorted.

Godric heaved a sigh, and bent to take hold of the beast's front legs. He began to drag it toward an overgrown thicket. "I have only my knife to dig with," he said, looking over his shoulder at Janna. "We need to find a place where the soil is moist and the growth thick enough to hide the evidence."

Janna nodded. Lifting her torch higher to cast a better light, she led Godric into the shadows under the trees.

She knelt beside him and helped him dig the grave, using a stout stick and her bare hands as tools. A silence fell between them as they concentrated on their task. Janna was acutely conscious of his presence beside her. She recalled her mother's teasing words, and her cheeks burned. If Godric had taken a fancy to her, it would be true to say that she had also found him worthy of inspection. She stole a quick glance. How old was Godric? Eighteen summers, maybe nineteen. Not much older than her, anyway.

As she dug deeper into the earth, Janna's thoughts went back to their first meeting only a few weeks ago. He had come, in a fright, for a cure for his mother. She was shaking with ague, he'd said. She could hardly breathe. He didn't know what to do for her. Could someone please come at once?

Eadgyth had sent Janna to gather fresh herbs, and Godric had followed her out into their herb garden, looking as if he wasn't quite sure where to plant his feet. Fearing for the delicate herbs, which were her responsibility, Janna bade him stand still and hold what she picked. Although he'd stayed where she'd put him, there was a contained restlessness about him that told her Godric was a man more used to action, and that he chafed at standing still. She was conscious that he watched her, and she tried to make sure he didn't catch her looking at him. Yet he was pleasing to look at, being tall and well built, with the fair hair and blue eyes of the Saxons. She'd been disappointed when Eadgyth bade her stay home to keep an eye on a mixture she had simmering over the fire, rather than allowing Janna to accompany them to the sick woman's cottage.

"What do you know of Godric and his mother?" she'd asked, when her mother returned home. Eadgyth had chuckled, not deceived by the casual question or the real focus of Janna's interest.

"They live over at Babestoche Manor," she said. "Godric owes his allegiance to Dame Alice and her lord."

"Not to the abbess?" Janna was surprised. The Abbess of Wiltune owned vast tracts along the Nadder River, including the land their own cottage was on. Godric must have walked several miles across the downs to seek them out.

"The manor's lands adjoin those belonging to the abbess. Godric's mother has told me about his position there, and his prospects. He sounds like a good and honorable man, Janna."

"He's not married then?"

"No. But his mother would be glad to see him take a wife." Janna wondered now if Eadgyth shared that ambition, and if she'd been left behind on purpose, so that her mother could check on Godric's suitability as a husband. Yet Eadgyth often left her behind while she went out to minister to her patients. It was an old grudge, and the injustice of it angered Janna anew.

"How is your mother?" she asked Godric, thinking that she should make use of this time to find out more about him while Eadgyth wasn't around to interfere. "Is she quite recovered now?"

"She is very well, I thank you." Godric paused for a moment and studied Janna. "It was a blessed day that brought me to your door."

And what did that mean? Was he thankful for his mother's cure, or was he glad of their meeting? Janna wanted to ask him, but was afraid where the question might lead. To a proposal of marriage? She smiled in the darkness, telling herself not to let her imagination run away with her.

"This is not how I imagined our second meeting would be." Godric continued to dig while he elaborated on his earlier observation. "I had intended to ask your mother if I might call on you."

Panic prompted Janna to deliberately misunderstand Godric's meaning. "Do you need more medication for your mother?" At once she wished she could retrieve her words. He'd already told her his mother was well. He'd think her a witless idiot.

Godric laughed. "I think you understand my meaning, Janna," he said cheerfully. To her relief, he straightened then, and said, "The hole is deep enough. Hold up the torch so I can see what I'm doing."

He grabbed the boar. "What a waste of good meat," he said as he tugged and pushed it into the hole they'd dug. Suddenly hopeful, he whipped his knife out of its sheath. "Couldn't I just slice off a little...?"

"Don't even think about it." Before he had time to put the thought into action, Janna scooped up a handful of earth and threw it over the animal. With a shrug of resignation, Godric sheathed his knife and set to helping her cover the boar.

Godric wanted to come calling on her! As Janna heaped earth over the dead animal, she reflected on what that meant.

Courtship. Marriage? No! Although she liked Godric—liked him a lot—she did not want to wed, not yet anyway.

True, she was well of an age to marry. Most of the young women of her age in the hamlets nearby were either betrothed or already wed. One was even expecting her second child, and wore the bump of her belly like a badge of honor.

Janna knew well enough how men and women found comfort in the marriage bed. She knew what needed to happen to cause the birth of a child, but she utterly rejected it for herself. She was not yet ready to share either her body or her life with anyone else. There was still so much she wanted to experience for herself, so many new places she wanted to explore. She could not—*would not*—plight her troth to Godric, nor to any other man, nor would she settle to keeping a home and bearing children at the price of her own freedom, and her own dreams for the future.

Yet what were those dreams, exactly?

Janna couldn't say, knew only how restless, how dissatisfied she sometimes felt; as if there was a world beyond the forest awaiting her, a world full of promise for the future. At such times a great longing seized her, a longing for adventure, a longing to be gone. She and Eadgyth eked out an existence from their small plot of land, and knew hunger if the season went against them. It was a hard life, but they were free to leave, to go anywhere they wished, whereas Godric, like all villeins, was bound to a liege lord and had to spend his days in service on the land so that he might have enough food to eat, and sufficient left over to pay his dues. If she wed Godric, she too would have to stay here forever. She would never know if there was something else out there, waiting for her.

Common sense told Janna she was nothing, a nobody. Her only identity came from being Eadgyth's daughter, while her occupation, her reason for living, lay in tending their garden and animals, growing the vegetables that fed them, and the

flowers and herbs for the concoctions that made up their livelihood. It was unlikely she'd ever go anywhere. In fact, she'd
be lucky to find a husband at all, let alone someone as kind
and brave as Godric.

Lost in her thoughts as she was, Janna was startled when
Godric wiped his muddy hands over a patch of grass to
cleanse them, and rose to his feet. "Do you know where we
are?" she asked, as she also stood.

"Of course. I told you, I know this forest." He plucked
off a small leafy branch of hazel and swept it around the
grave to hide all trace of their illicit activity, while Janna
scattered armfuls of dead leaves over splashes of blood to
further disguise the spot.

"Stay close to me. I'll look after you." Godric picked up
the resin torch, and took Janna's hand to guide her. He began
to push his way through the trees. It seemed to Janna that
they were setting off in the wrong direction, but she held her
peace, trusting him. Fallen logs and hidden tree roots tripped
her. Several times her feet sank into boggy patches, unseen
traps under the nettles, dock and bracken that carpeted the
forest floor. She would have fallen without Godric's hand to
steady her. Did he really know where he was going? He didn't
seem to be following a set path; in fact she was sure they had
turned through at least one circle. Once or twice he stopped,
holding up the torch so he could see the way ahead. He was
following the signs of his passage, she realized, understanding the significance of bruised and trampled plants, a muddy
footprint, broken twigs. At last he bent and picked up a dead
hare. He slung it over his shoulders and took her hand once
more, this time walking ahead in a straight, sure line.

Janna was pleased that saving her hadn't interfered with his
real night's work. All the same, she felt uneasy. She should say
something, just to have things clear between them. How could
she let him know how she felt without hurting his feelings?

It's not my fault I don't want to marry yet, she thought crossly. *Why can't he court Elfreda instead? Or Wulfrun? They would surely be pleased to have an offer of marriage from someone such as him.*

The memory of her ordeal did little to add to Janna's peace of mind as she trudged along. Her heart pumped faster and she broke into a clammy sweat as she relived the terror of the chase. She could have died tonight. Without Godric, all her fine dreams for the future would have counted for nothing. There was no getting around the fact that she owed him her life, and that she would always be in his debt. She hated that feeling of obligation, and what it might mean for her future. In fact, Janna was thoroughly uncomfortable by the time they came to a part of the forest she recognized. She was not so very far from home after all.

"Thank you, Godric." She stopped and let go of his hand, wanting to put an end to her indebtedness to him, and to her own uneasy thoughts. "Thank you for saving my life tonight. I know where I am now. I can find my way from here."

"I will see you safe home." He kept walking in the direction of the cottage.

"I know this part of the forest. I'm used to walking it alone," Janna protested.

Godric smiled at her. "I just want to make sure you are safe," he said simply. With a sigh of resignation, Janna followed him.

The cottage was in darkness when they reached it. Janna pushed open the door, hoping to find her mother returned home and sleeping within. But the only sign of life was the black cat, which stirred and blinked one sleepy eye at them. A faint warmth came from the turfed-down fire; thin wisps of smoke added to the already choking atmosphere. Janna flung open a shutter to let some fresh air into the smoky room, while Godric crouched down and blew on the embers, helping to bring the flame to life with a handful of dry leaves and twigs kept in a crock beside the fireplace.

As the flames caught and held, the small cottage became illuminated. Janna poured some water into a bowl and added a few leaves of soapwort to cleanse her filthy hands. She beckoned Godric to join her.

"Where is your mother?" he asked, once he'd dried his hands on the cloth Janna offered him.

"Gone to look after Dame Alice." Janna scowled at the memory.

"Is something amiss with my lady?"

"My mother has gone to help the dame recover from the birth of her babe," she said briefly, not wanting to fuel the situation with wild rumors.

"Will you be all right out here on your own? Shall I stay with you until your mother returns?"

"No! I'm quite used to being alone." Janna turned from him, willing him to be gone. Her thoughts were in turmoil, and he was standing far too close for comfort. She could feel the heat from his body, and shivered as his sleeve brushed hers.

The black cat uncoiled and began to weave around Godric's ankles. He nudged it aside with his boot. "Don't!" Janna remonstrated as the cat gave an affronted growl.

Godric looked up then, his expression serious. "I know your mother has skill with herbs, and I have good reason to be grateful to her. Dame Alice's patronage must also be seen as a mark of respect. But take care, Janna. There is talk in the village and in the hamlets around here, much talk about this cat—and about your mother."

"What nonsense is this?" Janna snatched up Alfred and stroked him, soothing his dignity along with her own agitation.

"The new priest speaks against you for refusing to come to his church. He says that your mother meddles in matters which should be left to God."

"I suppose he'd rather a woman die in childbirth than seek help," Janna said scornfully.

"I understand that you and your mother seek only to heal, to bring relief to those in need, but there is a midwife at Berford. Why not leave such things to her?"

"My mother has far more skill and knowledge than Mistress Aldith," Janna retorted. "She says the midwife knows more about burying mothers than bringing babies into the world. That's why Master Fulk was summoned to the manor house. And that's why he came to fetch my mother and not Mistress Aldith tonight."

Janna stopped abruptly as she remembered Godric's position at the manor house. "If Aldith has been speaking against us, it is because most women respect my mother's knowledge and seek her out rather than place their safety in the hands of an ignorant woman!" she added hastily.

"I have not heard Mistress Aldith blacken your mother's name, but others do. There is talk that your mother communes with the dead, and that she is even able to take on their appearance." Godric pointed at the cat in Janna's arms. "'Tis also said by some that this is the devil in your home."

"Alfred?" Janna's arms tightened around the cat. "You can't be serious!"

"And that's another thing," Godric said awkwardly. "They're angry that you've given your cat the name of the greatest king that Wessex has ever known." He smiled then. "Couldn't you just call it Fluffy, or something?"

"No, I could not." It was because of what had happened to the cat that she'd come to name it Alfred. She wouldn't change the name for anything.

"Well." Godric moved to the door. "I mean no harm in repeating what people are saying. It's nonsense anyway. I just wanted to warn you. But perhaps a warning isn't necessary if

Dame Alice has called on your mother's skill to aid her. That should be enough to stop any ill-natured tattle."

He opened the door, then quickly turned, seized Janna's hand and kissed it. "Farewell," he muttered. "God be with you, Janna."

"God go with you, Godric. Thank you for saving me tonight." Janna put her hand behind her back, feeling the mark of his lips burn like a brand on her skin.

"Shall I ask for a reward?" he said cheerfully. His face brightened. "Shall I ask for more than just your thanks and a kiss on the hand?"

Janna's face flamed scarlet. Godric grinned at her. "We shall meet again, Janna, and soon," he promised, and padded off into the night.

Chapter 3

The cottage seemed too quiet after Godric had gone. Janna stared into the golden heart of the fire, reflecting on his words. Did the villagers really fear them, fear Alfred? She set the cat down, then collapsed onto a stool, for her legs were trembling and weak. She still felt shaken after her encounter with the boar, but her encounter with Godric had left her even more unnerved. There was no doubt as to his intentions, but what did she really owe him for his deed this night? Was she willing to pay with her heart, her body, her life and loyalty?

Alfred nudged her hand, his intention plain. Janna bent to stroke him and he purred loudly. She smiled down at him, remembering how, so many months ago, she'd found him struggling in the river, along with the rest of the litter that had been thrown in to drown. She had tried to save them all. This was the only kitten to survive, so she'd decided to call him Alfred after the great king who had never given up, who had continued to fight the Danes until he'd succeeded in driving them out of Wessex.

Patiently she had set out to befriend the cat, and tame him. Step by step, Alfred had allowed Janna to touch him, to stroke his fur, to pick him up for a cuddle. Shut in on the long winter evenings, he had finally come to Janna in the midnight hours, when the fire had died down and the cottage was cold. Together and warm, they had slept through the night, and for many nights thereafter.

She picked him up and stood to place him on the straw pallet where she and Eadgyth slept. Next, she unfastened her girdle of plaited fibres and laid the purse of strawberries upon the table. They had cost her dear—how dear she could not tell her mother, for she knew the questions that would follow if she spoke of her encounter with Godric. She would not answer to her mother, or to Godric, until she knew the truth of her own heart, she decided.

She removed the long, gray, coarsely woven kirtle that covered her under-tunic and lay down beside the cat. She shivered, and pulled an old moth-eaten fur coverlet over her body, snuggling into its folds for warmth and comfort. The black cat curled up beside her, purring loudly. She raised a hand to stroke his glossy fur, then gave a sudden snort of laughter as she recalled Godric's warning. Could the villagers truly believe that Alfred was the devil? How could they be so ignorant, so superstitious! She longed to be free of them all, free to follow her destiny. What fun it would be to take to the road and have adventures, maybe even go as far as royal Winchestre. She could find work along the way. It wouldn't matter what she did, so long as she could earn her keep. And if she worked hard, perhaps she might become a somebody instead of a nobody. She might meet a handsome nobleman...or perhaps the king himself...

Janna's hand stilled upon the cat's soft fur. There was a half-smile upon her face as daydreams dissolved into the phantasmagoria of sleep.

*

The cottage was empty when she awoke. She sat up, feeling a moment's alarm until she realized that her mother must still be with Dame Alice. It meant things must be going badly for, with an important visitor to see this morning, her mother would surely have returned by now. Unless she and Fulk were busy making plans for their new partnership? Janna scowled at the thought, but it was followed quickly by another, more interesting idea. If Eadgyth spent most of her days in Wiltune looking after Fulk's patients, wouldn't that give her, Janna, more freedom to look after the villagers here on her own?

Janna was excited by the prospect. She began to regret her hasty exit the night before.

Alfred was waiting by the door. She jumped up to let him out, then followed him outside to peer across the green downs in the direction of Babestoche Manor. An approaching figure told her that Eadgyth was on her way home. She set about rekindling the fire, and hung a pot of water to boil, while she waited impatiently to question her mother about their future.

"And did you gather the strawberries after you left us so rudely last night, Janna?" Eadgyth's tone, as she opened the door, was cool, unforgiving. She did not look at her daughter but instead busied herself untying her cloak and hanging it from a peg. Janna's face flushed with embarrassment.

"And are you now in partnership with Fulk the apothecary, Mother?" She mimicked Eadgyth's tone, sulky with resentment.

"Hold your tongue, foolish girl." Her mother caught sight of the purse and moved to the table to inspect its contents.

The night's adventure was still vivid in Janna's mind. She wanted to tell her mother how dangerous gathering strawberries had proved, and ask her advice about Godric. But her mother had cautioned her to be silent and so she would. She, too, could keep secrets.

"I have spent the night with Dame Alice, although Fulk would have been present in my lady's chamber if he'd had his way, if I had allowed it."

"How is it with the lady? And the new babe?" If Eadgyth was trying to make peace, then Janna was prepared to meet her mother halfway.

Eadgyth frowned. "Dame Alice is recovering her health and her spirits, but I worry that the baby may not survive. He is weak after the lady's long labor and will not suckle. I suspect there may be more wrong with him even than that. I've done what I can to make him comfortable, and I shall make up a special tonic for him and call in after noon to see how they both fare. Indeed, I would rather have stayed on at the manor and made my physic there if it were not that I have agreed to see—" She caught herself before she said the name.

"You must go to the mill at Bredecumbe, Janna," she said instead. "We are in need of flour. You may take the usual crock of honey in payment." She considered for a moment. "It would be best if you seek out the miller's wife to conduct our business. I'll give you a balm of comfrey for her ulcers, for I know the poor woman suffers sorely."

"And why may I not stay and meet Mistress Whoever-she-is?" Janna said hotly, resentful at being sent away when her errand was not so very urgent.

"Because she has impressed upon me the need for the greatest secrecy. No-one must know of her coming, she told me. No-one. That includes you, Janna. Instead of being quarrelsome, make yourself useful. Go out and pick me some pennyroyal and also some houseleek. And bring me some sprigs of tansy and lavender to freshen the rushes on the floor."

"What of Fulk? How do matters rest with him?"

Eadgyth gave a short laugh. "Dame Alice knows my true worth, even if Fulk does not. I discovered that it was she who sent Fulk to fetch me. All that talk of wanting me to work in his shop was to cover his ignorance and bolster his pride. The man is a turnip head. I could never work with him, I have far too much to lose. So I've sent him on his way, with a flea in his ear for how he has treated his patient and instructions to summon me earlier next time he is called on to deal with such problems." She gave her daughter a brief, bright smile. "You and I will continue as we were, Janna, as we have always been."

As we have always been. Janna felt a sharp stab of disappointment as her brief dream of independence was snatched away. "I had thought, with you in Wiltune, that you might trust me at last to take care of the villagers on my own," she ventured.

"You are young, untrained. They would have no respect for you."

"Of course they won't respect me if I don't know what I'm doing. And I'll never find out if you won't let me try!"

"I've already taught you everything I know," Eadgyth protested.

"About plants and their properties, and how to utilize them—yes. Now let me use that knowledge to help people. You may be the greatest healer around here, but I could be too if you'd only give me a chance."

"I swear that tongue of yours has been sharpened by the devil!" Eadgyth gave her daughter a good, hard shake. "Soon enough you will marry, have children, be happy. That's the future I wish for you."

"And what about my wishes? I don't want to marry, at least not yet."

"Why not? You are certainly old enough to wed. Far better a life with a good husband like Godric than the hard life we live here."

"I want something more than to become some man's drudge and a nursemaid to his children."

"There's much more to wedlock than that!" Eadgyth retorted. "As well as bedgames, a good husband would give you security. Safely wed, you'd be both respectable and respected."

"And how would you know, Mother?" Janna seized the opportunity Eadgyth had given her. "Were you ever safely wed? What was between you and my father? Why will you never speak of him? Are you ashamed of him, or is it your past that shames you?"

"It is because of him that I would see you wed."

Janna read the pain in her mother's eyes, but the devil snapped at her heels. She had to go on, to push for answers to the questions that would not go away. "Tell me about him, please," she begged.

It wasn't the first time she'd asked. Her father had died just before her birth, or so her mother had told her. Janna had often wondered if Eadgyth was telling the truth, or trying to cover the fact that she'd never been wed—that Janna's birth, in fact, had been an accident. This thought nagged Janna like a sore tooth, but after she'd seen how talking about her father so distressed Eadgyth, she'd stopped asking after him. She knew anyway that Eadgyth never answered her questions.

Nor did she now. She turned to her task, dismissing Janna with a brief, "See to the herbs, Janna."

Frustrated and resentful, Janna stamped outside. Their garden was a small, awkwardly shaped piece of land that had come with the cottage because it didn't fit into the long strips of fields worked by the villeins. The hives that provided honey for her mother's salves and potions were tucked into one corner. Janna was protective of her bees and took good care of them, for their honey was like liquid gold when silver was always in short supply. The bees lived in straw skeps, woven and crafted by Janna herself, and usually she stopped and talked to them, following a long tradition of telling them about the doings of the household. Today she did not take her usual comfort from the soothing buzz that marked their industry. Instead, she slapped angrily at a lone bee that circled close to her nose, and seethed with the injustice of being treated like a child when she considered herself no longer to be one.

She stomped on past the dew pond that provided them with water, past rows of turnips, cabbages, leeks and broad beans that put food on their table, past bushes of alecost, which they used to flavor ale, and past flax plants, which were boiled into decoctions to ease various ailments, or were stripped and woven into cloth.

Janna looked to the wattle fence that penned their two goats, Nellie and Gruff, along with Fussy, Greedy, Rusty and Laet, their hens. The goats bleated anxiously, reminding her that they still needed to be fed. She stooped over the clusters of herbs that formed the basis of her mother's healing mixtures, forgetting her sulks for the moment as she concentrated on her task. She could not afford to make any mistakes if she wanted her mother to treat her like an adult, someone more fitting than Fulk to be her partner.

First, Janna stripped off several leafy sprigs of tansy and put them in her scrip. It was a useful plant: the flowers made a fine golden dye, while the bitter, aromatic leaves served as a repellent for lice and fleas. Janna turned next to the fleshy leaves of houseleek and the other herbs her mother had requested, but once they were gathered her mind returned to her grievances. Why would her mother not speak of her father? Was it sorrow that kept her tight-lipped, or was it the shame of bearing a daughter out of wedlock? Janna knew her mother's lips would stay stubbornly closed unless she could come up with some new strategy to persuade her to unlock the secrets of her heart. Could she perhaps threaten to go elsewhere for information? Who might know the truth?

Her mind ranged over possibilities. They were few indeed. Her mother had no close friends, no-one in whom she might confide if she would not confide in her daughter. For the first time it occurred to Janna how lonely her mother must be. Where was her own family? She didn't think Eadgyth had always lived here, on the edge of the forest, yet this place was all Janna could remember, so her mother must surely have come here before giving birth. That being so, people might have seen or heard something, might remember something of that time. If so, why had they never spoken? Had her mother sworn everyone to secrecy? Who was she trying to protect? Her daughter—or herself? Janna knew that Eadgyth was proud, and that she kept her secrets well. Yet if Janna was old enough to marry, she was surely old enough to be told the truth!

Janna rushed indoors, determined to try out this new argument.

She found Eadgyth, cheeks flushed from the rising steam, stirring a decoction over the fire. Absorbed in her task, she was humming quietly to herself. The tune was familiar and sounded rather solemn and sad. She'd once asked Eadgyth to teach her the song, but her mother had silenced her with a sharp look and an angry refusal. Janna had never asked again, thinking there must be something shameful in the song, for Eadgyth had looked so guilty when caught. Yet she'd heard her mother sing the same tune several times since; it seemed that she sang only when she was preoccupied with something else.

"Tell me about my father." Janna dumped the herbs in front of her mother. "You say I'm old enough to marry, so that makes me old enough to know the truth about my birth."

Startled, Eadgyth stopped humming and glared at her daughter. "I haven't got time for another argument. The lady will be coming shortly. You must go now."

"I still have to feed the hens and goats."

"I'll do it." Eadgyth jerked her thumb in the direction of the door. "I want your promise that you'll not linger to watch, but that you will go directly about the business I have given you, and speak to no-one of my business back here." She eyed her defiant daughter, and sighed. "As well as visiting the miller, you have my permission to walk on to Wiltune. You have experience enough to trade on your own, for today is market day. Take the beeswax candles and some of our special scented creams and rinses to sell there. They'll fetch a few pennies, so you may buy a hot pie for your dinner. I don't want you to leave Wiltune until you hear the abbey bells ring the hour of None."

Janna's face brightened. Going to the market was a rare treat, even if she knew her mother's offer stemmed from a need to keep her away for most of the day.

"I don't want to argue with you. I just want you to tell me my father's name," she said, refusing to be diverted from her purpose. She avoided her mother's eye, instead collecting up the goods she would sell and setting them carefully in a woven basket. She hoped that the beeswax stoppers were thick and tight enough to prevent the precious liquids from leaking out but, to make sure, she wedged fat scented candles around them to keep them in place. All the while, she waited for her mother to speak, but Eadgyth remained silent. Janna hefted the strap over her shoulder. The basket was heavy but she would carry it without protest, so long as her mother gave her something in return. Determined not to leave without an answer, she confronted Eadgyth.

"There may not be time to talk now, but I insist that you tell me my father's name at least."

"Janna!" Her mother threw down the spoon and, hands on hips, turned to glare at her.

"Who was he? Where did you meet him?"

"That's enough, Johanna!" Her mother only called Janna by her full name when she was in serious trouble. Otherwise Janna was known by her baby name, which was what she'd called herself when she was just learning how to talk. Being called Johanna made her feel uncomfortable, as if she was someone different, someone who didn't belong in the only world she knew. Now Janna felt torn between her usual obedience to her mother's wishes and a wild impatience to know more. She opened her mouth, then quickly closed it as she struggled to find a compelling argument to change her mother's mind.

Dismissing her daughter, Eadgyth turned back to the fire and picked up the spoon to give her decoction another stir. Janna pulled a face at her mother's back, then instantly regretted her action. She wasn't a child any more. How could she convince her mother of that if she still behaved like one? She scooped up the crock of honey and jar of healing salve her mother had placed on the table, then paused at the doorway, determined to speak her mind.

"I am sorry if the memory distresses you, Mother, but if you won't tell me about my father then you force me to ask others for information."

Eadgyth's hand stilled. Her whole body went rigid with shock. "Questions, questions!" she snapped. "Why do you always plague me with questions?"

"Because you taught me to question everything! Why, then, should I not question the mystery of my father?" Janna met her mother's hard stare, determined that this time she would not back down. For a long moment they defied each other. Finally, Eadgyth nodded slightly. "If you must hear of it, then 'tis better I tell you in my own words. Those who do not know the truth of the matter might not be so kind." She paused, weighing her words carefully. "You believe your father to be dead, but in truth and for all I know, he may still be alive."

"My father lives?" Janna's eyes widened in amazement. "Why did you not tell me this before?"

"I wanted to protect you." Eadgyth touched Janna's cheek in a rare gesture of affection. "I have many regrets in my life, but the one thing I shall never regret is giving birth to you. I'll do anything to save you from making the same mistakes that I made."

For a moment Janna was silenced by her mother's unexpected tenderness. Yet her will to learn the truth was strong; she was impatient with her mother's desire to protect her.

"All my life I have kept silent, thinking my father was dead and that it grieved you to speak of him. For all these years, you have let me believe a lie!"

"It does grieve me to speak of him. I loved your father. I still do. That's why I—"

A timid knock interrupted Eadgyth. Startled, she glanced from Janna to the door. "Wait here," she said, and went quickly outside, slamming the door shut behind her. Janna heard the soft murmur of voices. She moved to the door, listening hard. The door was suddenly flung open, catching her by surprise.

"Go now." Eadgyth was in too much of a hurry to reprimand her daughter for eavesdropping. "We will speak later." She pushed Janna outside, then followed her out and went toward the back of the cottage. "Go!" she shouted, as she noticed that Janna had stopped to watch.

Having secured her mother's promise, Janna did as she was told, but she couldn't resist a last look behind. Too late, she realized, as she heard the door slam. Her mother and the visitor were now both safely inside and out of sight. She turned then and walked on toward the small village of Berford. The day was cloudy; there was a hint of rain, but Janna's spirits rose as she sniffed the fresh air, smiled at peacefully grazing sheep and listened to the melodious whistle of a lone blackbird.

Her path followed the contours of the gently sloping downs, taking her toward the Nadder River and Berford. A straggle of thatched cottages came into view, set along a track of beaten earth close to the river. Like Janna's own home, the cottages were made from panels of woven wattle fastened between wooden posts and pasted over with a mixture of clay, dung and straw daub to keep out wind and rain. While still having only one room, these cottages were larger than the small cot Janna shared with her mother. Most of them boasted henhouses, vegetable gardens, goats and sometimes even a cow or pig. Beyond the settlement and above the water meadows were the open fields where villeins grew crops in their allotted strips, both for themselves and for the abbey.

The track was littered with human and vegetable waste. Pigs, goats, hens and ducks walked free, noisily scuffling among the rotting vegetation. Pools of scummy water added their stench to the ripe air. Janna picked her way past the worst of it, following the path that would bring her to the water mill and, by way of several small hamlets, to Wiltune itself. Near Bredecumbe she forded the river, splashing through clear pebbled shallows to the water meadows on the other side. She walked on to where the chalk stream divided and pooled into a small lake, turning the swiftly flowing tributary into the rushing torrent that powered the mill when the waters were released. Two low stone arches spanned the frothing water; above them was a thatched wattle-and-daub building where the grinding of the grain actually took place. Janna could hear now the thunder of the great wheel churning below.

She stopped, charmed by the sight of a mother duck paddling upstream with a string of babies behind her. Janna's pleasure in the sight quickly changed to alarm as she noticed that one of the ducklings had lagged behind and become caught in the undertow. In spite of its frantic efforts to swim away, it was being dragged closer and closer to the powerful wheel. She looked about for a net or a bucket, anything to save it, but even those few seconds had taken all the time that was left. As she turned back to the river, the duckling disappeared from view.

Janna swallowed hard, and hoisted up the honeypot so that it fitted more snugly under her arm. This was nature's way; it was stupid to get upset about it, she told herself as she walked up to the open door and peered in. The miller's wife, hand to her back and heavy with child, stood beside the chattering pit wheel, watching as brown, gritty flour poured down through the chute into the meal bin. Above her head, Janna could hear the heavy tread of the miller as he hoisted another sack of grain to feed into the hopper. The millstones ground the wheat with a dull roar. Janna sneezed as a spray of flour dust tickled her nose. The sound alerted the miller's wife to the fact that she had company.

She swung around. As she recognized her visitor, an expression of alarm flitted across her face. She took a quick step backward, and crossed herself.

Surprised, Janna held out the jar of salve, fixing a smile on her face as she did so. "I have here some ointment for you, Mistress Hilde. For the sores on your skin. My mother said I was to bring it to you."

The woman made no move to take the jar. Instead she scratched her arm while she took the time to look Janna over. Janna felt sorry for her. It was common knowledge that the miller strayed from home, and that he spread his favors among several women.

"Her jealousy is eating away at her skin as well as her heart," Eadgyth had said once. "I can soothe her sores, but she will never be free of them unless her husband stops straying or she ceases to care about it."

"But surely he will stay at home now that his wife is with child?"

Eadgyth had given her daughter a cynical smile. "It's at this time, when wives are large with child and become unwilling partners in bedgames, that most men are tempted to look elsewhere. Unfortunately for Hilde, her husband has already had a lot of practice in the art of straying. Nothing is likely to change him now."

Her mother must have thought her comments naive, Janna realized, yet she truly believed that a marriage should be for love, and forever. She would never settle for a husband who strayed, whose tomcatting left her vulnerable and despairing, and an object of pity and scorn to others. Janna felt a great sympathy for this hurting, discontented woman.

"Please, take the salve," she said, thrusting it into Hilde's hand. She kept her eyes fixed on Hilde's face so that she wouldn't have to look at the weeping sores on the woman's arm. Her mother had told her that there were sores on Hilde's legs as well—another reason for the miller to stray.

Hilde's fingers closed around the rough, home-made pot.

"I have also this crock of honey." Janna placed it on the table. "My mother wishes to exchange it for a bag of flour as usual, if you please."

The miller's wife gave a grudging nod. Janna wondered if she might ask a final favor.

"I am bound for the market at Wiltune, mistress," she said. "May I fetch the flour later?"

Undecided, the miller's wife looked up, as though seeking advice from her husband. Janna heard a loud rattling noise as the miller fed grain into the chute; the millstones began to grind once more. Coarse flour poured down into the meal bin. For the moment, the miller was safely occupied. Hilde's tight expression eased somewhat.

"You may come for it on your way home." She gave Janna a push toward the door.

With a light heart, looking forward to her treat, Janna turned and left. It was going to be a wonderful day, she just knew it. Whether it rained or no, the birds sang and whistled about their business, the river chattered merrily beside her, and the frights of the night seemed long ago and far away.

Chapter 4

Although Janna had been to Wiltune several times in the past, it had always been in the company of her mother. Now she enjoyed a new sense of freedom as she looked about her, fascinated by all that she saw. The abbess held the barony over just about all of the land she was walking through. Her villeins were out in the fields, working her lands and paying rent for the privilege of having a home and employment. Some, like the miller, paid rent and rendered services, while others paid their dues in labor. Every year Janna's mother grumbled about having to find the fee for the abbess for, although they were free to leave if they wished, while they stayed they must pay for their cottage and the land that came with it. In bad seasons, payment caused hardship for everyone. Fortunately, this year had started well and promised fair, unless the civil war between the king and his cousin came close enough to upset smiling nature and wrecked the harvest to come.

The sun was peeking through the clouds. It warmed Janna's face and dried her mouth. She shifted the strap of her basket from one shoulder to the other; her back ached from carrying it. She put it down and turned toward the river, squelching through mud and pushing apart sharp reeds to reach the water's edge. There, she bent to scoop a handful of cold, clear liquid into her mouth, relishing the moisture as it slipped down her parched throat. She drank her fill, picked up her basket, and set off once more, coming at last to the high stone walls that encircled the abbey. Janna followed them around, heading for the market square outside the abbey's main portal.

She heard the noise long before she got there: shouts of pedlars, shrill cries of children, yapping dogs and squealing, clucking livestock, and the rise and fall of voices as shoppers and traders bargained hard to get the better of each other. Janna sighed with pleasure. This is where I want to be, she thought. This is where real life is going on!

Pleasant odors wafted toward her—hot pies, spiced wine and gingerbread—but they were offset by the stink of sewage, newly tanned leather and salted fish. Traveling merchants had set up stalls among the more usual goods for trade. Janna stopped to admire a display of soft leather gloves and slippers, then moved on to inspect trays of ribbons, cheap trinkets, bone combs and buttons, strings of amber and glass beads and finely wrought brooches. She fingered her empty purse, imagining how it would feel to have enough money to buy whatever she wanted.

With a small sigh, she moved on to join a group gathered around a juggler. As she came closer, two women stepped out of her way, neither acknowledging her nor meeting her eye. Janna recognized them and was puzzled. One of them, the wife of a weaver from Berford, had made the journey to the edge of the forest several times to consult her mother. Surely she would not be influenced by the priest's prejudice against them?

"I give you good day, Mistress Bertha," Janna said, as she came closer.

"God be with you, Janna." Bertha didn't look at her, seeming absorbed instead in the antics of the juggler, who had now added a flaming sword to the three balls he was keeping in the air so skilfully. Janna scowled at Bertha's back as the woman walked away, then chided herself for being silly. She would not allow anyone to spoil her pleasure in the day. So she watched the juggler, and clapped his performance when he was done. She wished she had a coin to put in his cap, for he'd entertained and delighted her with his skill.

She was about to move on when she recognized another face. There, in the marketplace, his black cloak flapping around his short, thin frame so that he looked like an old crow as he swooped about, was the priest from Berford. What was he doing here? Probably making sure none of his flock managed to enjoy themselves, Janna thought with a grin, and edged away out of his notice. There was so much to see and do; she had no intention of being waylaid and lectured by the priest.

She ambled on, fascinated by all the products for sale: fruits and vegetables, sparrows, pigeons and hens, woven cloth of varying quality, fresh bread, candles and soap, crocks of honey and blocks of cheese. Her nose twitched as she smelled once more the fragrance of hot meat pies. She had come out in such a rush that she'd not yet broken her fast. Her empty stomach rumbled to remind her of the fact. As soon as she had sold her wares, she would visit the pieman. She looked for a space to set out her scented candles, creams and rinses, enjoying her new feeling of independence.

The thud of a horse's hooves and the jingle of a bridle alerted her to the presence of a stranger coming toward her. The first detail Janna noticed was the horse, a huge black destrier such as a soldier or a crusader might ride into battle. It was a sleek beast, quite unlike the shaggy ponies and plodding carthorses she usually saw in the fields. The horse's glossy

coat shone, and Janna shielded her eyes from the bright sunlight the better to admire it.

She became aware of its owner next, as he reined his
mount to a standstill and surveyed the market scene before
him. Dark, shoulder-length hair and clean-shaven face in the
old Norman fashion. A long and decorated tunic, the sort
worn by the nobility. A faint smile curled his mouth. Seeing
it, Janna clenched her fingers into fists, feeling hot indignation
on Wiltune's behalf. Condescending *bricon*, she thought,
automatically assigning to him the Norman word for fool. He
must surely be a Norman, for no Saxon would sneer at the
villagers as he was sneering now.

As if becoming aware of Janna's gaze—and her judgment—the man glanced down at her. The smile died on his
lips, burned away perhaps by her furious expression. Feeling
no fear, for she had nothing to lose, she continued to glower
up at him. A smile twitched his lips once more as he nodded to
her from his horse and called out, "*Bonjour, ma belle petite.*"

Janna bridled anew. She tilted her head back and glared at
him. Pretty little girl indeed!

"Can you give me directions to the manor house at
Babestoche?" The man continued his careful inspection of
Janna. There was warmth in his gaze; a smile of appreciation
curved his mouth.

For a moment, Janna thought to send him off in the wrong
direction entirely, but she had the sense that the stranger
already knew the way and was using this merely as a ruse to
speak to her. Telling herself she wasn't in the least flattered,
she said, "Follow the river to Berford, then ask again."
Although the stranger had asked directions in her own
tongue, pride prompted Janna to answer him in the language
of the Normans, taught to her by Eadgyth. She jerked her
head in the direction the stranger should ride, and walked
away, conscious that his eyes still watched her. Belying her

cool manner, her mind was full of a jumble of impressions, not least of which was the stranger's easy assurance, his fine tunic and hose and, yes, she was forced to admit it, his handsome face and strong physique.

Frowning, Janna considered the matter. Some years older, perhaps in his twentieth year, she thought. She could sense the experience behind his ease, the experience that told him his worth in terms of his birth but also in matters of life—and death. This was a man sure of himself, someone not to be disregarded or put aside. A scar down one cheek spoke of his having tested himself in combat, either of a personal nature or on the battlefield. A man of courage, then. A man's man. A lady's man too. Janna felt herself grow hot as she recalled how his bold glance had raked her body. He'd called her a pretty girl, but she was a Saxon serf and therefore unworthy of his notice; he was merely teasing her. This was a man who could pick and choose among women—and most probably did so, for who could not fail to be impressed by that proud, handsome face, that confident demeanor?

Janna was surprised how much she had noticed—and remembered—on such a short appraisal. Who was he? And what could he want up at the manor? These were troubled times for travelers—and for all of England. King Stephen had usurped the throne and was now forced to defend his position against his cousin, the Empress Matilda. Janna had a secret admiration for the empress. It seemed that, enraged by Stephen's action and determined not to give up the throne, Matilda had gathered her own army of supporters and come to England to fight for her rights. Her claim seemed just, for she had been named heir by her father, King Henry. He himself was the son of the Norman bastard, William the Conqueror, who had taken England for his own and established the line of Norman rule. There had already been several skirmishes between Stephen's army and Matilda's supporters. Was the stranger here on Stephen's behalf, to demand from the abbess and the manor house the knight service due to the king?

Telling herself his business was none of her concern, Janna found a space near to a traveler, a spice merchant. She pulled a clean linen cloth from her pack and spread it on the ground, having first cleared straw and assorted rubbish out of the way. Carefully, she laid out her goods for sale, all the while keeping a sharp lookout for the abbey guards or the shire reeve, for she had no permission to sell her wares. "Creams to perfume your skin, ladies!" she called, gesturing to the pots on the ground. "Smell like a rose for your husband tonight! I also have rosemary and chamomile rinses to cleanse and lighten your hair. I have fragrant lavender for your linen, and a mint rinse to freshen your breath. Only a ha'penny a jar."

The spice merchant leaned over and inspected the pots, perhaps calculating whether or not their presence would damage his own business. In turn, Janna stared at his portable table, fascinated by the strange seeds, berries and plants upon it. She stepped closer, then bent over and inhaled, savoring their fragrance. "What are these?" she asked, pointing at a pile of light brown sticks.

"Cinnamon."

"And those?" Janna gestured toward a crock of small black balls.

"Cloves." His manner thawing in the face of Janna's interest, the merchant kept on pointing out various spices, perhaps hoping that she might buy something. "My wares come from across the sea, from the east," he told her, speaking loudly so that his voice might be heard above the hubbub of the marketplace. "It is a long journey, and my spices are highly prized because of it. See—I have yellow saffron, cardamom, peppercorns and caraway seeds." While he answered Janna's questions, the merchant kept a sharp eye out for passing trade. She became aware that he was using his answers to her questions as a means to tempt others to inspect his wares. His ruse was working, for first one and then another woman drew closer. There was quite a crowd of observers around when Janna pointed to a small phial of brownish oil, and asked its purpose.

"It is a marvel, a miracle cure, most efficacious for aching joints. A little of this oil rubbed in at night, and you'll be as agile as a young spring lamb come morning." His eyes twinkled. "Not that you'll need it for quite a while yet, lass."

"But what is in the oil?" Janna persisted, refusing to be either diverted or beguiled by his flattery.

The man hesitated for a moment, then said, "It is a substance of such danger that I am loath to sell it to any other than those who are skilled in the art of healing and who know well the care that must be taken in its employment."

Was he sincere, or was he merely building up the mystery and therefore the desirability of his liniment? Janna wasn't sure, and didn't really care. Curiosity drove her on. "My mother is a healer, and would be interested to learn more of such a substance. Pray tell me what is in the oil?"

The man tapped the side of his nose, but stayed silent.

"Answer the lass," said Bertha.

Janna hid a smile. No doubt Bertha was after the secret ingredient so she could cure her own aching back rather than continue coming to Eadgyth for a special liniment.

A sergeant-at-arms had joined the swelling crowd around the spice merchant, and now he stepped closer. "Give us your answer, trader, and tell it true or I'll send you on your way. There's no place for quacks and charlatans here in Wiltune."

"I mean no harm, I mean merely to warn." The spice merchant stood his ground, looking self-righteous.

"Then warn away, and tell us what it is we need to fear." The sergeant moved even closer, dwarfing the spice merchant by many inches both in height and girth.

"It contains *Aconitum napellus*. The root is ground and mixed with oil and hot mustard and then rubbed into aching joints. It brings almost instant relief. It really is a wonder cure—but it is for external use only. Ingested, it may well prove fatal." The man was anxious to ingratiate himself now—and perhaps to make a sale in spite of his warning.

Aconitum napellus. Aconite. The man was making the herb sound more important by giving it the Latin name—unless it was a ploy to keep a common plant a secret? Janna was willing to wager that no-one present knew what it was but she knew what he was talking about. Her mother had instructed her well in the properties of herbs and the art of healing. The merchant could not bluff Janna with fancy Latin names. *Aconitum napellus* was known by several common names: monkshood, blue rocket, wolfsbane, helmet flower. Janna suppressed a shudder as she recalled the last time she'd seen it. It was the plant that grew near the strawberries she had risked so much to pick.

There was no secret here, for her mother already knew the properties of aconite, and no doubt the weaver's wife had felt its benefit on more than one occasion. Janna felt some satisfaction in thinking that Bertha would have to continue relying on Eadgyth for relief if she wasn't prepared to ask any more questions.

The sergeant nodded, and walked away. Janna breathed a sigh of relief that her own modest wares had not attracted his attention. Perhaps the sergeant had assumed that her pots were part of the merchant's display.

The trader was busy with other customers now. They all wanted to finger his spices, and smell them before making a purchase. Taking advantage of the crowd, Janna sang out a temptation to the women to inspect her own wares. As she did so, she noticed that Bertha had taken her turn to hand over a coin, receiving from the spice seller a small phial of the rubbing oil. Had things come to such a pass that Bertha would rather hand over good silver than visit the *wortwyf*, who would treat her in return for a piece of woven woollen cloth or the gift of a few eggs?

Bertha hurried off, but several other women turned to Janna after making their purchases from the spice merchant. She congratulated herself on choosing such a good position as she smeared a dab of cream perfumed with violets onto her skin so that the women might smell it. Judging from the stench of perspiration and unwashed clothes emanating from some of them, they might well benefit from its application, she thought, as she held out her wrist to a new customer to take a sniff. "The cream is good for your skin; it'll make it soft as a baby's cheek," she said persuasively when the woman hesitated.

Strangers bought from Janna; some who knew her hurried on, crossing themselves or making a sign against her to ward off evil. Janna assuaged her annoyance by calling out, "Buy my special perfumed candles for the church. Real beeswax, they'll burn for hours and hours and save your souls from damnation!" As her purse swelled and supplies dwindled, Janna's thoughts turned again to the handsome man on horseback. Would she ever see him again? The thought stirred her blood, bringing an unexpected heat to her cheeks and body. Blushing, although she knew not why, she sang her song of temptation once more, loud enough to drown out the thoughts that would not lie quiet in her mind.

"Lavender and roses to perfume your skin! Mint balm to refresh tired feet and hands! Comb out the tangles and add sunlight to your hair with a chamomile rinse."

When the last jar and the last candle were sold, Janna folded the linen square, now filthy from the dirt and dust of the street. She placed the fabric carefully in her empty basket. It would have to be washed and bleached before it could be used again.

Coins and tokens jangled in her purse as she stood. She smiled, feeling well pleased with the day's trade.

Her stomach grumbled, reminding her that she hadn't yet broken her fast. She pulled a token from her purse and set off toward the pieman.

Munching ravenously, she walked on then to the sundial in the center of the market square and inspected the shadow cast by the marker. Only a little past the hour of one. She was tired and she had a raging thirst. She was ready to go home, but dared not until she heard the abbey bells ring the three hours of None. She would not risk her mother's anger—not when there was so much at stake. If she annoyed her mother by coming home early, then the secret of her father's identity might well stay locked in Eadgyth's heart. Nor would she need to hurry home at None either, she realized with some dismay. Once her mother's visitor left, surely Eadgyth would go straight to Dame Alice, to take her the physic she'd been busy preparing for the new infant. It could be hours before she came home to answer questions as she'd promised.

Janna decided that she might as well relax and enjoy her small holiday. She glanced about the marketplace and the small shops that hedged it in. Master Fulk's shop was closed. Dame Alice must be paying him well for the business he was losing by attending her. Close to his shop was an alehouse, its purpose made clear by the bush tied to a pole outside the door, the same sign that marked the premises of several other alehouses in Wiltune. She fingered her bulging purse, and nodded to herself. She had never been to an alehouse before, but was curious to see inside. If she was old enough to wed, she was surely old enough to brave the louts who were hanging around outside, and who seemed to have made the alehouse their headquarters. She would go in, sit down, and have a jug of cool ale to slake her thirst. While she was resting, she would listen to the market gossip. Perchance she might overhear the identity of the man on horseback, and the mission that had brought him to Babestoche Manor.

Her first thought when she stepped over the threshold was to turn and run. The room was dark, having only a couple of window spaces to let in the light. Although there was no fire, stale smoke hung heavy in the air. It was mixed with the smell of sweat and unwashed clothes, and a lingering odor of animal waste brought in on boots and smeared over the already filthy straw strewed across the earthen floor. Janna placed her hand over her nose and coughed, debating whether she should leave. The bold glances of the patrons inside, and a lewd invitation for her to join some drinkers at their table, eroded her confidence even further. The only other women in the alehouse seemed to be whores looking for business. Yet pride made her defiant. She was not a coward; she would not turn and run. She had as much right to be there as any of them. She would find a seat and take some refreshment and the devil take them if they didn't like it. So Janna forced herself to keep on walking past the crowded tables until, mercifully, she spied an empty stool at the back of the room.

The alewife appeared from the brewhouse behind. She paused at the door to let her eyes grow accustomed to the dim light. She bustled over then and looked Janna up and down, mouth pursed in disapproval.

"I bid you good day, mistress," Janna said, continuing in a rush before she lost her nerve, "bring me a jug of your good ale, if you please."

The alewife didn't budge. Quickly, Janna produced a token and slapped it down on the rough wooden tabletop.

The woman waited until Janna produced another token. Then she nodded, slipped the tokens into a purse at her waist and disappeared through the crowd. Janna wondered if she'd ever see her again. She stretched out her legs and leaned back against the rough plastered wall of the alehouse, glad to rest as she waited to see what would happen next. Realizing that they would get no fun out of her, the other patrons of the alehouse stopped their stares and resumed talking among themselves and flirting with the harlots.

Janna relaxed further when a wooden bowl was shoved in front of her. The alewife filled it from a leather bottle, the liquid sloshing over the brim. Janna muttered her thanks and bent over to slurp up a mouthful so that she could then lift the bowl without wasting any more ale. The alewife kept on circulating around the tables, refilling and clearing as she went. Janna wasn't sure if the woman had taken against her because she despised her, thinking her another whore come to do business in the alehouse, but if so, Janna didn't care. She was determined to enjoy her drink. She lifted the bowl and gulped down a couple of mouthfuls.

She smacked her lips, savoring the cool liquid as it slipped down her dry throat. She swallowed again, and then again more slowly, holding the ale briefly in her mouth as she thought about its taste. Janna helped her mother brew their own ale from the barley and herbs growing in their garden and, like most villagers, they broke their fast each morning with ale and a hunk of bread. She sipped again. The difference was subtle, but it was there: this ale was flavored with some different herb. It was not nearly as sweet as their own ale, for Eadgyth tended to have a liberal hand with the honey, but was there something else added that gave this ale its different flavor?

Janna sipped and sipped again, trying to decide what it was that left the faintly unpleasant aftertaste in her mouth. Could it be that the water used by the alewife was not quite so fresh as the water Eadgyth always insisted that they collect from the most swiftly flowing stretch of the river for their own brew? In the past Janna had grumbled about having to carry the water some distance in heavy buckets, but she thought now that the effort was worthwhile if it made such a difference.

Having analyzed the ale to her satisfaction, Janna sat back to survey the room. Her eyes had adjusted to the dim light, and she found that a couple of the drinkers were known to her. She wondered if Fulk the apothecary was among the crowd, but after a careful scrutiny she concluded that his new patient must be keeping him occupied up at the manor. She just hoped he was not undoing all the good her mother had done.

In need of diversion, she began to listen to the conversations going on around her. To her surprise, almost the first thing she heard was a reference to herself.

"...the *wortwyf's* daughter. I'm told she's grown into a real beauty." The man gave a grunting laugh, unaware the subject of his conversation was listening in. "I'd be more than happy to take her on, if it wasn't for—" He stopped abruptly as his companion gave him a hard nudge and jerked a thumb at Janna. Undeterred, the man turned to wink at her before taking a thirsty swig of ale.

Janna looked away, not sure whether to be amused or upset. She knew that Torold the blacksmith was recently widowed, and had a number of motherless children. No wonder he was in the market for a wife. She wondered what stopped him from approaching Eadgyth to speak of the matter. "If it wasn't for..." What? The priest's denouncement of her mother? Eadgyth's reputation for shape-shifting and communing with the dead? Or was it because of Alfred, the devil cat who lived in their home?

"...on his way to Babestoche Manor." Another voice came to Janna's ears. "Did you see him, Eadric? Anyone would think he was King Stephen himself, mounted on that big black horse of his."

Janna shifted her stool closer to the speaker, eager for news of the handsome stranger.

"Does he come to rally support for the king?" Eadric was a dark, ill-featured man who seemed to be taking no pleasure from either his companion or the drink in front of him. "Does trouble come our way?"

"I think he comes only to visit his aunt, Dame Alice. He is quite often at the manor."

"I hope you speak the truth of it, for if he has come to raise an army for the king, there will be trouble." Eadric gave a loud belch, then patted his stomach. "His liege lord, the abbess, must surely side with the empress, not the king. After all, the Empress Matilda's mother spent part of her childhood here at the abbey."

"But the abbess risks everything if she supports the empress. If Stephen can arrest Bishop Roger, throw him into prison and seize his palace at Sarisberie, he most surely can arrest our abbess if she supports the wrong side. Mark my words, the abbess will put the abbey's interests first and go with the king. But you are right: if my lord Hugh comes to raise an army, there *will* be trouble."

"Why?" Eadric plonked an elbow on the table and leaned forward. "What do you know of Dame Alice's nephew then? Where does his allegiance lie?"

"I had it from that traveler, him with the fancy leather goods for sale, that he has witnessed the lord Hugh in the company of Earl Robert of Gloucester."

"Then that makes him the king's man."

"No, it does not."

"But Earl Robert has pledged his allegiance to the king."

"That was after the king seized the throne, but the earl has since changed his mind. After all, he's half-brother to the empress. 'Tis said he's now Matilda's strongest supporter and the leader of her army."

"So, if our fine lord is here on Matilda's behalf, he'll likely be clapped in irons and handed over to the king." Eadric smirked. It was the first time Janna had seen him smile.

"Aye, that's what I told the traveler. But his uncle, Robert of Babestoche, is the king's man."

"Is he, though? Are you sure of that?" The two men buried their faces in their beakers of ale and drank deep as they considered the question. Eadric's friend was the first to put down his pot and voice his concern. "'Tis a fact that Robert of Babestoche hasn't traveled even as far as Sarisberie to pay homage to the king, so who knows where his loyalty lies? Or ours, for that matter?" He cast a quick look over his shoulder to check whether any had heard his words, for they could be construed as treason. Janna quickly averted her gaze and instead studied her hands as if red, chapped skin and ragged nails were the most important things in her life.

Eadric drained his beaker and set it down with a determined thud. "I don't care who supports what, so long as the fighting don't come any closer," he said. "I've heard tell there's terrible hard times for those who are in the wrong place at the wrong time. Whole villages burned, crops and beasts destroyed, people murdered in their beds or left to rot in dungeons. Tortured, even." He shuddered. "May the king, his ambitious cousin and those murdering barons keep as far from us as the moon itself, that's what I say. The devil can take them all!" He pushed his stool back and stood up, then lumbered slowly out of the room, followed by his companion.

So the stranger's name was Hugh and he was Dame Alice's nephew. Janna sat back, finding more questions to replace those that the drinkers had already answered. When had Hugh been seen with Robert, Earl of Gloucester—before or after Matilda's half-brother had changed sides? Were they in agreement or at odds over the king? And what was his true purpose in coming to the manor? A small shiver of fear ran down her back at the thought that he might be running into a trap. Hastily, she consoled herself with the notion that Robert of Babestoche must have his mind on more urgent matters than affairs of state, like the birth of his new son and the health of his wife.

The crowd in the alehouse was thinning now as, refreshment taken, people went outside once more to bargain, buy or sell. Janna heard the bells ring out, and counted them: one, two, three. It was time for her to change her market tokens into good silver, and go.

On the way home, preoccupied as she was with questions about Hugh, and the more pressing matter of her father's identity, Janna almost walked past the mill, but, recalling her errand of the morning, she turned aside and went to the door to collect the bag of flour promised her by the miller's wife. Hilde was not there, but the miller was, and he smiled a welcome as he noticed his visitor. Stockily built, he had the fair hair and beard typical of Saxon men. Some women might find him irresistible, Janna thought, as she noted his cocky demeanor, but for herself she'd rather keep company with Godric—or even Hugh! The thought of the handsome stranger brought a rosy blush to her cheek. Hastily, Janna tried to compose herself. "I...I have come for the bag of flour promised me by Mistress Hilde," she said.

The miller stood by the door, unmoving. His smile grew broader.

"I left the usual crock of honey and some ointment for Mistress Hilde in return for the flour." Janna waited, wondering why he did not answer.

He made no move to fetch the flour, but instead let his gaze roam over Janna's body. "I believe I hold the toil of my labor more dearly than my wife does," he said at last, and stepped closer. "However, I am sure we can come to an arrangement agreeable to both of us." Before Janna had time to move, his hand was at her breast. He stroked her shrinking flesh through the fabric of her kirtle.

"No!" Janna backed away, crossing her arms over her chest to protect herself.

The miller laughed softly. "You are still a maid, are you not? It is time for you to grow up, Johanna; more than time. I am willing to teach you what it means to be a woman."

"Save your instruction for your wife!" Janna said tartly, and backed off further. "Just give me the flour and I'll trouble you no more."

"I told you—I want something more than honey in return for my labor. Something much, much sweeter."

"You'll have my silence—and your wife's good humor—in return for not tormenting me further."

The miller glowered at her. Feeling more confident, she stared back defiantly. With a scowl, he turned and walked away. Janna lingered by the door, savoring her victory. As the miller returned with the sack, she held out her hands to receive it. The weight of it dragged down her arms, leaving her defenseless as the miller suddenly pulled her close and kissed her hard on the lips.

With a cry of outrage, Janna jerked up her knee. The miller's face darkened with anger as he doubled over in pain. Janna swung around, ready to run. She found Hilde waddling toward her, grim-faced, holding her hands over her belly as if to protect her unborn child.

Janna tried to find the words to explain the scene that Hilde must surely have witnessed, but she had no chance to say anything for the woman shouldered her aside with an oath and stormed into the mill, hurling a torrent of abuse at her husband as she did so.

Janna was sorry that Hilde now had further proof of her husband's nature, yet she was also relieved that the woman had arrived in time to prevent the miller from chasing after her to vent his anger, and also his lust. She was a maid, yes, and determined to remain so until someone far more worthy than the miller captured her heart and, along with it, her body.

With a wry grimace, she hoisted the heavy bag of flour onto her shoulder and set off once more along the path for home.

Chapter 5

Once home, Janna kept busy with chores while she waited for her mother. She dug up some precious carrots and turnips for their dinner and fed the tops to the grateful goats, along with a handful of dock, dandelion and other weeds hastily gathered from the forest's edge. Seeing the tansy and lavender she'd picked that morning still lying on the table, she strewed the aromatic herbs over the floor rushes. Their fragrance scented the smoky room, adding to the rich smell of the vegetable stew she'd set to bubble in a pot over the fire. Janna had already used some of the new flour to make two flat breadcakes on the griddle, and now she ladled some of the vegetables onto one of them, too hungry to wait any longer for Eadgyth. Alfred mewed, and batted her with his paw. She put some of her dinner down onto the rushes for him, and he ate it hungrily.

Why was her mother so late returning? Janna yawned, and wondered if she should go to her bed. Yet she knew she'd be too restless to sleep. Curiosity would keep her awake until she finally found out the truth about her father.

She sat down in her mother's chair beside the fire. Alfred jumped up and turned in a circle. He dug his claws into her kirtle and kneaded her lap, purring loudly as he made himself comfortable.

Janna stared into the flickering flames and pondered her mother's surprising admission. She felt deeply angry that Eadgyth had bought her silence with a lie designed to shut her mouth. Her father might still be alive! Who was he? A common laborer who had moved on, perhaps impelled on his journey by news of her mother's pregnancy? Or did he still live in Berford or Babestoche, or even Wiltune, with a wife and children of his own? Janna sifted through all the men she knew, peasant, merchant and laborer, rejecting each one almost as soon as his face came into her mind. She would surely have sensed a bond when they met, or intercepted a special look between her mother and father when they thought no-one was watching. Besides, if he was a local man, Eadgyth would know for sure whether or not he lived.

He must be someone from her mother's past, from a life lived somewhere else. Either that, or her father had moved on rather than deal with the fact of her birth. Would she want to acknowledge someone like that, someone so cowardly that he would leave a maiden—either wed or unwed—to face her ordeal alone?

No, she would not! Neither would her mother—and yet Eadgyth had confessed that she loved him still. What could have gone so wrong between them that he'd abandoned them?

Janna's thoughts were interrupted by the faint drumming of hooves. As she listened, the sounds became louder. A horse from the manor house, bringing her mother home? She tipped Alfred off her lap, then unhooked the pot of vegetables and laid it aside in readiness.

The cat's back arched and its black fur stood on end as it faced the door. "Scaredy-cat!" Janna scoffed. The sound of hoof beats died. A loud knock thundered against the door. Not her mother then. Janna knew a moment's alarm. Surely not Fulk! Could it be Godric? No, he wouldn't come on horseback. Just like her, like most of the villeins, he wouldn't know how to ride a horse. She hurried to the door and opened it.

A man stood outside, solidly built and clad in the garb of a servant. Janna's first instinct was to close the door on him, but he jammed a foot against it. "I am sent to fetch you, mistress," he said. "You must come at once." Janna's heart plummeted as she noticed the compassion in his eyes.

"What has happened?" Instinctively, she took a step backward, as if to distance herself from what was to come.

"Your mother is taken so ill she is like to die. Dame Alice hopes that you might yet be able to save her." Without waiting for her reply, he turned and hastened toward his mount.

"But...how? What is amiss with my mother?" Dazed and confused, Janna stared after him.

"I know not." He did not check his stride, nor did he turn to look at her. Thrown off-balance, too upset even to close the door behind her, Janna scurried after him. Before she had time to protest, the man put his hands around her waist and swung her high onto the horse's back, then vaulted up in front of her. "Hold on." He dug his heels into the horse's flanks and the beast took off across the downs in the direction of Babestoche.

Janna had never been on horseback before. Excitement and terror overrode her modesty. She'd landed astride the horse but she had no time to cover her legs with her kirtle, no time for anything but to throw her arms around the stranger, lean close and hold on for her life.

Her mother so ill she was like to die? Eadgyth had seemed perfectly well when Janna had said goodbye to her. She couldn't believe it, yet the proof was in this race across the downs. Silently, Janna berated herself for not taking the time to select some healing herbs, but how could she know what to bring when she didn't even know what was amiss? Would she have the skill, the ability to save her mother? Janna closed her eyes as she recalled their argument. Yes, she had a knowledge of herbs and how to make up medicaments, but unless her mother was still lucid enough to speak, she would not be able to tell what was wrong, nor would she know how to treat the malady. Yet who else was there to help, if she could not? Perhaps she should have questioned the servant more closely, rather than allowing herself to be swept up by the urgency of his message. The knot of anxiety tightened in Janna's stomach. "Hurry, hurry," she whispered in time to the horse's galloping hooves. "Hurry, hurry!"

They pelted on through the night until they came at last to the gatehouse of Babestoche Manor. The gate was already open and the horse galloped through, not breaking its stride. Janna caught a brief glimpse of the gatekeeper standing by as they rushed past.

The manor house loomed large before them. Made of stone, it was the biggest house Janna had ever seen. She had only a confused impression of bulky darkness below and a faint gleam of candlelight shining through window slits high above, before the servant reined in and dismounted. Without ceremony, he reached up to Janna and swung her down. Trembling, she stared about her.

"Come." He set off at a fast pace across the courtyard, and Janna hastened after him. He bypassed the door that seemed to lead into the manor house, and instead raced up a stone staircase outside the building. Janna followed close on his heels, her heart thumping with fear.

The servant stopped abruptly, and hammered on a door. It was flung open and there, standing dark against the light of the torches behind him, stood the handsome stranger from the marketplace. Surprise flared in his eyes as he recognized Janna, but his face quickly creased into lines of concern. "You must be Johanna," he said gravely, dismissing the servant with a flick of his fingers. "I am Hugh fitz Ranulph. Please come with me."

Janna hardly had time to make her obeisance before he turned and strode quickly through a long hall with a high, beamed ceiling. A fire blazed in a huge fireplace, shedding a soft, dancing light on stone walls and the decorative tapestries that partially covered them. Flaming torches, slotted into sconces, added a glow to the rich colors of the hunting scenes woven across the walls, but Janna was too preoccupied to do more than glance at them. She followed her guide through the hall and into a smaller room screened off by a leather curtain at the far end.

"Please wait here," Hugh said. He pushed aside the heavy curtain and disappeared from view. "Alice?" he called. Janna heard a murmured reply then Hugh's head poked out. "Come," he said, and vanished again. Janna hastened to obey.

A woman lay upon the large bed that dominated the bedchamber, her figure partially obscured by a number of people gathered around her.

"Mother!" Janna sprang forward without thinking, only to freeze in embarrassment as she realized the reclining figure was a stranger to her.

"Here is Johanna, my lady, as you requested." Hugh's deep voice made the introduction. The figure on the bed raised a feeble arm. Just as Janna was debating whether or not she was supposed to kiss the lady's hand, Dame Alice made a dismissive gesture.

"Your mother is through there." She indicated a small alcove off the bedchamber. "Pray do what you may for her, and quickly, for I have great need of her services."

Dread settled on Janna's heart. She rushed into the alcove, taking in the situation with one agonized glance. With a half-stifled sob, she fell to her knees. She didn't need to be told that Eadgyth was dead. She'd read it instantly in the blueness of her mother's lips and the absence of light in her eyes. Fighting grief, she placed her hand on her mother's chest, willing the heart to pulse beneath her fingers. She forced herself to concentrate so that she could mark off time to the rhythm of her mother's heartbeat—but there was no movement, no indication of life. Janna bent her head close to Eadgyth's mouth, listening for a breath, for anything that might give her hope. The silence, the waiting, seemed to stretch into eternity.

"Mother!" Desperate now, Janna grasped her mother's arm and shook her hard. There was no response. Janna noted that her arm was limp, her body still quite warm, not yet stiffening into death. She had arrived too late, but only just. Bitterly, Janna reproached herself for not insisting that she accompany her mother on the long journey to the manor house. If she had seen with her own eyes what had gone amiss, perhaps she might have been able to prevent her death.

Dry-eyed, numb with grief, Janna raised her head and looked about her. The smell of vomit assailed her nostrils. Now she noticed traces of foul matter down the front of her mother's kirtle. Beside the straw pallet lay a basin of stained water and a cloth. Someone, then, had cared enough to wash her mother's face, and try to help. Janna glanced around, catching the gaze of a young woman standing beside Dame Alice's bed. The girl's face was deathly pale. She looked strained and ill at ease. She knows, Janna thought. She knows my mother is dead. The girl colored a delicate pink under Janna's gaze. She turned away and murmured something to the man at her side. Janna bobbed a hasty curtsy as he cast an appraising glance over her. "Pray see to the *wortwyf*, Master Fulk," he said curtly.

"Of course, my lord Robert. Right away." Fulk had been bending over Dame Alice, encouraging her to sup a little broth, but now he straightened obediently and came into the alcove. He peered over Janna's shoulder to look at Eadgyth.

"The *wortwyf* is dead," he confirmed, and turned to Janna. "I am sorry for your loss." His face was tight and cold, yet there was a gleam of triumph in his eyes. With a cursory nod, he swaggered back to Dame Alice's bedside and picked up the bowl of broth.

Cold fury seized Janna. Only last night her mother had saved Fulk's skin, and his reputation. Now, when she was most in need, his concern was all for his wealthy patron. "You claim to have such great knowledge of the art of healing, Master Fulk," she snapped, springing to her feet to face him. "Surely you could have done something to help my mother, to save her life!" Her voice choked on the last word.

Fulk made no reply. He turned his back on Janna and lifted a spoon of broth to Dame Alice's mouth. She pinched her lips together and turned her head away. Fulk hesitated, then put the bowl down and, instead, picked up the lady's hand and felt the pulse at her wrist.

"You might pretend you don't care about my mother, but last night you were so desperate for help you offered to make her a partner in your shop!" Janna hissed.

"The girl is hysterical. Ignore her." He gave Dame Alice's hand a reassuring pat.

"Tell me what happened to my mother! How did she die?"

"I expect she took one of her own foul potions." Fulk carefully rested his patient's hand on the fine linen bed sheet. "It is lucky for you, my lady, that I came in time," he told Dame Alice. "You, too, might have suffered the same fate but for my intervention."

"Don't be absurd!" Dame Alice raised herself up against the bolster and beckoned Janna forward. "I am sorry that you did not get here in time to save your mother," she said. Her voice was high; she sounded somewhat peevish as she continued, "Eadgyth spoke highly of you. I had hoped you might be able to help her."

Janna was less than flattered by the implied compliment. She was beginning to understand that Dame Alice had an entirely selfish reason for summoning her so urgently. "Fulk was here!" she retorted. "Why didn't you ask him to save my mother?"

"Keep a civil tongue in your head, girl," Robert warned. "I bade Master Fulk leave his practice in Wiltune to tend my wife; I didn't ask for your mother." He clicked his fingers, beckoning one of Dame Alice's attendants to his side. It was the young woman Janna had noticed earlier. She stepped forward and stood with bowed head before him. "Ask the steward to arrange for a litter to carry the *wortwyf* down to the church at Berford."

The girl bobbed her head and hastened from the bedchamber.

Robert walked back to his wife's bedside and bent to kiss her cheek. "Try not to upset yourself, Alice," he murmured. "For the sake of our child, you must stay calm and recover your health."

Unsure what she was supposed to do, Janna sent a glance of appeal at Hugh.

He moved to her side and took her arm. "Johanna has had a bad shock. Small wonder that she's upset. Why don't I take her to the kitchen for a hot posset?"

"But I need to—" Janna cast a glance at her mother's still form lying on the pallet in the alcove. Before she went anywhere, she wanted to say goodbye and ask her mother for forgiveness. Even more important, she wanted to be sure that her mother's body would be treated with the respect she deserved.

"Come." Hugh's firm grip shifted Janna from the room, propelling her through the solar and out into the hall. Feeling his grip slacken slightly, Janna jerked free and faced him.

"If Master Fulk was anywhere near as good as he pretends to be, he could have—"

"You'll achieve naught by accusing the apothecary of neg-
lect," he cut across her protest. "Your mother died a hard
death. I doubt anyone could have saved her."

"But that—that quack didn't even try, did he?" Janna
steeled herself, knowing she could not rest until she heard
the worst.

Hugh shrugged apologetically. "I know not what
happened before I arrived, but I heard that your mother
poured scorn on Fulk and his treatments on her return after
noon. It seems he insisted that Dame Alice drink an infusion
of his own making, but your mother threw it out. They had
a fierce argument about it. Of course, as soon as Fulk heard
that your mother was taken ill he lost no time in returning
to the bedchamber and putting it about that your mother had
brought this illness on herself and that she was not to be trusted. He has his good name to salvage, Johanna, you must
understand that."

Yet Dame Alice had quickly put Fulk in his place when he'd
tried to suggest that Eadgyth's potion might have killed her.
Janna took some comfort from that, but knew that she must
also use her own persuasion to counteract Fulk's accusations.

"My mother was always careful with her mixtures, sire,"
she said. "I have never known her make a mistake, not ever.
Besides, if the mistake lay in my mother's potion, it would be
Dame Alice lying dead now, not—" Janna swallowed hard,
unable to finish her sentence.

"What you say makes sense. It may be that you speak the
truth of the matter."

"Then what happened to my mother? She was perfectly
well when I last saw her. There must be a reason for...for..."

"I'm sorry, Johanna, I really don't know. All I can tell
you is what I saw toward the end, after Jeanne, one of my
aunt's tiring women, came in search of Fulk and Robert. I
was with Robert at the time and I accompanied him to Alice's

bedchamber, for I am her kinsman and so have great concern for her wellbeing. It is fortunate I was present, for Robert fell into such distress that I thought he might lose his senses altogether. His face blanched of all color; he trembled as if with the ague and I feared he might collapse. We thought his wife was beyond all care, you see. It took some moments before we realized that, in fact, it was your mother who was taken ill. Dame Alice insisted that a groom be sent to fetch you. Robert stayed to reassure and comfort her, while Cecily looked after your mother. She gave her water and washed her clean, but alas, nothing seemed to help."

"And Master Fulk? What did he do?"

"He sent Jeanne to the kitchen for one of his possets. Really, he did his best to help your mother."

Janna made a rude noise at the back of her throat, knowing that Fulk's best wasn't worth a dirty straw. She looked up at Hugh and struggled to put her suspicions into words. "Did my mother say anything of what ailed her before she died?" she asked, hoping for some sort of clue. She didn't believe for one moment that Eadgyth had been affected by one of her own mixtures, yet something unexpected had caused her mother to die so quickly and in such distress.

"Let us ask Cecily. She may have spoken to your mother while she tended her," Hugh said, as the young tiring woman entered the hall in company with the steward she had been sent to fetch. He beckoned her forward; she stopped dead momentarily before approaching them slowly. Janna plaited her fingers together and squeezed them hard as she struggled to keep her emotions under control. She could not give in to grief, not yet. She needed all her wits to find out the truth of her mother's death, and all her courage to get through it.

"My lord?" Cecily bobbed a knee in front of Hugh and waited, her eyes cast down in humble submission. Full of gratitude and forgetting her place, Janna took the young woman's hands in her own.

"Thank you, mistress," she said. "Thank you for taking the time to ease my mother's passing."

Cecily nodded, not speaking. Janna noted that she was much younger than the other attendants. In fact, Cecily looked no more than a year or so older than Janna herself. She had delicate features, set in a heart-shaped face, which was framed by a cloud of dark hair. For all that she must be highborn to be a tiring woman to Dame Alice, she seemed as miserable as a wet cat. Janna wondered what was troubling her.

"Can you tell us, did the healer say anything before she died, Cecily?" Hugh asked the question before Janna could, and she was glad of it, for surely the girl would respect him and so would answer truthfully. Janna felt a rush of warmth toward him as she realized he had called her mother a healer, acknowledging her true worth.

Cecily stole a quick glance at Janna, then looked down. "Mistress Eadgyth complained of feeling cold," she whispered. "She said her lips felt numb. She could barely speak or swallow. It was hard to hear her, and to understand her words, but she said your name, Johanna. She called also for a monk, I suppose to give her absolution before she died."

A monk? Janna frowned, utterly rejecting the notion. If her mother had known she was dying, if she'd wanted absolution, she would have called for the priest. Even that seemed unlikely, given her mother's reaction to the priest when, at the first—at the *only* service they had attended after the new church opened at Berford, she had turned her back on him and walked out, dragging Janna behind her.

"Thank you, Cecily."

The tiring woman bobbed a curtsy and hastened back to the bedchamber. Hugh shot a glance of concern at Janna.

"Come." He put his hand under her arm and propelled her down the stairs and out into the night. The dark shapes of other buildings spread out before them under the star-filled sky. Janna hardly had time to wonder as to their purpose before Hugh hurried her on and into a small stone building set close to one side of the timbered palisade that enclosed the manor.

Two great fires heated the room to an almost unbearable temperature. The cook's sleeves were pushed up to her elbows; her face was red, dripping with perspiration. She was rolling pastry, pressing it down with hard, determined thumps of the rolling pin. Rich scents flavored the air: fresh bread, and the smell of stew from a cooking pot hanging over one of the fires. A joint of beef was being turned on a spit by a scullion who crouched beside the second fire, sweating heavily as he labored. In spite of her distress, Janna's mouth began to water.

The cook paused, as did two maids and a young boy who was busy washing vegetables. They all stood to attention as Hugh came forward, gently pushing Janna ahead of him.

"This is Johanna, daughter of Mistress Eadgyth, the *wortwyf* and healer," he introduced her. "Treat her kindly, for she's had a great shock. Her mother has died most suddenly and unexpectedly. Give her a hot drink and find her a pallet and somewhere to sleep tonight." To Janna he said, "You shouldn't be alone. Stay here and I'll escort you home in the morning. You'll also need to make burial arrangements with the priest in Berford, but I can help you with that."

Janna didn't know why he was being so kind, but was grateful for his understanding and care. "Thank you, sire," she whispered, and bobbed a curtsy. He nodded to her and left the kitchen.

At once everyone relaxed. But they did not resume work. Instead they crowded around, staring at Janna as if she'd come down to them from the moon and riding on a broomstick.

"Don't think you can come in here and start telling me what to do like your mother did." The cook was the first to speak. She smeared huge floured hands down her stained apron in a vain effort to clean them, then stuck them on her hips. "Giving me all manner of strange berries and roots and ordering me around in my own kitchen. 'Boil this, soak that,' as if she was Lady Muck of the Manor herself."

"In truth, I do believe the *wortwyf*'s mixtures helped Dame Alice," one of the kitchen maids ventured timidly.

The cook flashed a glare in her direction. "Not according to Master Fulk! Now there's a gentleman. We were in absolute agreement over what was needed to help my lady. In fact, he paid me many compliments on my preparations." She shot a triumphant glance at Janna. "Master Fulk threw out your mother's vile potions and 'tis just as well he did, seeing as the woman has now died by her own hand." She shook a fat finger under Janna's nose. "You'll not brew any concoctions in my kitchen while you're here," she warned. "I'll be watching you."

Janna drew in a breath, almost too indignant to speak. "I'll not stay here to be watched," she retaliated. "My mother was quite well when she left home this morning. Who is to say it's not something from *your* kitchen that has poisoned her!"

The words were out before she'd thought them through. Poison! Yet Janna knew instinctively that she'd spoken the truth. Her mother must have been poisoned; there was no other explanation for her sudden and untimely death.

The cook's face flushed dark red. She drew herself up, large bosom heaving so hard it seemed she might burst through the fabric of her kirtle. "How dare you!" she spluttered. "I keep a fine kitchen and a fine table. My lady has told me so herself." She picked up a twiggy besom and gave Janna a hard poke in the chest. "Get out of my kitchen! I'll not stand here to be insulted by an ill-bred brat like you!"

Janna retreated. The cook kept coming, jabbing the besom at her until she turned and fled out into the quiet night. Once outside, her steps slowed. She breathed deeply, trying to settle her agitated spirits. Where was the gate? She looked at the bulky shapes of the buildings around her, trying to make sense of them, to remember the way in. From the smell, Janna judged that some of the buildings must be used to house pigs and other animals. She spied the gatehouse, and hurried toward it. To her relief, the gate was still open, while the gate-keeper was nowhere in sight. She scurried outside. Not for anything would she stay at the manor through the night. She was exhausted, shattered by grief, as she started the long walk home, her path lit by the rising moon. Questions tormented her. Who and what had killed her mother? How had she come to die such a hard death? Janna drew a shuddering breath. Now was not the time to give in to sorrow. She must be strong. She must concentrate, ask questions, find answers. She would not rest until she had found out the truth.

Eadgyth would never poison herself, not even by accident. Someone must have given her poison; someone must be responsible for what had happened. Someone who held a grudge—like the apothecary, whose position at the manor had been threatened by her mother's greater knowledge and expert treatment of her patient. Or Aldith, who must know that women—even Dame Alice herself—would rather seek help from clever, knowledgable Eadgyth than an ignorant village midwife.

Perhaps she should talk to Cecily again. She'd seemed anxious. Perhaps there was something she did not want to say in front of Hugh? Janna resolved to win her confidence and find out all she knew. She must also question the cook, who had run her out of the kitchen in spite of Hugh's instructions to take care of her. Why? Did the cook have something to hide?

No-one would believe her if she spoke her suspicions out loud; she must find proof before she could accuse anyone. So she would ask questions, and find out what she could. And she would not stop until she had discovered the truth, along with the evidence she would need to bring to justice whoever was responsible for her mother's death.

It was a solemn vow, one that Janna knew she must keep if ever she was to know peace of mind again.

Chapter 6

The journey that had flown by on the back of a horse was long and frightening on foot. Spooked by shadows and plagued by dark suspicion, Janna was shaken and sick at heart. As she came to the cottage she'd shared with her mother, she was surprised to find the door open. She remembered, then, her hasty departure. She walked into the cottage, half-expecting to find her mother stirring something over the fire, or perhaps drowsing in her fine chair. Grief shook Janna anew as she surveyed the empty room. She felt especially wretched as she recalled their argument.

She'd never been so angry, so outspoken before. Through her childhood she'd trusted and respected her mother's wisdom and her skills with herbs and healing, and had been keen to learn all she could. It was only lately that she'd begun to feel constricted, to suspect that she could do more with her life, for there was so much of the world outside their cot for her to learn about and see. Now, when it was too late to explain how she felt, or to make amends, she must live forever with the knowledge that she and Eadgyth had not parted on friendly terms. It was too late to apologize, and beg forgiveness. Worse, it was too late now to learn the secrets of her mother's past and her father's identity.

Hot tears welled in Janna's eyes and spilled down her cheeks. She dashed them away, but they continued to fall until at last she crumpled into the large chair and buried her head in a cushion to smother her sobs. Even though there was no-one around to hear her, she needed to hide the sounds of her own distress from herself. If only she could stifle her cries and pretend that all was as it should be, then perhaps life might continue as it had always done. The truth of her situation was much too huge and frightening to think about.

Janna cried until there were no tears left to shed. She had never, ever, felt as lonely as she did now. There was no-one she could talk to, no-one to whom she could turn for help. Finally, exhausted, she blew her nose and mopped her sore eyes one last time. Then she stood up, knowing that she could postpone the future no longer. She would have to face it, no matter how bleak. One day at a time.

But a day seemed too long and too hard; even an hour was too much of a trial.

Moment by moment then, at least for now.

Janna took up the tinder box and produced a spark from flint and steel, to ignite the kindling and start the fire again. Light and warmth seemed a good way to begin the rest of her life. Her task accomplished, she glanced around the room, seeking Alfred. The cat was nowhere to be seen. She was surprised he hadn't already come to greet her.

Janna remembered her hasty flight, the open door. He would have escaped outside, delighting in the opportunity to go hunting at night. Janna felt a cold frisson at the thought that, in turn, the cat might find himself hunted. They always kept him shut in at night for that very reason. But Alfred was a survivor, just like the king after whom he'd been named. She went to the door. "Alfred!" she called.

She listened intently, but there was no answering miaow.

"Alfred! Tssss-sss-sss-sss."

Silence, broken by the lonely hoot of an owl. Janna comforted herself with the thought that, like the owl, Alfred would be busy chasing field mice and voles and other small creatures, and stuffing his belly full of wild food. She looked into the silent forest, its silvered treetops, its dark and secret depths. Soon enough a new day would dawn, marking the beginning of her new life. Briefly, passionately, Janna wished that she could turn back time. She would rather face the boar without Godric than face the future alone.

She called the cat again, searching the inky blackness for a gleam of silky fur. Through the noises of the forest she strained to catch any sound of the cat's presence.

The crunch of leaves made her heart quicken.

"Alfred!"

"Janna!"

For one wild moment Janna wondered if the cat had answered her, until reason told her that even if Alfred could talk, he wouldn't have answered with Godric's voice.

"Godric?"

He came out of the darkness. "I'm so sorry to bring you bad news, Janna. Your mother has been taken ill up at the manor."

"Oh, Godric!" She stretched out her hand to him, then hurriedly snatched it back as she recalled their parting words. It was not fair to encourage Godric to believe he had a chance with her. "News travels fast, it seems," she said warily.

"You already know about your mother's illness?"

"I've been to Babestoche and back tonight."

Godric looked surprised. "My informant told me that your mother has been poisoned by one of her own potions," he said awkwardly. "But I've told him he is mistaken."

"Of course he is!"

"But you have the knowledge and skill to aid her recovery, I am sure of it."

"My mother is beyond help, Godric. She is dead." Janna's throat ached with the pain of saying it.

Godric drew in a quick breath of surprise. "I am so sorry, Janna. I am so sorry." Not giving her time to retreat, he threw his arms around her and held her tight. Secure in his embrace, Janna began to cry once more.

"Shh. It's all right, everything's going to be all right," he soothed. "You mustn't worry about anything, Janna. I am here, and I'll do all in my power to help you."

Even with Godric's help, Janna knew that nothing would ever be all right again. She broke free and wiped her eyes.

"You've seen your mother? You are certain there's no hope?"

She nodded, unable to speak.

"But this is so sudden! Was she ailing?"

"No. I believe she was—" Janna stopped abruptly. Should she tell Godric of her suspicions? No, she thought, remembering the vow she'd made to herself. She would trust no-one until she could prove the truth of her words.

"She was...?" Godric prompted.

"...quite well when she left to go to the manor house. You're right. Her death was very sudden."

Godric stood back so that he could study Janna more closely. Then he walked into the cottage and fanned the fire into brightness. Once set, he added pieces of wood to keep it burning high. He filled a pot with water from a bucket, and hung it over the fire to boil. Then he looked through the few provisions set on a shelf close by. "You need a hot drink and something to eat," he said, and held up the leftover griddle cake.

Janna picked up a jar and pushed it forward. Godric inspected the contents, then pulled out his knife and spread the cake with a paste of honey and crushed hazelnuts.

"Eat," he commanded.

She gave Godric a shaky smile as she took the cake from him. She took a bite and chewed, relishing its sweetness.

He smiled back at her, and settled down on a stool beside the fire, sneaking glances at Janna as she ate. A soft rustle sat him bolt upright, straining his ears to listen.

"What is it?" Janna's voice was indistinct through a mouthful of cake.

"I heard a noise outside."

"My cat?" Janna jumped up and went to the door. She peered out into the dark night. "Alfred?" she called.

Godric stood up and looked over her shoulder. "Fluffy!" he bellowed.

Janna was surprised into laughter. "He won't come if you insult him like that," she said. They stayed by the door, looking out into the faint light of early dawn. All was silent and still. There was no sign of the big black cat. Finally, Janna shrugged and sat down again. "There are always noises in the forest at night." She took a large bite from her cake, and began to chew once more.

Not satisfied, Godric ventured a few paces outside, searching for movement, for the source of the sound. But there was nothing to see and nothing to hear. He waited a few moments, then came back in and closed the door behind him.

"A squirrel, a deer. It could be anything," Janna said, still chewing.

Godric nodded, and settled down beside the fire once more. Janna stuffed the last of the griddle cake into her mouth. Too late, she wondered if Godric might also be hungry. There were only crumbs left now to offer him. She licked her sticky fingers, then jumped up to attend to the pot of water steaming over the fire. She picked up the dipper and scooped water into two mugs, flavoring the hot drinks with crushed herbs and a spoonful of honey for sweetness.

Godric cleared his throat beside her. "Janna," he said, and took hold of her hand. "I came to escort you to the manor house to see your mother. I'm so sorry I arrived too late. Now that I know your mother is gone, I'm worried about you. You are so far from help, should you need it. We don't know each other very well, but I wonder if you'd consider—"

"Please don't ask me to be your wife!" Janna snatched her hand away. "I don't want to marry you, Godric."

The surprise on Godric's face was quickly masked by a guarded expression that told Janna she'd hurt him.

"I don't want to marry anyone—not yet, anyway," she added hastily.

"I wasn't going to offer marriage," Godric retorted. "This is certainly not the time for such a question. But it seems, from what you say, that I would be foolish even to consider such a thing." There was a rough edge to his voice. Janna deeply regretted her thoughtless outburst. Eadgyth always said that her quick tongue would get her into trouble, and she was forever being proved right! But Eadgyth would never say such a thing to her again, Janna remembered. Utterly cast down, hardly knowing what to say to redeem the situation, she studied her boots intently.

Godric broke the silence. "I was actually going to suggest that you come and stay with my mother and me for a while. For your own safety."

"Oh." Janna couldn't look at him for shame and embarrassment. "This is my home," she mumbled. "This is where I wish to stay."

"Then I'll trouble you no further." Godric's earlier warmth was gone, replaced by a cool courtesy. He set down his mug, stood up and moved to the door.

"Thank you for your offer, Godric. I'm sorry if I—"

"I thought we were friends, Janna. After last night and tonight, I hoped that one day we might become something more.

A fool's dream, I see that now. I shall not trouble you again." He walked out of the cottage and slammed the door behind him.

Godric had every right to be annoyed. Janna remembered how she had clung to him for comfort, and how tenderly he had held her. She wished now that she had gone with him. But she didn't want to give him false hope, nor did she want to be beholden to him and his mother. She didn't want to be beholden to anyone. Even though it was frightening to face the world on her own, she knew she would have to get used to it. Only hours before she had longed for freedom, yet now it had come to her, and so unexpectedly, she shrank from it. She lay down on the straw pallet and pulled the covers over her head. If only she could sleep a little, perhaps things would look better in the morning. This thought was followed by a desperate wish that she might wake to find out that this was just a bad dream.

She closed her eyes. Tears began to flow once more. She sniffed and tried to wipe them away, but they continued to flow until, at last, she fell into a troubled sleep.

Chapter 7

The sun was already up when Janna awoke. A beam of light slanted through the window slit, brightening the room and warming her face. Joyously, she sprang from her bed to greet the day.

Memory struck her with the force of a body blow. She crumpled back onto the straw pallet, holding her stomach and gasping with the pain of it. Not for one moment would she accept that her mother had been poisoned by one of her own potions. So who could have given the poison to her, and why did her mother not recognize it for what it was? Surely she would have known the truth when she was dying. Why did she not speak out?

Perhaps she did! Janna tried to recall Cecily's words. Eadgyth had complained of feeling cold. Numb. She'd had difficulty speaking, but had called for a monk. Why?

Cold. Numb. Janna searched her memory for her mother's instructions on the herbs she used, particularly her warnings about poisonous plants. Hemlock was one. It caused paralysis and loss of sight, but Cecily hadn't said anything about her mother going blind.

Deadly nightshade? Her mother sometimes ground the tiniest portion of the plant into a powder to relieve a toothache.

Janna knew there'd been no call for such a remedy recently, so it was unlikely that she'd had it to hand—but others might. The plant was common enough, and most people would know that it could be dangerous. If too much was ingested, rapid breathing was followed by convulsions and death. Not nightshade then. Cecily hadn't mentioned anything about panting or fits. She'd said her mother had complained of feeling cold. Numb. And she was vomiting. Cecily had said she could barely speak, but it seemed she'd stayed conscious until the end.

The spice merchant's face flickered into Janna's mind. Why was he important? He'd had a whole selection of herbs and spices on display, some of them exotic substances she'd never seen before, but which were on sale to any who could afford them. Could her mother have been poisoned by something like that up at the manor house; something unfamiliar and therefore dangerous?

The only substance the spice merchant had warned about was his rubbing oil. Aconite was common enough. Prized for its pretty blue flowers, it grew in gardens everywhere. Most people would know its poisonous properties, although they would be more likely to call the plant by its common name: wolfsbane or monkshood.

Monkshood! It caused numbness of the face and tongue, making speech difficult. It also caused nausea and severe pain, leading to death. Eadgyth hadn't called for a monk at all. She was trying to tell someone she'd been poisoned!

Anguish jerked Janna upright, and she cried out as she recalled how she'd gone into the forest, how she'd been so afraid of the boar that she'd grabbed at the strawberries and stuffed them into her purse. Had she been so hasty that she'd also pulled off bits of the poisonous plants growing alongside them, not noticing what she was doing in the darkness of the night? Her mother might well have eaten the fruits that were left over from the potion, not knowing that she was also swallowing bits of the monkshood that grew close by.

In her mind, Janna had accused everyone but herself. Now, she was faced with the knowledge that she alone was responsible for her mother's death. Time and again Eadgyth had warned her of the need to be careful; warned her that she should never underestimate the power of the herbs they used. Now her mother had died as a result of her carelessness.

Janna didn't know how it was possible to feel so much pain and fear, and still be able to breathe. She jumped up from the pallet and rushed over to the shelf that held Eadgyth's medicaments. Her hands shook as she began a desperate search for any sign of the strawberries or the potion that may have contained them.

A new horror forced itself into Janna's consciousness. Her mother's important visitor! Had she also taken poison along with the strawberry mixture? Was she also lying dead somewhere?

Janna almost dropped jars and dishes in her haste to open stoppers and sniff the contents. Some she tasted before setting them aside to continue her search. Her heart gave a sudden lurch as she spied a rough earthenware dish pushed toward the back of the shelf. It contained several small, ripe strawberries. Janna inspected them carefully. Their bruised and torn flesh bore testimony to the haste in which they'd been collected and bundled into her purse. Yet they were quite clean, sitting in a small puddle of water that indicated they'd been washed.

Relief swept over her, leaving her feeling dizzy. She sagged onto a stool, blinking back tears of gratitude. Her mother had washed the strawberries before using them. Of course she had! How many times had Janna witnessed that very act, the careful washing of all roots, leaves, flowers, seeds, fruits and nuts she'd gathered. Her mother had always insisted on it.

Nothing took away from the fact that her mother had been poisoned, though, and not by anything unfamiliar either. Monkshood! Why had her mother not recognized its taste after the first mouthful, and taken steps to protect herself?

Janna poured a beaker of ale to break her fast. The first mouthful reminded her of the ale she'd supped at the alehouse, and how she'd wondered why it tasted slightly different from their own. What if that ale had contained poison and she knew not how ale should taste? She might well have drunk it down and died as a result. Was that what had happened to her mother: that the taste of the poison had been masked by something else? Janna sniffed the ale, then took a cautious sip. It smelled the same, and tasted as it always did. She quickly slaked her thirst and ate the remaining strawberries. Feeling somewhat more composed, she raked her fingers through her long hair to tidy it, then walked to the door and opened it.

"Alfred!" she called, expecting to find the cat waiting for her, miaowing and hungry. There was no sign of him, so Janna stepped outside to look around. "Alfred!" she bellowed, startling a woodlark. Its sweet trilling ended abruptly, replaced by the fluttering of wings as it flew away.

A glimpse of something hanging from a tree in the distance caught her eye. The dark shape shifted and changed as she watched. For a moment she stared at it, not fully comprehending what she was seeing. As her brain finally made sense of the image, she let out a long, ragged cry and began to run.

Alfred was tied to the tree, the cord looped around the tree trunk several times so that he was stretched out as if crucified. His limbs were stiff, and his fur was stained with blood. A swarm of flies buzzed around him, grouping and regrouping as they searched for wounds to feed on. Frantic, Janna brushed them away.

She saw that Alfred's throat had been cut. He must have died sometime during the night. She began to shiver. Her teeth chattered as she forced herself to touch her pet. The cat's fur was matted and sticky. The flies she'd disturbed buzzed around her in a thick black cloud and then settled once more on Alfred's body. Looking down, Janna saw that she'd stepped into a puddle of blood that lay directly beneath the dead animal. Her thoughts splintered into fragments of grief as she tried to come to terms with Alfred's fate.

It seemed clear that he had been killed right here, next to the tree, and then strung up straight away. She looked at the smudged footprints around the dark red puddle congealing underneath the cat's body. Her own, or did some of them belong to whoever was responsible for Alfred's death?

Janna examined them carefully; the prints of her own small boots were superimposed on prints made by other, larger boots. Whose? It was impossible to tell. Staining a patch of leaves nearby was another splatter of dark red blood. Head bent, Janna traversed the ground in a widening semicircle around the cat, searching for signs of disturbance. The path to their cottage bore the faint marks of boots: hers and her mother's, and probably their visitors too: the groom from Babestoche Manor, Fulk and Godric.

She looked back to where she'd found the cat, some twenty paces away. Had the killer first cut Alfred's throat, and then looked for a tree from which to hang the dead body so that it would be the first thing Janna saw when she walked out of the cottage? Suddenly anxious, Janna swung around to scan the forest in case the killer was still lurking somewhere nearby. She could hear only the churring of turtle doves as they puffed and preened in the warmth of the sun.

Dry-mouthed, trying not to panic, Janna hurried back to Alfred and began to wrestle with the tight knot around his neck. As she tugged and pulled at it, tears ran down her face. She was crying for the kitten with the will to live, who had struggled so hard to survive. The cat would have had no chance against a man with a knife in his hand, and hatred in his heart. Who could have done such a thing? Who could have anything to gain from Alfred's death?

Godric! The thought was sudden and shocking, and Janna immediately tried to push it out of her mind. It would not go away. Yet she couldn't believe it, didn't want to believe it. Could he really be so cruel? Surely it wasn't possible! Yet the evidence hung before her, grisly and gory and only too real. Who else could have done such a thing, if not Godric? He had visited her in the night, had held her tight and offered help and comfort. And instead of being grateful, she'd flung his kindness back in his face and made it quite clear that she wouldn't consider him for a husband.

Had he taken out his anger on Alfred? Janna remembered how he'd nudged the animal aside with his boot, and how he'd slit the boar's throat without even blinking. Perhaps, like the villagers, he believed Alfred was the devil and that it would be wise to kill him. Tears almost blinded Janna as she tugged and pulled at the knots binding her cat, but a new thought filled her with a scalding anger. With such an act, did Godric think to frighten her out of the cottage and into his arms? She would rather scratch out his eyes! How could he have done such a thing to a defenseless animal? She would never forgive him—never!

Unable to vent her anger on Godric, she fought with the knot instead, until finally she managed to untie Alfred and bring him down from the tree. She laid the body carefully on the ground and went off to fetch a spade to dig a grave.

When she returned, a sudden thought made her pause: Should she save the body as evidence, in case she could call down justice on Godric's head? She leaned on the spade while she reasoned it out. To whom could she report this crime? Godric's liege lord would not punish him for the killing, not if it came down to Godric's word against her own. The villagers certainly wouldn't support her; she was an outcast, and they thought the cat was the devil. No doubt they would agree with Godric that it was better dead than alive. No, it seemed to Janna that if she wanted justice, both for the death of her mother and for Alfred, she would have to find it in her own way.

Starting with Alfred. She didn't need his body to challenge Godric. He would know what she was talking about—and she would make him suffer in every way she could. She began to dig, attacking the earth with angry jabs as she thought of how she might make Godric pay for what he had done.

She had cried all the tears she could cry. Now she felt achingly empty and sad. And angry. Her anger added iron to her backbone and gave her the strength to do what had to be done. She rubbed her cheek against Alfred's soft fur, then tenderly laid him down into the hole she had dug. The cat stared up at her, his wide eyes clouded now by death. Janna leaned down and gently closed them. She stroked Alfred's black fur one last time, then covered him over with damp, dark earth. As a last gesture, she gathered up some late bluebells and red poppies to brighten the grave. So, too, would she find something to place on the grave of her mother.

Her mother! Janna straightened hastily and scanned the sky, noticing the sun's position. By now her mother's body would be lying in the church, probably unguarded and certainly unmourned. Janna knew it was up to her to see that her mother was washed, anointed and prepared for burial with the proper rites. Although she shrank from the task, it was her duty. But first and foremost, she wanted to keep vigil beside her mother's body, to ask for her forgiveness, and to pray for God's grace to go with her mother on this, her final journey. She ran inside to wash her dirty hands then snatched up a basket into which she placed leaves of soapwort and a jar of oil scented with roses, and hurried outside again.

Her mother's livelihood had come from the herbs and flowers that she cherished, so it was only fitting she have some on her grave for her last journey. Janna made a careful selection: poppies and creamy purple pansies for consolation and loving thoughts; they would also provide a splash of bright color to mark her mother's final resting place. And last, a healthy sprig of rosemary to mark forever what was in her heart. Regretting that she hadn't left earlier, Janna set off at a run through the fields toward the village.

Although the sun was shining just as it had the day before, this time she could take no comfort from its warmth. Everything seemed black, full of shadows; her heart was full of anger and despair. She hurried on, not pausing to draw breath or ease the pain in her side, until she came at last to the small stone church in the center of Berford. She raced inside, pausing only to cross herself before looking about.

There was no sign of her mother's body. As Janna bent over, trying to catch her breath and ease the stabbing pain in her side, the light from the open door was blocked by the batwing form of the priest. He advanced on her.

"Johanna," he said. His narrow face was closed and hostile. Janna instinctively recoiled. "Your mother's body lies outside, beyond the pale. You must go outside the churchyard walls if you wish to say your last farewells to her."

"Beyond the pale?" Janna could hardly speak for horror.

"I cannot bury your mother in consecrated ground. You remember, I am sure, what happened the last time you and your mother came to church."

Yes, Janna remembered only too well. The trouble with the priest had started as soon as he was appointed to the new church at Berford. She and her mother had attended his first service. Before the church was built, a preaching cross had served as a place of worship as well as being a focus for the exchange of news and gossip. An old priest had come regularly from Wiltune to hold a mass in the open air. Gentle and mild, he had welcomed them all and had happily absolved them from sin and given them his blessing every month. But at the new priest's first service, he had gazed around his small congregation, taking their measure. It seemed he had taken the trouble to find out about his parishioners, for his gaze lingered longest on Eadgyth.

His knowledge of the nature of his flock became certain when he began to address them from the pulpit. It was a long rant against the dangers of breaking God's commandments, and it seemed to be aimed directly at Eadgyth. Janna's mother had kneeled on the hard stone flagging, listening as the priest warned his flock about those who lived outside God's laws, which he then itemized. Small choking sounds told Janna how her mother regarded the priest's rules, especially when it came to the servitude of women and their absolute subjugation to their husbands' will. But it was on his injunction that the villagers must bend always to the will of God and not question it that Eadgyth had come to the end of her patience.

"Surely God gave us a brain in the expectation we would use it," she hissed under her breath to Janna. "After all, He gave us the capacity to choose right or wrong, and to acquire and use knowledge for the benefit of mankind. If God wanted us to wait around for him to fix everything, we'd have been called 'beetles', not 'humans.'"

"Shh." Janna agreed with Eadgyth, but she wished her mother would just let it go for now.

Eadgyth frowned at her. "Don't tell me you agree with what he's saying? I brought you up to have a mind of your own, Janna. I taught you to question everything."

"Shh!" Others now turned on Eadgyth, annoyed that her sibilant whispers were interrupting their devotions. Janna felt embarrassed. The trouble with her mother was that she never let anything lie until she'd argued her own point of view, but now was not the time or place for it.

"...and if God should cast affliction on us, we must be like Job and bear our troubles with patience and courage, and with prayer." It seemed almost as if the priest had heard Eadgyth's protests, for he fixed her with a gimlet stare as he continued: "There are some who would set themselves above God, who believe they have the power of life and death over others. There are some who will even do the devil's work, breaking God's laws to carry out their foul deeds. To you, I say, beware, for God is watching and great will be your fall. On the Day of Judgment, when sinners are called to—"

"I've had enough of this." Eadgyth grabbed Janna's arm. "Come!" To Janna's intense embarrassment, her mother pulled her to her feet and marched her down the aisle and out of the church. A tense silence had marked their passage, but Janna heard the priest's voice raised in exhortation once they exited.

"You don't need to go to church when God's great cathedral is all around you, Janna," her mother had said once they reached their cottage. She'd pointed then at the bright flowers in their garden, the dancing butterflies and furry bumblebees, and the green forest beyond. "I follow God's law in my own way. I certainly do not need the priest to tell me how to behave, and what I may or may not believe."

Hearing her mother's voice in her mind brought tears to Janna's eyes. Determined not to give in to grief in front of the priest, she blinked them back.

"Your mother didn't believe in Christ and she didn't come to church. And I know there were times when she broke God's law," he said now, as he grasped Janna's arm and led her outside. She suspected that he was referring to the abortifacients Eadgyth sometimes administered to the desperate women who came to her. She kept silent, knowing that in truth there was no defense against most of his accusations.

"She was a sinner, a heretic, and I will not allow her to lie in my church, nor will I bury her in consecrated ground." The priest turned from Janna, indicating that their conversation was over.

"That's not true! She believed in God." Outraged, Janna stood her ground, silently damning him to the hell he was wishing upon her mother.

"She condemned herself out of her own mouth. Indeed, they were almost the last words she spoke to me."

"When did you see her? When did you speak to her?"

"When I asked to hear her confession before she was admitted into Dame Alice's bedchamber."

"You were up at the manor yesterday?"

"Indeed I was. I'd been told of my lady's troubles, and I was ready to administer the last rites should I have cause to do so. It was only fitting that your mother should be in a state of grace before being allowed into the presence of Dame Alice."

"If my mother said her confession to you, why do you deny her burial now?"

"She did not make her confession. Instead, she told me to get out of her way for she had more important matters to attend."

"Like saving Dame Alice's life!" Janna was having difficulty reining in her temper. Only the importance of changing the priest's mind stopped her from shouting at him.

"Nothing is more important than communion with God."

"I am sure my mother would have made her confession if time had allowed it." Janna wasn't sure of any such thing, but she had to fight on her mother's behalf. Not to be buried in consecrated ground would leave her mother condemned by everyone. And if people condemned her mother, they would surely condemn Janna herself.

"She would not!" the priest contradicted sharply. "She told me to take my blessings and prayers elsewhere, for Dame Alice had no need of them."

"By that, surely she meant that she believed she could make the lady well again." Janna hated pleading with the priest, but she had no choice.

To her surprise, he smiled at her, baring the brown stumps of his teeth. "I bid you good morrow, sire," he said.

Realizing the smile was not for her, Janna swung around to find Hugh advancing toward them, leading his destrier. His voice was full of concern as he asked, "Why did you run from the manor? I meant to escort you here today, but they told me you left last night and they haven't seen you since."

I'll wager they didn't tell you why I left. Janna wasn't prepared to enlighten him either. She bobbed a curtsy to him, and said, "I thank you for your care of me last night, sire, but my place was at home, not up at the manor."

Hugh studied her for a moment, then turned to the priest. "I have been especially charged by Dame Alice to see about the burial arrangements for Mistress Eadgyth. Where have you laid her body?"

The priest looked down at his toes. "I was just informing Johanna that her mother lies outside the churchyard, beyond the pale. She will be buried forthwith."

"What?" Hugh sounded incredulous. "Mistress Eadgyth's death was an accident! The healer did not knowingly take her own life."

Hugh's words confirmed that he, too, believed that her mother had been poisoned—and by one of her own concoctions. Before Janna had time to protest, the priest began to defend his decision.

"If the lady died by her own hand it is suicide, and suicide is a sin against God. Even if her death was an accident, as you claim, she died unshriven. She did not come to church. In fact, almost her last words to me were that she had no time for God."

"She said no such thing!" Janna wouldn't be silenced a moment longer. "She was in a hurry to see Dame Alice, you told me so yourself."

"She was in a hurry to go about her devilish practices," the priest said darkly. "I have spoken time and again from the pulpit, warning my flock of the dangers of submitting to ancient beliefs about *aelfshot*, and the conviction that diseases may be cured by magic and leechcraft. My flock now repent the error of their ways. They know that they must bend to God's will and seek Christ's blessing on the ills that befall them. Only your mother continued to defy me, brewing her potions and communing with that black cat to summon the dead."

"She sought merely to heal, to bring comfort and relief!" Janna could hardly speak for rage.

"She took the power of life and death upon her shoulders." The priest glowered at Janna, silencing her.

Hugh's expression was grave as he turned to the priest. "Let me remind you of Dame Alice's wishes in this matter, and add my own plea for Mistress Eadgyth. No matter what you may believe, the herbwife was a good woman and as such I ask you to give her the benefit of your Christian charity, to relent and accord her a decent, Christian burial."

"Never." The priest drew himself up to his full height, which took him as far as Hugh's shoulder. "A Christian burial for that woman would contradict everything against which I have warned my flock. Besides which, it would be an abomination in the sight of God." His glance at Janna was both spiteful and triumphant. "You must hurry if you want to see your mother, for her burial will take place shortly."

'No! I have not had time to prepare her."

'You have come too late."

Janna seethed with the injustice of the priest's judgment. She turned to Hugh, hoping for his help, but the quick shake of his head made her realize that further argument was futile.

With a muttered exclamation, she pushed past the two men and ran through the churchyard. The warmth of the sun fell on her face like a blessing, but Janna was unaware of it, could hardly see for the tears streaming down her cheeks as she hurried past the graves with their rough stone markers, and out through an archway in the stone wall. A shrouded bundle lay in the wasteland beyond. It was a weedy, unkempt piece of ground which housed the unmarked graves of felons and those poor itinerants who had died without kin to identify them, and was littered with rubbish strewn by idle and uncaring passersby.

The grave had already been dug, a gaping hole that looked like a greedy mouth waiting to be fed. Eadgyth lay beside it, wrapped in a roughly woven cloth. Janna fell to her knees and gently removed part of the wrapping so that she might see her mother one last time. It seemed important to say goodbye and ask for forgiveness.

Eadgyth's face was calm in repose. Janna kissed the tips of her fingers then put them to her mother's lips. "I'm sorry I was angry with you," she whispered. "Forgive me." She gazed down as a lifetime of memories crowded into her mind. Her mother had raised her, and had taken the trouble to pass on her knowledge of herbal lore and leechcraft even if she hadn't allowed Janna to practice it. But she was not given to praise, nor to demonstrative acts of affection. Janna couldn't remember ever being kissed or comforted by her mother, not even as a child. Perhaps, she thought now, Eadgyth's ability to show love had died when Janna's father had abandoned them? Now, her mother's hard and lonely life was over, and she would take her secrets with her into the grave.

With bitter regret for all that had come between them, Janna took one last look at Eadgyth, noticing again the traces of vomit on her kirtle and cheeks. Could her mother have taken, by mistake, some of the aconite mixed with oil that she made up as a rubbing lotion? It hardly seemed possible, particularly as her mother only made it fresh when it was needed and always threw out whatever remained, rather than risk keeping such a deadly poison close to her other preparations.

Janna tried to still her fears with the memory of her search earlier. She'd checked all the jars and had noticed nothing untoward, certainly nothing that resembled the rubbing lotion. The poison must have come from outside, and in a form unknown to her mother, for she would never have taken it willingly. Lost in thought, Janna carefully draped the russet cover over Eadgyth's face once more. "Goodbye," she whispered, and rose to her feet.

She was startled to find that she was no longer alone. Hugh was standing some distance away, watching her. As she caught his glance, he approached her. She gave her eyes a hasty scrub with the back of her hands, and faced him.

"I've done all I can to change the priest's mind," he said. "I even offered him payment, but it seems to have become a matter of principle with him that he will not allow your mother to lie in consecrated ground. I'm so sorry, Johanna."

Janna nodded sadly. "He's been preaching against us ever since he first arrived here. He knows he will lose face among the villagers if he gives her a burial with all the rites."

"Was your mother not a Christian, then?"

Janna hesitated, wanting him to be on her side against the priest, wanting him to be sympathetic to her cause. Yet she didn't want to lie to him either. "My mother believed in God, who created our world and who watches over us," she said at last. "She believed that true goodness lies in how we live our lives, and that was how she lived her life—because she believed that healing the sick was God's work, and a good thing to do. She told me she followed God's law, not the priest's. She disagreed with what he said about women, and she hated the way he told the villagers that anyone who questioned what he said would go straight to hell. The priest spoke against my mother's healing powers and her skill with herbs, calling it the devil's work. The villagers listen to him and some of them stopped coming to my mother when they were ill and in need of help. She was very angry about that. She blamed the priest for making the villagers suffer needlessly, when she could have given them relief."

Hugh nodded in understanding. "I know that she saved my aunt's life, for Dame Alice told me herself how your mother helped her when the apothecary could do nothing more." He tapped the purse hanging from his belt. Janna heard the jingling clink of coins. "Dame Alice gave me silver to give to the priest for your mother's burial. As he has proved so uncooperative, I will also make arrangements for the bishop to say a mass for your mother at the abbey. It's the best I can do."

"And I thank you from my heart, sire. Please also give my thanks to Dame Alice." No matter how hostile the priest was to her mother, Janna knew that he would still expect payment for her burial. It was kind of Dame Alice to relieve her of that burden. Now, she struggled to find the words that might yet save her mother's soul.

"Please, tell the bishop there was never anyone so good as my mother. She helped so many people with her healing skills; she saved their lives. She did not deserve to die, nor does she deserve to lie out here in the wasteland. My mother will go to heaven, for certes, and I hope the priest may rot in hell for his deeds this day!" She turned away, gulping down sobs as she fought to regain composure.

"I will speak to the abbess about the priest," he said firmly. "And I will make sure your mother has a mass said for the repose of her soul." He looked at her with kindness. "God keep you, Johanna," he said, and stepped back to join the priest and a small group of villagers who had now gathered nearby.

Janna's glance swept over them. Her face hardened when she saw Godric. He was standing a little apart from them all. She turned abruptly so that she would not have to look at him. With head held high, she waited for the priest to approach the grave, and the funeral rites to commence.

The priest beckoned Godric forward. Aghast, Janna watched as he carefully lowered her mother's body into the gaping hole and then bent to pick up a spade. She was filled with rage and contempt. Not content with trying to frighten her into his arms, he was now going to earn a penny or two as a gravedigger. She had once thought him honorable, kind and brave. How could she have been so completely wrong?

It seemed to Janna that there was no more desolate sound in all the world than the scrape of the shovel and the soft thump of falling earth as slowly, so slowly, the cloth-wrapped body of her mother began to disappear from view. Her throat ached from unshed tears. "I will seek out the truth. I will make sure that justice is done." She whispered the vow as Godric dropped another shovelful of dark earth into the hole. In spite of her good intentions, her eye was drawn to the sun-burned skin of his neck, the knotted muscles of his arms as he drove the spade once more into the earth piled beside the grave. Anxious for distraction, she glanced around the assembled villagers, curious as to why they had come. Mistress Hilde, the miller's wife, stood among them, looking sullen and resentful. As she caught Janna's gaze, she gave her a vicious glare. The woman really seemed to hate her. Could she truly believe that Janna was a threat to her happiness?

Torold, the blacksmith, and his three children had also come to witness the burial. He was paying no attention to the grave; instead, he was staring at Janna, his eyes hot and hungry. Uneasy, she shrank into herself, knowing she no longer had her mother's protection from unwanted suitors—anyone could come calling. And if they wouldn't go away there was nothing she could do about it, for she was but a young woman, no match in strength for any man determined to have his way with her. The village was too far away from the cottage for her to run for help; it was too far for anyone to hear her cries.

Janna was appalled as she came to a full understanding of her predicament, and how vulnerable she now was. Godric had understood. He had offered protection, and she had refused it, had flung his offer back in his face. But it was too late to unsay the hasty words that had led to such a shocking outcome. After what Godric had done she wanted nothing more to do with him. He was beyond her forgiveness.

Torold was smiling at her now. Leering at her. Janna hastily looked away, but not before she caught him licking his lips. Her glance fell on the village midwife. Mistress Aldith had no reason to be here; in fact, she had every reason to rejoice in her rival's death. Eadgyth had made no secret of her contempt for the incompetence of the village midwife. She had certainly taken away some of the midwife's business. Had Aldith come to make sure Eadgyth was truly dead and safely interred? Janna watched the woman for a moment, searching her face for any show of triumph or pleasure, but the midwife continued to contemplate the earth steadily piling up in the grave, her expression serious. Perhaps, like so many mourners at these times, she was not thinking of the recently deceased but contemplating instead how brief and fleeting was life on earth, and how long a death awaited them all.

Next to the midwife stood Hugh, with a lady by his side. Cecily. Her small face was pale. Was she clinging to Hugh's arm for comfort, or to show possession? Janna felt an unexpected pang of disappointment at the thought of Hugh being already attached and out of reach.

He'll always be out of my reach! Janna knew she would do well to remember it. Yet he had been kind to her and she valued that, while acknowledging it was a kindness he might have shown to anyone, even a stray dog. She eyed Hugh and the tiring woman thoughtfully, and came to the conclusion that he supported the lady from necessity. She seemed ill, and in some distress. What was she doing here? Why had they both come to witness this sorry scene? Janna could not pride herself that Hugh had stayed on for her sake. It was his commission from Dame Alice to ensure that her mother was properly interred. And Cecily? It must be kindness that had brought her to the graveside, the same kindness that had prompted her to wash Eadgyth's face and try to ease her dying moments.

Janna became aware of silence. She looked from Godric, red-faced and sweating after his exertions, to the newly dug patch of dark, damp earth. Her mother was covered from sight now. She was truly gone.

Cold misery shuddered through Janna, but she tilted her chin, defying the motley collection at the graveside. She did not want their pity, she wanted acknowledgment of her mother's true worth. "*Requiescat in pace*," she prayed quietly, and waited for the priest to echo her words, to commend her mother's soul to God so that she might rest in peace. Surely he could not refuse her this small comfort? But the priest remained silent.

His silence goaded Janna to action. She had meant her ritual to be private, but his petty meanness spurred her to make a public farewell to her mother, to show them all that she honored her mother's life—and death. She stepped forward, holding the bright flowers that now seemed inappropriate for this sad, rubbish-strewn wilderness. She laid them carefully at the place where she judged her mother's heart to be. Then she straightened and held aloft the rosemary so that all might see what she carried.

"This is rosemary, for remembrance," she called, her voice sounding high and clear above the quiet murmurings of the assembled gathering. She knelt down and carefully inserted the plant into the soft, damp earth. She pushed the stem in deeper and patted the earth firm around it to keep it secure, so that it might take root and grow, and mark forever the site of her mother's last resting place.

The assembly had fallen silent, waiting to hear what she might say next. Janna rose from her knees and faced them. Willing her voice not to tremble, she said, "With this rosemary, I pledge to remember my mother, just as all of you who knew her will remember her for her healing ways, and for the aid and comfort she has given you over the years." It was a command, not a wish. Janna hoped they recognized the difference. She took a deep breath.

"My mother's death was an accident." She looked directly at the priest, daring him to contradict her. Wisely, he kept silent. Janna wished that she knew more, so that she could tell them the truth of what had really happened, and still their wagging tongues forever. But it was too soon; she didn't know enough yet. She looked down at the rosemary on her mother's grave. This was her pledge to herself: to find out the truth, and bring whoever was responsible for her mother's death to justice.

She had one last thing to say. She gave herself a moment to marshal her thoughts. "Here, under the open sky, I commend my mother's spirit to God, for I know that she believed in Him and in His great mercy. I know also that she will rest peacefully out here in His green garden. My mother always told me that God was everywhere around us, and I would rather she rest out here in open space, and in the sunlight of His love, than be confined within the demesne of a mean and narrow spirit." Janna's last words were addressed to the priest, her intent unmistakable.

"How dare you show so little respect!" His eyes bulging with fury, the priest stormed away in the direction of the churchyard gate. Seeing that the priest was leaving, the villagers hastily crossed themselves and set off after him. Torold lingered momentarily, perhaps hoping to press his claim.

"Go away!" Janna tried to keep the fear from showing in her face. He hesitated, took a look at Godric and hurried off, dragging his children behind him. He was followed by Hugh and Cecily. Janna was left alone to face Godric across her mother's grave.

"I suppose you were paid well for your toil this morning." Her voice was sharp with contempt.

Shocked, Godric took a step backward, recoiling as if her words had been a physical blow. "Janna, I thought it would be some small comfort to you if I dug...if I..." Unable to spell out his intentions, he stuttered into silence.

She faced him down. "I don't want your comfort, Godric. Not after your deeds last night!"

"But...but..." Now his face showed only bewilderment. "But my offer was kindly meant, Janna. And my mother would have welcomed you, I am sure."

"I'm not talking about that!"

"What then? I don't understand."

"You crucified my cat!" Janna could not stem the rushing torrent of anger as she relived the horror of finding her pet's dead body. "You cut its throat and strung it up on a tree, knowing I would find it hanging there in the morning. My cat. A poor, defenseless creature that never did anyone any harm! How could you do that, Godric? How could you?"

"In truth, Janna, I don't know what you're talking about."

"Don't try to pretend you are innocent of this crime! I found Alfred's dead body this morning. You warned me about him, and when you left my cottage in anger just before dawn, I suppose you thought killing him would be a good way to punish me for not bending to your will."

"This is dreadful news, Janna, but I know nothing—"

"Of course you do! Who else would do such a thing if not you?"

"Janna, I swear to you on your mother's grave that I—"

"Don't you dare swear on my mother's grave. You are not worthy even to speak of her!" Janna drew a sharp, agonized breath. "And I never want to speak to you again, either. Go away, Godric. Stay out of my life. I hate you for what you've done." She whirled around and set off toward the arched doorway in the stone wall of the churchyard, walking with fast, determined steps.

It was over, all over. She'd never felt so alone, so miserable. She wanted to throw back her head and howl like a dog. Instead, she scratched up the tattered remnants of her courage, and marched steadily on.

Chapter 8

"I would speak with you, Janna." The hissed whisper startled Janna. She stopped, wondering who had addressed her.

Aldith stepped out from behind a clump of bushes at the side of the church and put her hand on Janna's arm to draw her behind the bushy screen. Curiosity prompted Janna to follow her.

"What do you want with me?"

"What are your plans for the future?" the midwife asked in turn.

Janna blinked. She had no plans. There'd been no time to think of the future, no time to think beyond trying to fathom the mystery of her mother's death.

"I had great respect for your mother's knowledge," the midwife continued, perhaps hoping to ingratiate herself. As Janna stayed silent, she continued. "I know you helped your mother prepare her herbal potions. You must have learned a great deal?"

Janna dipped her head in acknowledgment, wondering where this was leading. The midwife sighed.

"Your mother was a proud woman, and arrogant with it. She put me in the wrong whenever she could for I have only a midwife's knowledge, whereas she seemed to know almost as much as any skilled physician!"

As Janna sucked in a sharp breath, ready to spring to her mother's defense, the midwife continued, "My business is birthing babies, and Eadgyth had knowledge of herbs and healing practices that would have helped the mothers and babies in my care. When I asked if she would teach me, she said only that I should wash more often and keep myself clean. In fact, she brushed me off as if I was no more than a fly come to irritate her." An old resentment soured the midwife's voice. "I hope you have not inherited your mother's arrogance, Janna. I'm asking you to share your knowledge with me, just as I am prepared to share my experience with you. I'm hoping that perhaps we may work together in the future?"

"But..." Janna struggled to find the words to defend her mother. "But..." She remembered the impatience and contempt her mother had shown both Fulk and the priest, and the way she had spoken of the midwife. Could there be some justice in Aldith's accusation?

"I suppose Fulk will make much of helping Dame Alice with the birth of her child," Aldith observed. "But I suspect they'll be calling for my services soon enough—once they've discovered for themselves his ignorance of women's troubles."

"It was my mother who saved the lady and her child—not that weasel!" Janna said hotly.

The midwife nodded in agreement. "I believe you, but 'that weasel' is doing all in his power to take the credit, while laying blame on your mother for trying to poison Dame Alice."

"My mother would never poison anyone!"

"I believe you," Aldith said again. "And I'm sure that, whatever the cause of her death, it was not by her hand."

Hearing Aldith's words, Janna could have wept with relief. Here, at last, was vindication for her mother.

"But that will not stop Fulk from telling everyone what he would like them to think," the midwife continued. "Be careful, Janna. No man cares to be seen as a fool. He was a danger to your mother while she was alive; he may yet be a danger to you."

Fulk! He was top of her list of suspects. It was a comfort to have her suspicions echoed by the midwife.

"I advise you to stay in your cottage for a few days, keep well away from him," Aldith continued. "He'll be returning to his shop in Wiltune soon enough. With his new exalted opinion of himself, he may even move on to Winchestre to ply his trade!"

Janna's lips twitched to hear her mother's opinion of the apothecary repeated by the midwife. Curiosity prompted her to ask, "And once Fulk is out of the way, what then would you have me do?"

"Become my assistant," Aldith answered promptly. "I'm aware that you lack experience so there is much I can teach you, just as I believe that your mother will have taught you much that I do not know. We can learn from each other."

Janna hesitated, tempted by Aldith's offer. It seemed far more genuine than Fulk's offer to her mother, and its benefits were manifest. Under Aldith's protection she would find a place and acceptance in the community, as well as gaining the experience she needed. Yet Aldith had been Eadgyth's rival, and was about to reap the benefits of her death. While her offer might be kindly meant, Janna cautioned herself to stay on guard. Aldith was not off her list of suspects yet.

Aldith was waiting for her answer. Undecided, Janna wondered what her mother would have advised her to do. She looked down at the midwife's apron. It was clean and freshly laundered for the occasion, but the kirtle underneath was somewhat grubby and stained. There was her answer—or was it? If Eadgyth had only bothered to explain, the midwife would have understood why cleanliness was so necessary for the health of mothers and their babies. Aldith seemed more than willing to learn—and so was Janna. If sharing their knowledge would benefit the villagers, her offer was surely worth consideration. About to say yes, a further thought stopped Janna. If she accepted, it would tie her to this place just as surely as she'd been tied by her mother and their life here. Was that what she truly wanted?

"It's kind of you to think of me, and I thank you," she said, searching for the words to frame a more gentle refusal than her mother would have done. "Please give me time to think about it, for I know not what the future holds for me. It's too soon to make plans. Who knows, I may even find someone to wed, and move away from here."

It was an attempt to sound light-hearted, but Aldith nodded in immediate understanding. "Eadgyth told me that it was her dearest wish that you would find happiness with a good man."

"Why should my mother wish for me what she never knew herself?"

"I think it's because she wanted to keep you from making the same mistake that she did," Aldith said quietly.

"Did you know my father?" Janna could hardly breathe from excitement.

Reluctantly, Aldith shook her head. "I never met him," she admitted. "I only know the very little your mother confided to me when first she came here, swollen with child and needing somewhere to stay."

"Where did she come from?"

Aldith shrugged. "I don't know. She never said."

"Why did she come here? Did she tell you why she chose this place?"

"She came to see the abbess, I believe. She had little money or jewelry to give in return for shelter, but the abbess did well out of the exchange for the cot you live in was derelict, and the small piece of land beside was not large enough to support a villein and his family. Not only did your mother repair the cot and render that land fruitful, she also paid rent to the abbess in return for that act of charity. Your mother was no beggar, Janna."

"Did she ever speak of her family, or her past? Please, please tell me everything you know," Janna begged.

"I can't tell you much. Your mother and I weren't close, as you know. I gave her shelter while she repaired your cottage, for she had no money to hire a laborer for the task. We exchanged some confidences then, but I think she later regretted even the little she'd told me. And she repaid my kindness by stealing my patients!"

Janna was silenced by the bitterness in Aldith's voice. Her mind teemed with the questions she wanted to ask, questions that Aldith probably couldn't answer. She became aware that Aldith was studying her intently. "You have your father's eyes," she observed.

'How can you know that? I thought you'd never met him."

"I didn't. But your mother was a Saxon beauty with her fair hair and gray eyes. You have your mother's fair hair, but your eyes are dark brown."

"Then I must be ugly. I would rather look like my mother than a father I don't know and who doesn't want to know me!"

"I suspect he doesn't know you even exist."

"Did my mother tell you that?" Janna was worried now that she'd utterly misjudged her father.

"No. From the very little she told me about her circumstances, I gained the impression that your father might be someone wealthy, important. Perhaps too important to wed a woman of no consequence like your mother?"

"Surely, if my father was wealthy, he could have helped my mother live a better, more comfortable life than she did!"

Janna's anger blew like a straw in the wind as it shifted between her mother and her father. She longed to know the true circumstances of her heritage and her birth.

"Perhaps he was already betrothed to another and would not—or could not—break off that alliance?" Aldith suggested. "Your mother may well have decided to leave rather than beg for his help when she discovered she was carrying you!" As she noticed Janna's stricken expression, her voice softened slightly. "Your mother did not hold a grudge against your father, for all of that. In fact, she spoke of him with great love—such a love, I think, that prevented her from taking any other man to her bed thereafter."

Janna nodded slowly as she came to understand the truth behind her mother's lonely life, and her desire for her only daughter to marry and be safe. "My father's name? Did my mother ever tell you it?" she asked.

To her utter disappointment, Aldith shook her head. "Your mother kept her secrets, Janna."

"From me, as well as from you. And now she's dead, I'll never know the truth about my father." Janna felt her throat clog thick with tears. With a huge effort, she struggled to stay dry-eyed and calm.

She took Aldith's hand. "I am grateful to you, more grateful than I can say."

"Think over my offer." Aldith pressed Janna's hand between her own. Janna felt ashamed of her mother's past treatment of the midwife, for she believed that the woman was kind, and that she meant to bring comfort. "We'll talk again," Aldith promised, and slipped away.

Head bowed, Janna stayed motionless, thinking over what she'd just learned. Her father was likely highborn, too important to wed her mother. Which meant that by now he would surely have wed someone else, a lady, and he would probably have children of his own. She longed to know more about him. Why had her mother kept his secret, never gone after him, never asked him for anything in spite of the hard times she and Janna had lived through? Pride? Or was it love and the need to protect his good name with his family that had kept her away?

Aldith had told her she had her father's brown eyes. She might have inherited more from him than that, Janna thought, for her fair hair and her skill with herbs were the only characteristics she shared with her mother. As well as resembling her father, did she have his temperament too? What sort of man could he be to inspire such love and devotion in proud Eadgyth, and yet abandon her so completely? Janna frowned, rejecting any part of her own nature that could ever be so brutal.

What would her father say if he knew he had a daughter? Would he welcome her, or was his own family so important to him that he'd deny her and send her away?

Saddened by her thoughts, Janna walked slowly along the narrow street that led through Berford. It seemed to her that several people turned aside as she passed, or ducked into doorways or down lanes rather than meet her face to face. She looked back to check if her suspicion was true, just in time to see a young boy making the sign of a cross with his fingers, as if to ward off evil. Acting on impulse, Janna made the sign back at him. His eyes widened and he scuttled off. Janna looked after him, feeling troubled and angry that the villagers seemed so against her when her mother had always done her best to help them.

The priest and his sermons, and the fact that he would not bury her mother in consecrated ground: that news must be out already. Truly the priest had succeeded in turning her and her mother into outcasts.

Lost in thought as she was, Janna did not at first pay attention to the slender woman in the long green gown walking ahead of her. It was only when the woman glanced behind her, and their gazes met, that Janna saw who it was. Not bound by any notions of maidenly modesty, she picked up her skirt and raced after her.

"Mistress Cecily!" she shouted. "Please wait for me!" There was no reason why a highborn tiring lady should pay any attention to her, Janna understood that, but her need to ask questions was greater than her need to worry about propriety. "I want to ask you about my mother," she called.

The young woman stopped. Slowly, reluctantly, she turned around. Her face was pale, her eyes red-rimmed as if she'd recently been crying. Janna wondered where Hugh had gone, and if the lady was weeping because of him. She quickly banished that disturbing thought from her mind. She needed all her wits to find out what she could from the last person to see her mother alive.

"Forgive me." She bobbed an awkward curtsy. "I called after you because I wanted to thank you again for looking after my mother while she lay dying. I'm trying now to piece together the last hours of her life, so that I may truly understand what happened to her." The tremor in Janna's voice was real, and Cecily responded with sympathy.

"I thought your mother seemed out of sorts once she came into my lady's bedchamber, but I put it down to the fact that there was a heated argument between her and Master Fulk over the best potion to help Dame Alice. Fulk had prepared a posset, you see, but your mother threw it out and told him to leave the room. Fulk appealed to Dame Alice, but she said he should do what he was told. He was very angry with Eadgyth. He blamed her for everything." Cecily cast a timid glance at Janna, then modestly lowered her eyes.

"Did my mother have anything to eat or drink after she arrived at the manor?"

"Dame Alice offered her a beaker of water. I suppose she thought your mother would be hot and thirsty after her long walk."

"That was kind of her." Janna hesitated, wondering how to phrase the question without offending Cecily. "Did my mother say anything about the water? About its taste?"

"No. She thanked Dame Alice, and drank it straight away."

"Could the water have been—" Janna was going to say "poisoned," but stopped in time. "Foul? Polluted in some way?"

"Not at all!" Cecily bristled in indignation. "It was poured from the very jug that Dame Alice herself uses. But your mother became sick soon afterwards."

"Who gave the water to my mother?" Janna had visions of Fulk slipping aconite into the beaker, but then remembered that he'd been banished from the bedchamber.

"I poured the water myself, and brought it to her. She thanked me. She said the water had cooled her. In fact, she soon complained of feeling cold." Cecily still looked indignant. Janna knew she could not press the matter further.

"Did my mother take any food or drink before she saw Dame Alice? Could she and the apothecary perhaps have taken some refreshment together?"

"I doubt it!" Cecily gave a brief snort of laughter at the idea. "There was no love lost between them right from the very beginning. He never wanted your mother to come, it was only that my lady insisted on it." She looked up at Janna, suspicion in her eyes. "Why are you asking me all these questions?"

Janna hesitated. She was being too blunt. "Forgive me. I believe my mother's death was an accident, and I'm trying to find out how it happened. Did she swallow any of the decoctions she prepared for Dame Alice?"

"No."

"So they could not have caused her death?"

"No."

"Yet Dame Alice took them—and they helped to stop the bleeding and they gave her strength?"

"Yes, indeed." Utterly serious now, Cecily faced Janna. "We'd heard of your mother's knowledge and skill in the matter of carrying and birthing babes from one of the kitchen maids. That was why—" She stopped abruptly, pink washing over her pale face.

"That was why…?" Janna prompted, curious to understand why Cecily looked so embarrassed and uncomfortable.

"Why…why Dame Alice sent Master Fulk to fetch your mother." Cecily had hold of her girdle and, with restless fingers, was busily shredding the delicate fibres. Janna wondered at her apparent distress. Before she could question her, Cecily hurried on. "It was my lord Robert who asked Master Fulk to attend my lady. She soon saw that he had even less knowledge than the midwife when it came to…to…and the maid had said—"

"I'm glad my mother was able to help Dame Alice," Janna intervened, taking pity on Cecily's reluctance to speak of womanly matters. "Did she say anything else before she died? Did she give any clue as to what ailed her?"

Cecily hesitated. "I wondered if her wits had gone wandering. She said there were ants in the bedchamber, but there never were!" Indignation sharpened Cecily's tone. It seemed she took the accusation personally. "'Ants,' she said. 'Ants.' Her words were quite clear."

Eadgyth's intention was clear to Janna too. Her mother had told her that symptoms of monkshood poisoning included feeling cold, and also having the unpleasant sensation that ants were crawling over your skin. To be sure, she questioned Cecily again. "You said my mother called for a monk?"

Cecily nodded vigorously. "That is true. I offered to send for the priest but she shook her head most violently. 'Monk,' she said. Even though she could hardly talk by then, she was most insistent about it."

"Are you sure she said monk, not monkshood?"

"You mean the plant with the pretty blue flowers?" Cecily frowned, puzzled. As understanding came, she clasped her fist to her breast in shock. "But...but it's poisonous!" she stammered.

"Yes. Yes, it is." Janna was torn between wanting to clear Eadgyth's reputation and keeping her suspicions a secret until she could prove them. "It was just a silly thought I had. Don't worry about it," she said quickly.

"Your name was on your mother's lips as she died." Cecily seemed anxious to switch to a safer topic. "Johanna." Her voice softened in sympathy. "I am so sorry you came too late to speak to her."

"She called me Johanna?" She was only Johanna when she was in trouble. Eadgyth must have taken the anger of their argument to her death. The thought, piercing as an arrow, was enough to bring Janna to tears.

"Actually, I thought Eadgyth was calling for 'John,' but when I asked one of the tiring women where he might be found, she told me your name. Your real name."

Janna felt sick with misery, sick that her mother had died without forgiving her for their quarrel. "I thank you for your time, for answering my questions." She turned away, too dispirited to ask any more.

A couple of small, grubby children were scooping mud from a puddle in the lane and carefully fashioning it into a castle. They reminded Janna of one last question. "Dame Alice's new babe? How does he?"

Cecily's face crumpled into sadness. "He does very poor. When she first arrived at the manor, your mother bade us wash him and rub him with salt, and then wrap him tight. The cord had been cut to separate him from my lady, but it was not tied and there was a great deal of blood. Your mother took care of that, and took care also to cleanse his mouth and rub his gums with honey. As soon as she was done, the priest came in to Dame Alice to baptize the child in front of his parents. The baby is now in the care of a wet nurse, but he does not thrive. Your mother brought back with her a mixture to stimulate the child and help him suckle, but she fell ill before she could do much more than instruct the nurse as to its use."

Cecily's voice echoed with misery. Janna felt a flash of warmth toward the tiring woman, who seemed so kind and compassionate. She wished Cecily could be her friend, even while acknowledging that the young woman was so far above her in station that this would always be impossible. Yet a friend was what Janna most desperately needed right now.

"Cecily!" Hugh's voice captured Janna's attention. She tried to still a sudden kick of excitement as they turned in his direction. Janna watched him lead the huge black destrier toward them, along with a smaller brown horse on a leading rein. The gleam of appreciation in his eyes was for Cecily, not her. She bobbed a curtsy as his gaze swiveled to encompass her.

"Johanna."

"Sire." She would have spoken her thanks for his presence at her mother's burial, but he forestalled her.

"I understand that grief may have unbridled your tongue, but it was rash of you to speak as you did beside your mother's grave. I fear you have made an enemy of the priest."

Janna flushed, shamed by his reproof, yet she was determined that he should understand her. "The priest is already my enemy," she said. "He made himself so when he refused to bury my mother in consecrated ground."

"Nevertheless, you should not jeopardize your position in the village with public displays of this sort. I understand there has been a lot of hostility directed toward your mother, which might now spill over onto you."

Janna's face darkened with resentment; she had thought Hugh an ally, but it seemed she'd been wrong.

"Don't misunderstand me," he said quickly. "I agree with you that the priest acted outside his duty and showed no charity toward you or your mother, and I have just told him so. I've also warned him that I'll be speaking to the abbess about it. She holds the barony from the king and has the bishop's ear. You must let them deal with this priest together. Meanwhile you should more properly show concern for your own position in the village now that you no longer have your mother to protect you."

"I am of an age to protect myself!"

"Certes you have the temper for it," Hugh retorted, but he smiled as he said the words. Janna blushed anew. Mercifully, he turned his attention to Cecily, who stood silent by Janna's side.

"I asked you to wait for me until my business with the priest was done so that I might escort you back to the manor," he said courteously.

"I...I thought a walk in the fresh air might revive my spirits, sire."

"But you are still ailing. Why do you not rest?" There was sympathy in Hugh's eyes as he surveyed the tiring woman.

"I had long enough to rest yesterday morning." Cecily looked down at her muddy shoes rather than meet his eye.

"Yet you did not rest," Hugh observed drily. "Dame Alice said you were gone from the manor all morning. She's worried about you, particularly as you looked so ill on your return. When she realized you had come out again today, she sent this palfrey to me with a messenger. She has asked me to ride home with you."

"Dame Alice is kind to think of me." Cecily looked stricken. Her face was so white, Janna thought she might swoon.

Hugh led the palfrey to a post nearby. Janna tried to suppress a flash of jealousy as she noticed the care he took while helping Cecily to mount. Did his hand linger unnecessarily on the lady's waist? He held the leading rein all the while, gentling the palfrey so that it would not startle and upset Cecily. Their journey back to the manor would be slow and decorous, utterly unlike the wild ride Janna had shared with the groom. She felt a flash of resentment over the lack of respect shown to her, but knew, had she been given a mount of her own, she would not have been able to ride it. She and the groom had been racing against time. When death awaited there were far more urgent considerations than the chance exposure of a lady's ankle or leg.

A lady! Janna made a disgusted noise in her throat. Truly she was reaching far above herself with these thoughts. All the same, she found it hard to smother a pang of envy as she watched how solicitously Hugh settled the young woman into the saddle.

"God be with you, Johanna," he said, and mounted his own horse. Slowly, they rode away.

Janna stayed still, watching them depart, her head crammed with questions. Cecily's description of her mother's symptoms had dispelled any doubts as to the poison her mother had ingested. Aconite was fast-acting. Janna knew that from what her mother had told her when warning her about the properties of various poisonous plants. So whatever Cecily believed, her mother must have had some refreshment on her arrival at the manor as well as the water she had accepted.

A thought stopped Janna: If her mother had taken only a little of the aconite in something well flavored, there might not have been enough in the taste to warn her, while a tiny amount of poison might take some hours to wreak its damage. If that was so, Eadgyth could have taken the poison even before she arrived at the manor house. Who then might have given it to her?

Janna frowned as she sifted through various possibilities. It was true Eadgyth had exposed Fulk as a charlatan and that he would have access to monkshood, but Janna now knew her mother was treated with suspicion by more people than the apothecary. She would have to cast her net more widely to encompass everyone her mother might have met on that last fateful morning of her life. She would start with her mother's mysterious visitor. Who was she? Certainly not one of the villagers. A lady, her mother had said. Up until yesterday they'd known no-one like that.

Janna stood stock-still, pondering who she might be. The woman visiting her mother had insisted on secrecy. Cecily had just revealed that she knew it was a long walk from their cot to Babestoche Manor, and also that Eadgyth's skill with women's troubles was known to the household. More, it seemed that she'd tried to fool everyone at the manor into thinking she was resting when, in fact, she'd gone out without telling anyone. If Cecily had visited her mother yesterday morning in a desperate attempt to get out of trouble, it could explain why, in return, she'd tried to look after Eadgyth in the last moments of her suffering, and why she'd come out to see her buried today. It would also explain why she looked so distressed and ill.

Janna decided she must find out from Cecily if she, or anyone else, had shared food or a drink with her mother. Someone must know something, and Janna vowed she would not rest until she had discovered it.

She set off to climb the downs toward the forest and home, but a hoarse shout stopped her before she'd taken more than a few steps. Turning, she found herself confronted by the miller's wife. Hilde's face was flushed dark red; her eyes were bright with anger as she waddled up to Janna.

"Whore!" she spat. "Ill-gotten harlot! Taking a man to your bed even while your mother was breathing her last!"

"What?" Janna felt like she had been slapped.

"I suppose you thought you were safe to do as you pleased, with your mother out of the way dispensing her potions and poisons up at the manor?"

"I-I don't know what you're talking about!" Janna didn't know how to defend herself against Hilde's wrath, but she couldn't let the smear against her mother's name go unchallenged. "My mother was working no poison up at the manor. She was helping to save the life of Dame Alice and her newborn son."

"Then how did she come to poison herself at the same time?" Hilde's eyes twinkled bright with malicious glee.

"She did not poison herself. She did not!"

But Hilde was no longer listening. She began to scratch at the rash of sores on her arm, unaware that she was drawing blood. "You leave my husband alone!" she spat. "He told me he was going out to check his eel traps last night and he didn't come home. I know he was with you and I'm warning you, you will join your mother in her grave if he visits you again."

"But…but I haven't seen your husband!" Janna remembered the scene at the mill, the scene the miller's wife had witnessed. "Well, I saw him when I went to fetch the bag of flour, but his actions were none of my doing."

"I don't believe a word of it! I saw you talking to him, leading him on. You invited him to come to you in the night, did you not?"

"No!" Janna was disgusted by the very thought of it. "If he was gone from your bed, mistress, I assure you he was not in mine! You must look elsewhere for someone to blame for his roving ways. Perhaps, indeed, you should ask your husband for an explanation!"

Hilde's hand, bloodied from scratching at her arm, moved down to her bulging stomach. She touched its rounded contours with soft fingers. Janna felt a twinge of pity, until she caught Hilde's expression. Stony and unforgiving, her glance raked over Janna.

"I saw you in his arms. I saw you kiss him!"

"He kissed *me*—and I kicked him in the bollocks in return!" Janna felt sick, poisoned by the woman's suspicion.

Hilde looked momentarily nonplussed. Then she gave a snort of disbelief. "I am warning you, miss. Do not entice my husband to your bed again." She pulled a small knife from the purse at her girdle, and brandished it in Janna's face. The blade glinted bright in the sunlight. "Tempt him again and it'll be your turn to feel how sharp this is!"

Janna blinked. Before she could respond, Hilde had shouldered her aside and lumbered back down the lane. Janna looked after her, shocked and upset by the unexpected confrontation. That the woman was unbalanced was obvious, yet her mother had told her it was not unknown for pregnant women to become unsettled and to take odd fancies. It was certainly true that the miller gave Hilde good cause to worry and fret. She resolved to keep out of Hilde's way in future.

As Janna walked on, she made an effort to dispel her disquiet by thinking back to the conversations she'd had with Aldith, Cecily and Hugh. Aldith had told her something of her father, but nothing that had shed any light on who had killed her mother. True, she had warned Janna about Fulk, but Janna already had her own suspicions about him. Posturing turnip head that he was, even Fulk would know about the poisonous properties of aconite. Everyone knew, although they might call the plant by another name.

Janna considered the midwife's position. She held a grudge against Eadgyth, that much had become clear. She also had much to gain from her death. Could the midwife be as blameless as she appeared? Janna had been so intent on learning what Aldith knew about her father that she'd neglected to question her about her own movements on the day of Eadgyth's death. At the very least, she should find out when Aldith had last seen her mother.

As Janna began to climb the grassy downs, she stared up at the great blue canopy over her head. God's realm, where truth and justice must surely prevail. It was comforting to think that someone watched over her, that someone cared what happened to her. She had a Father in heaven. She might also have a father right here on earth.

It was like an itch that wouldn't go away, this mystery of her father. To know so little was frustrating beyond belief. Yet already she knew far more than she'd ever known before. Why had her mother been so secretive? Because she felt shame? Because she could not bear to talk about the man she loved? Would her mother have honored her promise to tell Janna the truth, or had she learned more from Aldith than her mother might ever have confessed? The questions kept coming, questions without answer. She could not set her thoughts free.

Sad that she'd never been given the chance to know her father, or even to understand her mother, Janna entered her empty, silent home.

There were still vegetables left from the night before, the dinner her mother never came home to eat. Although tempted to throw them out, Janna put them in the pot, then hung it over the fire to heat for her dinner later. They were far too good to give to the goats. Instead, she cut some nettles and brambles from the edge of the forest, and grabbed up a handful of grain for the hens. "Nellie! Gruff!" she called, and the goats bleated and ambled toward her, ready to be milked and fed. The hens came running too. Janna waited until they were all busy eating before she produced an extra morsel for Laet, who always came last in the race for food. "It's a hard life," she told the small, scrawny hen. "You've got to fight if you want to survive." It was advice she herself should heed, she thought, as she trudged back to the cottage to fetch a pail.

The row of bee skeps under their woven covers brought a pang of remorse as Janna recollected how she'd stomped past them before, and had even tried to smack down a passing bee. Now she stopped beside them to make amends. "I need to tell you what's happened."

There was a relief in talking about it, she found. The bees were coming back to the hive; their murmurous buzzing soothed Janna as she poured out her misery. "I've sworn an oath," she confided. "I shall not rest until I find out where the poison came from and I've brought the person responsible to justice."

She needed first to work out who would want her mother dead, and who'd had the opportunity to translate desire into action. If she could fathom that, it should lead her to the identity of the killer. "I'm sure it's Fulk," she told the bees. "He has the knowledge, and I know he hated and resented my mother. I just need to find out if or when he had the chance to act against her. But Cecily hasn't told me all she knows. I shall talk to her again, even threaten her with telling her secret, if necessary." The bees hummed quietly about her. "There's also Aldith," Janna continued. "She'll know about monkshood. I like her, but my mother's death will certainly be to her benefit. I must find out when they last met."

The priest, Janna thought suddenly. He, too, had been at the manor house. He, too, wished her mother ill. Could a priest know such hatred that he would break God's law and kill someone he thought of as evil, even if it was done in the name of Christ? It was a disturbing thought, made more pressing by Janna's sudden memory of the market place in Wiltune. She'd seen the priest swooping about like the carrion crow he was. Had he been listening when the merchant spoke of the healing effects of his rubbing oil? As a priest, he would have an understanding of Latin and so would be able to identify the plant in question. By the end of the merchant's sales pitch, he would also know how dangerous it was. If he could overcome his scruples, he certainly had the knowledge and possibly also the opportunity to act. "I also need to question the priest," she told the bees.

Once inside, after milking the goats, she put the hot vegetables onto a griddle cake, and sat down to eat. There was no Alfred to share her meal this night. Janna felt immensely sad and immensely lonely as she took off her kirtle and lay down on the pallet to sleep. She missed the presence of her mother beside her, and the warm bulk of Alfred at her feet. Tears pricked her eyes, and she gave a forlorn sniffle. Knowing she had a plan for action brought her some comfort, and helped to settle the questions that tumbled endlessly through her mind. Instead of lying awake all night, as she had supposed she would, exhaustion claimed her and she fell into a deep and healing sleep.

Chapter 9

Janna woke late the next morning to find the sun already high in the sky. Her long sleep had refreshed her, so that although she felt lonely as she went about her morning chores, she also saw that this was how things were going to be from now on, and that, in time, she would get used to it.

She found herself humming the tune she'd heard her mother singing, and stopped. For some reason she felt as if it were forbidden, even though Eadgyth was not there to censure her.

She walked outside with an armful of feed for the animals. Their pen was getting somewhat smelly, she noted, as she looked about at the mounds of excrement. She dumped the greens in a corner to entice the goats and hens out of her way then, with a sigh, she took up a spade to shovel the mundungus out and over the garden.

"*Dirt and disease go together*," Eadgyth had said, when Janna had once questioned why their animals were not brought into the cottage at night for safety, as was common practice. "*The fence protects the animals; that is why I made it: to close them in. And their waste can be spread among the plants to help them grow, instead of fouling the rushes on our floor and making us both ill.*" The sound of Eadgyth's voice in her mind brought tears once more. Janna blinked hard, and kept on digging.

Once done, she came back into the cottage and washed her hands. She would have to do the work of two if she wanted to survive. She would need goods to trade for other necessities as well as for some of the foodstuffs that she was unable to provide for herself. Even with her mother by her side, they had often gone hungry. Janna felt a twisting knot of fear in her stomach. She had the coins from her sales at Wiltune market, but there were no lotions or potions left to sell; she would have to create more. In addition, she needed to think about Aldith's offer, although she would not commit herself to anything until she could be sure of the midwife's innocence. And in the meantime she should put the word about that she was able to physic the villagers just as her mother had always done.

It wasn't quite true, and Janna felt a flash of anger toward her mother. Then she shrugged. It was the way it was, and she would just have to make the best of it. She had her mother's knowledge. It was only a matter of time before she gained her experience.

The sound of galloping hooves alerted Janna to a horseman approaching the cottage. She opened the door and stepped out into the sunlight, recognizing the big black destrier and its rider.

"Johanna."

"Sire." She smiled up at Hugh and bobbed a small curtsy. He led a palfrey on a rein behind him, the same palfrey he'd brought for Cecily to ride.

"I am pleased to find you at home," he said, and hurriedly dismounted. "Dame Alice is distraught. The baby has taken a turn for the worse and is like to die at any moment. Robert has sent for the priest, but Alice won't give up the babe, not yet.

She begs you to come with me and do what you may to save him." Even as he spoke, he planted his hands around Janna's waist, ready to hoist her on to the palfrey's back.

Janna panicked. "I-I can't…I don't know how to ride," she stammered.

"I should have thought of that." Hugh kept his hand on Janna's waist as he pulled the destrier to him. "You can ride with me." Before Janna had time to protest, he hoisted her up. She landed awkwardly, her legs straddling the beast's back.

She felt a flash of resentment that she had no say in the matter, that in spite of all the tasks she must do to ensure her survival, she was expected instantly to abandon them and do as she was bid. Her protest was silenced by the urgency of Hugh's message.

"What ails the infant?" she asked instead, trying all the while to pull down her kirtle. Once again it had bunched up over her knees. She was aware of Hugh's appreciative glance at her legs as she tried in vain to cover them. In spite of the gravity of the situation, Hugh's eyes twinkled as he watched her endeavors.

"I know not. Dame Alice trusted your mother's knowledge, and hopes that she has taught you enough to save the child." He quickly tied the palfrey to a nearby tree, then pulled himself up in front of her. He turned the destrier and kicked it into a gallop.

As the full enormity of Hugh's words sank in, Janna subsided into a frightened silence. She was expected to save the baby's life, but she no longer had her mother's knowledge and expertise to draw on. If the child died, she alone would be held responsible.

This last thought tightened her grip on Hugh. Sensing the pressure, and perhaps seeking to reassure her, he turned his head to speak to her over his shoulder. "The baby has been baptized, and the priest now counsels Dame Alice that it will be God's will if the child should die. But Alice won't hear of it. She has had such ill luck since the birth of her first little boy. She had thought, having brought this child to term and borne him alive, that he would thrive. Will you be able to save him, Johanna?"

"No! I don't know how!" It was a cry from the heart, but even as she uttered her fear aloud, Janna knew that she could not give up so easily, not if she meant to honor her mother's name. Besides, if she could save the child, surely it would still the clattering tongues that spoke of poison and devils and such. "But I'll try. I'll do my best!" she said loudly, to contradict her denial. And then, as honesty prevailed, she muttered, "But only if I can tell for myself what is wrong with him." She tried to collect her frightened thoughts. Should she ask Hugh to turn around and go back to the cottage? What might she need to save the baby's life?

There was no point asking Hugh. He'd already admitted he didn't know what was wrong with the infant. Eadgyth had said that the babe was weakened by the long birth, and would not suckle, but was that all that ailed him? If so, Janna knew what steps to take to ease the problem. If it was something worse, however, she was in trouble, deep trouble and she struggled to decide what to do for the best. Finally she came to the reluctant conclusion that she would not know until she could see the child herself. Hopefully she would recognize the symptoms and be able to find the herbs to treat him in Dame Alice's own garden. Otherwise she would have to ask Hugh to take her back to the cottage.

Desperately, passionately, Janna wished that her mother was still alive. If only she had her mother's experience! She closed her eyes. "Help me," she whispered, her plea unheard against the drumming of the horse's hooves. "Please, help me." She wished the ride could go on forever, so that she would never have to confront the dying child and his distraught mother—and her own ignorance. But all too soon they were flying through the gateway and dismounting in the yard.

Almost the first person Janna saw as she hurried up the stairs and into the great hall was Aldith. She stopped, dismayed. The midwife's apron was clean, but Janna knew the dangers of the grubby skirt beneath.

Aldith gave her a reproachful glance. "What are you doing here? Tending mothers and their babies is the work of a midwife. Your mother knew that full well, although that didn't stop her pushing her nose in. Now that she's gone, you must allow me, as having more experience than you, Janna, to take care of Dame Alice and her new babe."

"Dame Alice has asked for me," Janna retorted. "That's why I'm here."

"But I am come prepared to help my lady." The midwife held up a flask, the movement accompanied by the sound of sloshing liquid. Her lips twitched up in a smile of triumph as she glanced at Janna's empty hands. "Go home," she advised. "There is naught for you to do here."

Hugh frowned at Aldith. "You'd better wait here. Dame Alice wishes to see Johanna without delay." He brushed past the midwife, not waiting to hear any further argument. Janna kept her head bent as she scuttled after him. All her suspicions had been aroused by Aldith's presence at the manor. The midwife had hardly waited to see her rival safely interred before hastening to take her place. Janna hoped the woman would wait in the hall, as instructed. She had questions to ask the midwife, questions that would reveal either her guilt or her innocence.

Her emotions were so close to the surface that tears came to her eyes when she entered the bedchamber. The lady, red-eyed from weeping, clutched the limp body of her baby to her breast. With shaking fingers, she was trying to guide his mouth in a desperate effort to make him suckle. "Please, help us," she implored as she caught sight of Janna. "If my child would only feed, I am sure he could be saved."

"Drink some wine, dearest." Robert of Babestoche was a handsome man, Janna thought, with his shock of dark hair and the ruddy complexion that spoke of a great enjoyment of all the good things that life at the manor had to offer. With great solicitude, he poured some red liquid from a glass bottle into a silver goblet. Janna looked at the bottle, fascinated by both it and its contents. She had never seen such a beautiful bottle before, nor had she ever tasted wine made from grapes. This looked so fine it must have come by ship from Normandy.

Robert held the goblet out to his wife. "This will strengthen your blood and, I am sure, give strength to our son as well."

With an impatient exclamation, Dame Alice knocked his hand away. The goblet fell, spilling its contents in a red stream. The wine looked like blood on the fine linen sheets. Janna gasped, horrified at the waste.

Robert's lips tightened in anger. He retrieved the goblet and set it carefully on a chest close to the bed. "Try not to distress yourself, my love," he said, and bent down to brush a kiss on his wife's forehead. "We are in God's hands now."

He left the room, acknowledging Janna's presence with a brief nod as he passed. It seemed that he, along with the priest, was ready to give up. But Janna was not; she was here to fight for the life of Dame Alice's infant. Although trembling with fear, she forced a confident smile as she approached the bed. First calm the patient, Janna thought, and cast her mind back to recall what Eadgyth did when faced with an angry or distressed villager. Although she knew she was taking a great liberty, Janna laid her hand on Dame Alice's arm and tried not to betray her fear.

"I will do all in my power to help you," she said, speaking low and slowly. "First, I need you to tell me all that you have seen and observed since the baby's birth." She looked down at the infant cradled in his mother's arms. He was swaddled tight in a woollen wrap. A strap kept the wrap in place; it was crisscrossed around his tiny body. His head, too, was covered. Janna could see nothing but his tiny face. What she saw did not reassure her. His eyes seemed blank, without life, and there was a bluish tinge to his lips.

"He was perfect! A beautiful, healthy child who was taken away from me." The lady sounded desolate, but there was an edge of anger beneath her words. At first, Janna thought the anger was directed at her mother, until she followed Dame Alice's gaze and noticed what she'd missed before. Fulk was standing in a shadowy recess, watching her, watching them both. Now he hurried over to the bedside, ready to defend himself.

"My lady, you know right well that it is common practice for ladies of high birth to appoint a wet nurse to suckle their babies."

"Common practice it may be, but I deeply regret that I did not follow the herbwife's advice to suckle the child myself. Now I fear I am too late, for he will not feed." Tears welled up in the lady's eyes and spilled down her cheeks.

"Who's been looking after the baby since his birth?" Janna queried.

A slight young woman stepped forward, looking haggard and careworn. Janna sympathized with her. She must also have a new baby of her own, if it lived, and would be in need of a husband or her family to support her. Should the baby die, she would carry the blame and would be dismissed. Without anyone to speak on her behalf, she would be unable to find work anywhere else.

"Tell me about the baby. What did you observe while he was in your care?" she asked. She was sorry to put the woman in a difficult position, but she had to know the answer. She already suspected part of it. Knowing Dame Alice's situation, Eadgyth would not have suggested that the lady suckle her own child unless she was worried that he might not thrive.

The wet nurse gave a nervous glance around the room as if testing whether or not it was safe to tell the truth. If she confirmed Dame Alice's statement, she would most certainly be blamed should the baby die. If she spoke the truth about its ailments, she risked the wrath of the mother, who believed her child perfect in every respect.

Fulk broke the silence with a cough. "You were in no position to suckle the child yourself, my lady," he said. "The birth was long, and very hard. There was an excessive amount of bleeding. Far better that you rest and recover your strength and leave the nourishment of your child to someone else."

Dame Alice glared at him. "Get out," she said. "Pack your bags and be gone. Had I listened to you alone, and done as you suggested, you would be getting ready to bury me along with my son."

"But I—"

"Go!" Dame Alice commanded, her voice rising in hysteria as she cried, "You have done enough harm. I will not see you again."

Angry and resentful, the apothecary shouldered Janna aside and left the room.

Janna felt her skin crawl at his touch, understanding the anger behind the violent movement. He was her enemy now, as well as her mother's. She turned her thoughts back to the more pressing problem. "Please, tell me everything you can about the baby," she prompted, hoping answers from the nurse might guide her to the truth of the baby's condition.

The woman glanced nervously at her mistress, then looked quickly away. "The child's skin was deadly pale, he was almost blue when I first saw him," she whispered. "After she tied the cord, Mistress Eadgyth bade us give him a warm bath and wrap him tight. His skin flushed more pink in the warmth, but he still seemed somewhat distressed. Your mother asked us to place some lavender next to his cradle, which she said would soothe and calm him, and she collected herbs for the cook to make into a syrup with some honey. She instructed us to give the baby a small sup of it every few hours."

"And did you do that?"

"Yes. At once when the mixture was given to me, and again in the morning. The lavender is still beside his cradle."

"Did you have syrup enough for only two doses?"

"The apothecary ordered me to throw it away. Your mother brought a different potion back with her, but Master Fulk told me to destroy that too." The girl looked uncomfortable. Janna wondered if she'd done what she was told. She must have a baby of her own, a child who might also be ailing and in need of a healing potion. Yet Janna was sure the nurse would not give her a straight answer in front of Dame Alice.

She tried another tack. "What was in the mixture? Did my mother tell you?"

"No." The girl shook her head, not meeting Janna's eye. Desperation forced Janna's hand. "And did you throw it away, as you were bid?"

The girl remained silent.

"Come now, Dame Alice will not punish you if you disobeyed Master Fulk's orders. In fact, I am sure she will reward you if you can bring the mixture to us now. For certes my mother knew exactly what was needed to save the baby's life." Janna flicked a glance toward the lady, mutely asking for her support.

Dame Alice leaned forward. "If you still have it, I beg you to fetch it immediately."

The girl nodded, and fled. Dame Alice fell back against the pillows, her sigh of relief echoing around the chamber.

Exhilarated by what she saw as a win, Janna called for a jar of honey to be brought. As soon as the girl had returned with the mixture, and the baby had swallowed a few drops of Eadgyth's healing brew, Janna dipped her finger into the honey and then, greatly daring, spread the sticky sweetness over Lady Alice's nipple. Another dip into the honey, and this time she picked up the baby and put her finger in his mouth.

He turned his head away. She could hear his breath rattle faintly in his chest. The sound alarmed her, for it was the sound made by the dying. But she could not give up, not yet, and so she persisted, dipping her finger into the honey once more. Eventually, the baby responded to the sweetness and began to suck, although with little enthusiasm. At once, Janna removed her finger and lowered him into the lady's waiting arms. Gently, she guided his mouth to the honeyed nipple, willing him to start taking nourishment. She held her breath.

At last his lips moved and he began to suckle. Janna felt her tense muscles unclench. The knot in her stomach began to dissolve.

"I thank you." Dame Alice didn't look at Janna. Her attention was focused on the small bundle in her arms. She bent to kiss the dark fuzz on top of the baby's head. Unsure if she should stay or go, Janna hovered beside the bed. She wondered if she could ask for permission to leave the bedchamber. The baby's rattling breath alarmed her. There were herbs that might alleviate the problem, if she could find any of them growing in the manor's own kitchen garden. Cecily was not here to give her advice; another tiring woman was in attendance. Perhaps Cecily was looking after Dame Alice's little boy? Janna wondered if he'd met his new baby brother yet.

A rattling cough brought Janna's focus back to the bedchamber. "May I take a walk in your herb garden, my lady?" she asked. "I hope to find something there to ease your baby's breathing."

"Yes, go at once. But don't leave the manor." Dame Alice glanced briefly at Janna. "I need you here."

"Yes, my lady. Of course. I'll stay for as long as you need me."

Janna hurried out into the hall, keeping a lookout for someone to give her directions to the kitchen garden. She hated the thought of asking at the kitchen and having to face the cook once more, but she had no time to waste and so she set off toward the outside flight of stairs.

Before she'd taken more than a few steps across the hall, she heard her name called—Aldith had been lying in wait for her to appear. Now she stood fast, blocking Janna's path. "So," she said, "you have managed to push your way in here just as your mother did."

A flash of anger heated Janna's blood. "It was none of my doing. You heard the lord Hugh. Dame Alice sent for me."

"A green, untried girl. What do you know of women's and children's troubles?"

"I know what my mother taught me. Which, I wager, is a great deal more than the apothecary knows, and probably more than you know yourself, mistress." Janna knew she was being rude. Too provoked by Aldith's accusations to guard her tongue, she continued: "You were very quick to take my mother's place here at the manor. 'Tis certain that my mother's death will be good for *your* business." She was about to hurry on through the hall, but Aldith's next words stopped her dead.

"Midwifery has always been my business. There is no blame in wanting to help a mother and her new child if they are in need. That's why I've now offered my services to Dame Alice, and before that to your mother, when she told me where she was bound. She refused my offer, of course. Wanted all the glory for herself, I dare say."

"You met my mother on her way to the manor?"

"Indeed I did. She was looking inordinately pleased with herself. I asked where she was bound and she told me." Aldith put her nose in the air and gave a contemptuous sniff, trying to hide her jealousy.

"And you offered assistance? Did you tell her what to do to help the lady and her babe?" Janna tried to placate the angry midwife with flattery—and in the hope that she, in turn, might also be offered some guidance.

"I gave advice, yes. After all, I have been here before to attend Dame Alice and I have witnessed her troubles." Aldith hesitated a moment, struggling between boasting or telling the truth. "Your mother wouldn't listen to me, of course. She told me she already knew all she needed to help Dame Alice and her babe."

Janna didn't like to point out that Fulk the apothecary had only been called because, under Aldith's care, the babies had all died. "Did my mother perhaps take any of your syrups or potions, even if she wouldn't take your advice?" Janna held her breath. The answer to her mother's death lay in Aldith's reply.

Aldith's face darkened. "She took no advice, and she spurned the tonic I offered. But she wasn't too proud to ask for some of my special cordial to drink."

"You gave her some cordial?" Janna kept her voice under control as she asked, "Did my mother drink it?" Her hands felt clammy; she sweated with the need to know the truth.

"Of course she drank it! My mint cordial is renowned for its cooling and reviving properties."

"Of course it is!" Janna agreed hurriedly. "What herbs do you use, mistress, to make it so special?"

Aldith looked coy. "It's a secret recipe."

"Mint. And perhaps a few drops of poppy juice?" Janna probed.

"I will not tell you my secrets."

"A little hemlock to dull the senses? A mite of monkshood, perhaps?"

"Are you accusing Mistress Aldith of poisoning your mother?" The deep voice of Robert of Babestoche startled both Janna and Aldith. They had not seen him enter the hall. Janna wondered how long he'd been standing there, listening to their conversation. Now he strode forward, and pinned Janna with a fierce gaze. Beside her, Aldith had sunk into a deep curtsy. Janna hastily copied the midwife's action.

"I-I know my mother was poisoned. I am trying to find out how it happened, sire," Janna stammered, as she rose to her feet once more. She was dismayed at having to explain herself when she'd hoped to keep her suspicions secret.

"If your mother was poisoned, it was certainly none of my doing." Aldith drew herself up, looking deeply offended. Janna silently cursed the lord's untimely appearance. She could understand Aldith defending herself, but knew she would come no closer to the truth while he was present. Still, she had to defend her mother's reputation in front of him.

"My mother knew and understood herbs and their properties—especially the poisonous ones. She was very particular with her potions; very careful when she collected the ingredients and especially when she mixed them. She would never knowingly have ingested monkshood, and yet she died of its poison."

"Just so am I particular with my mint cordial." Aldith glared at Janna. "You cannot hold me to account for your mother's death. I vow I will make you sorry if you try!"

Janna looked from Aldith to Robert, reading anger and condemnation in both their expressions.

"You do wrong to spread false accusations," Robert said coldly. "I can only thank God that my dear wife has suffered no harm at the careless hands of your mother. Let this be a lesson to you not to meddle with nature or the Lord's will.

It was at my wife's request that you were brought here, Johanna, but I will not have you spreading slander and lies about the manor. You may consider yourself dismissed!" Turning on his heel, he strode through the hall in the direction of the bedchamber, leaving the two women to confront each other.

"I offered your mother my advice and my cordial in friendship and as an act of Christian charity, hoping to ease her thirst and her fatigue," Aldith hissed as soon as they were alone once more. "I will not forget or forgive your accusations. They are made worse by the fact that you tried to blacken my name in front of the lord of the manor."

"I did not know he was there, listening to our conversation." Janna wondered how far she could trust Aldith's protestations of innocence. The cook, and everyone else, claimed that her mother had taken no food or drink on her return to the manor house. Aldith's cordial was the only clue to her mother's death that Janna could find, yet the midwife's anger and dismay seemed genuine.

"You are a silly, impudent girl. I understand that your mother's death has upset you, but you do your case no good by making these rash accusations." Aldith leaned closer, so close that their noses almost touched. "You would do well to follow my lord's advice. Go home, Janna. Do not meddle in what you don't understand." Cradling the jar with its liquid contents closer to her breast, she stepped away from Janna and went toward the bedchamber, casting a triumphant glance behind her.

"How much of your cordial did my mother drink?" Janna called after her.

"We shared a whole jug!" Aldith disappeared from Janna's view.

A whole jug? It was true Aldith was proud of her mint cordial, and rightly so. Janna had once tasted some herself, when the midwife had paid her mother in kind for a soothing cream. It was to Aldith's credit that she'd made no secret of the fact that she'd met Eadgyth on her way to the manor house, nor that she'd given her the cordial to drink. Even if Aldith was lying about sharing the cordial with her mother, Eadgyth knew its taste. If she'd had any suspicions about it, she would have spat it out and poured the rest of it away. And she would have broadcast her suspicions up at the manor house as soon as she started to feel ill.

Janna's thoughts led her to conclude that it was kind of the midwife to share her cordial, especially if she was carrying it to sell. And if she was carrying it to sell, she would never have added poison to it. She couldn't know that she would meet her rival, and that they would share a drink. It was far too great a risk to carry poisoned cordial when anyone might have stopped her along the road to buy some.

She had unjustly accused the midwife of poisoning her mother—and in Robert's hearing too! She felt a pang of remorse, as well as annoyance that she'd let her suspicions run away with her. Aldith had shown kindness, both to Eadgyth and to Janna. Now, because of her stupidity, she had one friend less, when friends were what she most needed. First Godric, and now Aldith. Soon she would have no friends left at all.

Janna cheered up slightly as she remembered the gallant Hugh. And Dame Alice. She had asked Janna to save her baby—but Robert had told her to be gone. It took only an instant for Janna to make the decision. Impatient that she'd already wasted time, she ran down the stairs and set off toward the kitchen in the hope of finding the garden nearby.

Her spirits revived somewhat as the sunlight warmed her. The sight of a well made her lick her dry lips; talk of Aldith's cordial had made her thirsty. She pushed the thought aside. A drink would have to wait until her mission was complete.

She hurried on past several low buildings whose functions she could only guess at, fascinated by this glimpse of a life so different from her own.

She'd guessed that the herbs and vegetables would be grown close to the kitchen for easy picking, and so it proved. The garden was situated in a sunny and protected spot between the kitchen and the timber palisade surrounding the manor house and grounds and apple, pear and plum trees formed a screen to provide shelter from the worst of the elements. The plants were set out in neat rows for easy identification and picking; many of them were familiar. She took a quick glance around, envying the abundance and variety of vegetables occupying the large space available for their growing. It must be wonderful not to want for anything, she thought, as she eyed the long rows of cabbages, lettuces, leeks, turnips, broad beans, peas and onions. She turned her attention then to the herbs, noting with some pride that there were fewer to choose from than in their own garden, nor did they look as healthy. Her garden now, she corrected herself. There was great sadness in the thought.

She spied the thin, fleshy spikes of ground pine, and broke some off. The fragrant steam from boiling its shoots should aid the baby's breathing. She looked about to see what else she could find to help him thrive.

With a heavy heart, Janna recalled her mother's words some years before when, after several miscarriages, one of the village women had finally succeeded in giving birth to a living child only to have it die within a few short hours.

"*I know not how to explain it,*" her mother had said. "*The fact that the mother has had such difficulty carrying other babies to term tells me that there is some deep, underlying problem that we do not understand and therefore cannot treat. Mother Nature's way is usually to expel the child before it has a chance to form properly, but in this case it seems that the baby's will to fight kept it alive, at least for a time."* Eadgyth's voice had been troubled as she'd concluded, *"But 'tis better, I am sure, to lose a baby early, before it resembles a living child, than to give birth and watch your son or daughter die in your arms."*

Did this child have the will to keep him alive through these early and dangerous days? A brief vision of Alfred flashed in front of Janna. The kitten had almost drowned, but his will had kept him alive until his throat had been cut. At least this baby had nothing to fear from a vengeful and rejected suitor. Janna wondered if that was really how Godric thought of himself. Here, in the peace of the garden, it seemed absurd to think he would go to such lengths just because she'd told him she wasn't yet ready to marry.

She remembered there was a lavender bush somewhere in the garden, for her mother had already plundered it. As she plucked the fragrant flowers, her troubled thoughts moved on. Godric's action went against everything she'd observed of him and that had been reported to her by her mother. Kind, decent, courageous: those were the words she would have used to describe him. True, he had seemed to dislike Alfred. Possibly he even feared the cat if he believed, like the villagers, that Alfred was the devil. But would he go so far as to kill it, and in such a brutal manner? Janna shook her head. Godric had seemed genuinely shocked and surprised by her accusation. Yet if he was innocent of the charge, who then was responsible?

Mindful of the need for haste, Janna scanned the garden for any other herbs that might prove useful. She spied the hoof-shaped leaves of coltsfoot. As she hurried to pick them she continued to puzzle over Alfred's death.

Godric had heard a noise that night, she remembered. He'd gone outside and looked around. Could someone else have come out to her cottage and seen Godric embrace and comfort her? Could that someone have waited until he was gone, and then killed her cat? But who would want to do such a thing?

Slowly, Janna answered her own question. Someone who hated her, who thought of her as a rival perhaps, and who may have mistaken Godric for someone else. Hilde's distorted face and her angry accusations came into Janna's mind, along with the memory of how Hilde had brandished a knife while uttering a final threat: "*Tempt him again and it'll be your turn to feel how sharp this is.*" In that moment Janna knew she'd accused an innocent man of a terrible crime.

For a moment she stood still, stricken to the heart. Godric! She had been so wrong about him, so wrong. How could she ever look him in the eye again? How could he ever forgive her?

There was no time to think of him now. Saving the baby's life was far more important, but Janna resolved that, somehow, she would find a way to apologize to him, and try to make amends. She took one last glance about the garden to see if there was horehound, or anything else that might help, and frowned as she noticed some bright blue caps of monkshood. They were growing close to a clump of parsley, a dangerous proximity when their leaves were so similar. Was it there by accident or design? Had someone at the manor discovered that monkshood eased aching joints and the pain of rheumatics when rubbed in with oil, or were the plants prized for a more deadly purpose altogether? Could it even have been a portion of one of these plants that Eadgyth had ingested?

She gave them a hurried inspection. Rough scars told her that leaves and stems had been harvested, and quite recently. A cold frisson of warning shivered through her. She resolved to keep asking questions, but for now her most urgent task was to relieve the child's breathing. In spite of Robert's banishment, she must return to the bedchamber. Janna looked down at the fresh herbs she carried. She had a good reason to be there, as well as Dame Alice's instructions not to leave. Surely no-one could refuse her entry if there was some small chance that she might be able to save the baby's life?

*

The first person Janna noticed as she entered the hall was Cecily. The lady was pleading with Robert, who seemed unmoved by her distress. A scowl marred his handsome face as he said something in return. Janna supposed Cecily was in trouble for leaving the house without permission, abandoning her mistress not once but twice and at a time when she was most needed. He broke off abruptly when he noticed Janna, and gestured for Cecily to leave him. Wiping away tears, she hurried into the bedchamber. Janna was left alone to confront the lord.

Robert scowled at her. "I told you to go."

Janna looked up at him, trying to conceal her dislike. Handsome he might be, but it seemed that the power of his position as lord of the manor had created a bully.

"I have picked some sprigs of ground pine, sire." She bobbed a respectful curtsy, then indicated the handfuls of herbs she carried. "If you will order these leaves to be boiled, the fragrance of the steam will help your new son breathe more freely."

"We want no more of your poisons around here."

Janna choked back her anger with difficulty. "This is not a poison, sire. It's common ground pine, picked from the manor's own herb garden. And these are the leaves of coltsfoot. They should be thrown on hot coals; the fumes will help to clear the congestion in the baby's chest and also aid his breathing. These herbs are not for the baby to swallow. They are utterly harmless." She recalled the monkshood growing so close to the parsley, as well as a number of other plants which, if used injudiciously, could cause pain or even death. But Robert was unlikely to have any knowledge of the contents of the kitchen garden, harmful or otherwise, and it was certainly not her place to enlighten him.

"Do not argue with me. I want you to go. Now!" Robert stepped closer to Janna, menacing and forceful. "No matter what my wife might say, I do not trust you with the care of my newborn son." He raised a hand to push her toward the flight of steps outside. From the expression on his face, Janna wondered if he would push her right down them if she didn't obey him.

A loud cry stayed his hand. At once Robert wheeled and rushed to the bedchamber. After a moment's hesitation, Janna followed him, still clutching the aromatic herbs.

"My baby!" Dame Alice wept as she held out the limp figure for Janna's inspection. "Help him! Save him, please!"

Janna took one appalled look at the child and knew that help was no longer possible. He was dead.

Robert had also summed up the situation. Now he clicked a finger at Cecily, and jerked his head toward the door. "Fetch the priest."

She rushed out, leaving a deathly quiet in the bedchamber. Janna stepped forward to take the baby but Dame Alice snatched him back. Cradling him to her chest, she faced Janna.

"I asked you for help, and you failed me."

Janna knew that the accusation was spoken in pain, from the desolation of losing a child. Nevertheless, the words cut deep. "I-I am sorry, so sorry, my lady," she stammered. "Truly, there was little I could do for him."

"You've done enough!" Robert's voice was edged with sorrow and anger. "I've already told you once to get out. I'll have you thrown out if you don't leave immediately."

"No. Wait." Dame Alice sounded sick to her soul. "She is not to blame. It is God's punishment for my sins that my babies are taken from me."

Janna kept silent, grateful for the reprieve. Yet she couldn't help wondering why Dame Alice thought God would want to punish her so. Her mother had told Janna that the love of God was everywhere, yet the priest would have everyone believe He was cruel and unforgiving; that the smallest misdemeanor would call down His wrath and that He had no room in His heart for love.

"The *wortwyf*'s daughter speaks true," Aldith affirmed unexpectedly. Janna hadn't noticed her standing at the back of the bedchamber. "I have seen other babies born and die in like manner, as well as your own, my lady. In spite of all my physic, there was nothing I or anyone else could do to save them." She held out her arms. "Let me take the child," she said, brisk and matter-of-fact after years of experience. "Let me prepare your son for burial."

"No!" Dame Alice's heartbroken cry filled the room.

"'Tis better so. There's naught you can do for him now." Aldith bent and quickly scooped up the baby.

Janna sucked in a breath. If she was going to do it at all, she should get it over straight away. "Mistress Aldith, a while ago I accused you unjustly, and in front of my lord Robert. It was very wrong of me, and I do most humbly beg your pardon."

Aldith gave a grudging nod. As she bore her small burden away, Robert sent Janna a hostile glance from beneath his bushy eyebrows.

"You accused an innocent woman when it was your mother's own foul concoctions that caused her death, as well as the death of my child," he said angrily. "I told you to be gone, and you will do as you are told!"

"But I…" Janna searched for the words to defend both herself and her mother. She cast a glance of appeal at Dame

Alice, willing the lady to speak up for her. But the dame lay still and tears trickled from her closed eyelids. In her grief, she had no thought for anything other than the loss of her child.

Janna recognized that this was neither the time nor place—she'd probably be wasting her breath if she tried to refute Robert's accusations—so she bobbed a curtsy and left the bedchamber. Let him think she was obeying his command. In fact, Janna had every intention of doing so—but not just yet. For the moment, she intended to stay on at the manor and question all those who might have knowledge of the truth behind her mother's death. She no longer suspected Aldith, but that still left Fulk, the priest and also Cecily.

She started off down the hall in search of them, but had taken only a few paces when she saw the priest swooping toward her. He made the sign of the cross when he saw her, but said nothing, nor did he check his passage as he rushed on and into the bedchamber. Cecily followed him. Hugh, who had also come in answer to the summons, stopped in front of Janna.

"I understand there is no need for haste, for the baby has died."

Janna nodded, hardly able to speak. To her surprise, Hugh took hold of her hand and led her to a long bench running the length of one wall.

"Sit down," he said softly. "Rest a while. You have endured a great deal these past few days."

Janna felt tears prick her eyes at the kindness in his tone. She sank onto the bench, conscious all at once of her aching limbs and the pain across her forehead that spoke of too much emotion and anxiety. She had wanted so much to save the baby, had tried her best, but her best just wasn't good enough.

She closed her eyes, trying to prevent her tears from spilling. She did not want to cry in front of Hugh. The bench creaked as he sat down beside her; she felt his light touch on her face as he pushed back the hair from her forehead. "The baby was ailing. You mustn't blame yourself for his death." He began to run his fingers through her hair, soothing her. Grateful, she leaned against him and started to relax. *If only I could stay like this forever*, she thought, lost in the darkness behind her closed eyelids and held in thrall by the light touch of his fingers. *If only I belonged here; if only I was the lady of the manor and Hugh was my dearly loved lord.*

Lulled by his gentle touch, Janna lapsed into a dream of her life with Hugh: they might take ship and sail away together, sail to the far off lands where the merchant bought his exotic spices. What sights they would see! What adventures they would have! And at night, in the marriage bed—a great wave of longing and desire washed over her; she felt as if she was drowning. It took all her will and all her courage to open her eyes and pull away from him.

Hugh looked down at her, surprised by the abrupt movement. "Feeling better?" he asked.

"Yes, I thank you, sire." Deeply ashamed of her absurd fantasy, Janna managed to dredge up a shaky smile.

"You look a little happier," he said, observing her flushed cheeks and the brightness of her eyes.

"You're an excellent physician, Hugh!" Not for anything would Janna confess to him the real reason behind her apparent recovery. Suddenly recalling the difference in their position, she added a hasty, "I beg your pardon, my lord."

He smiled back at her, seeming to forgive her cheeky remark as he paid her a compliment of his own. "I am sure your knowledge of the healing powers of herbs far outweighs any small skill I may have." He surveyed her thoughtfully for a moment. "And yet you know little of the world outside, I think."

"You speak the truth, sire. My mother and I live—lived a quiet life together." Honesty prompted Janna to add, "But I've had a suitor."

His eyebrows lifted in an amused quirk. "And?"

"I turned him down." It wasn't quite true, but it would serve to let Hugh know that she wasn't quite the innocent he took her for.

"I shall take that as a warning, shall I?"

Janna couldn't tell if he was mocking her or not. She kept silent, wishing she'd had more practice at this sort of thing.

"A child of the forest, naive and ignorant of the ways of the world, yet able to speak the language of the nobility. In truth you intrigue me, Johanna."

"I can also write letters! I can sign my own name." She resented his assessment and was anxious to impress him.

"Can you indeed?"

"I may have lived a quiet life, but it doesn't mean I'm incapable of learning about the world should the opportunity come my way," she said angrily, scratching her memory for something to prove her words. "For instance, I know that our country is at war, and that you support the claim of the Empress Matilda to the throne."

"What?" Hugh looked momentarily stunned. "Such talk could get us both into great trouble," he warned. "I suggest you keep that pretty nose of yours out of my affairs. They are none of your concern."

"I assure you, sire, my concern is only for your safety," Janna said hurriedly, embarrassed by his reproof. He'd warned her against upsetting the priest, and now she'd gone and upset him too. To convince him of her good intentions, she decided to pass on the conversation she'd overheard at the alehouse. "'Tis known that you have been seen with the empress's half-brother, Robert of Gloucester, and that he now supports the empress against the king. I know not where the lord Robert's allegiance lies, but the Abbess of Wiltune is the greatest landowner in these parts. Her allegiance must surely lie with King Stephen now that he has stripped all land and property from the Bishop of Sarisberie. The king's action is surely too close for our abbess to ignore, nor will she defy him. I do fear that you might find yourself entrapped, sire."

Hugh surveyed Janna, looking thoughtful. "I suspect I may have misjudged you," he said. "Thank you for your warning. I shall certainly keep it in mind, but I assure you that I come here only to visit my aunt and report on my custodianship of her property."

"I know also that you visit her quite frequently, which confirms my suspicion that you did not need to ask me for directions."

To Janna's intense delight, Hugh looked somewhat discomforted at being caught out. Then he grinned. "That nose of yours seems to have a way of sniffing out the truth—and yes, I made the most of the opportunity to talk to a pretty girl."

"And I'm not a girl either!"

"True enough." Hugh's admiring glance swept over her. "You are indeed a comely young woman. I apologize if I have given you offence, *ma belle*."

Janna blushed anew. "Your visit to your aunt was timely on this occasion," she said, anxious to change the direction of their conversation.

"Yes, indeed. I've been worried about her, for I know how hard she takes these failed pregnancies. As for Robert—" He checked abruptly. "And now, Johanna, I must go and comfort Dame Alice, though I wish with all my heart that this had turned out differently, and that comfort wasn't necessary." He smiled at her, bringing new warmth to Janna's troubled spirit. "Wait here in case Dame Alice has further need of you." He walked on through the hall and into the solar.

Janna looked after him, intrigued by the sentence he'd left unfinished. What had he been going to say about Robert? True, the lord seemed a man given to sudden tempers. Janna found him rather frightening. So did Cecily, she thought, remembering the scene she'd witnessed. But even if he bullied his servants, he was hardly likely to intimidate a man like Hugh. And he certainly didn't intimidate his wife! Janna shook her head over the wine that the dame had spilled. What a waste!

She shrugged. The lord of the manor was none of her concern. But Hugh...He'd been so kind, so understanding. A dreamy smile stole over her lips as she imagined how her life would be if she and Hugh were husband and wife. They would drink wine at every dinner. They would eat roast swan, as well as the king's venison. She would have a different gown for every day of the year, and wear bright jewels of every hue to match. She would ask him to teach her all he knew, so that she could be his equal in every way...

A sound disturbed Janna's musing. She blinked, and saw that the priest had come out into the hall. He came right up to her. Janna resisted the urge to shrink back against the stone wall.

"You are still here?"

"Yes. As you see."

"Where is the baby? I have come to pray for his soul."

"I do not know. The midwife has taken him."

"I knew that the baby would not thrive under your care." The priest sounded as if he'd won a victory. Janna wanted to rip his gloating tongue out of his mouth.

"The baby was ailing ere he was born." She curled her fists and dug her nails into the palms of her hands to remind herself not to attack the priest. "It was a miracle he survived even as long as he did."

"God's miracle—whom you destroyed."

"I did all in my power to keep him alive—and so did my mother!"

The priest sighed. "This won't do, Johanna," he said unexpectedly. "You are young, and impressionable, and your soul may yet be saved if you'll only seek the path of righteousness.

I must not blame you for your mother's wrongdoing, nor her wrong beliefs, for you have been a dutiful daughter. You have honored your mother as you were taught, not knowing that your honor was misplaced and your mother not worthy of your love and trust."

"You are wrong, so wrong!" Janna had taken Hugh's reprimand to heart, but still it took all of her self-control to hold on to her temper. She must try to convince the priest with the sincerity of her words; she would achieve nothing by shouting at him, or attacking him. She took a deep breath. "My mother was an honorable woman, dedicated to using her skills to cure people of the ills that afflicted them. Surely her skill with healing came as a gift from God?"

The priest opened his mouth to answer, then closed it again. He seemed to be having difficulty finding a response. At last he said, "I will not hold your mother's deeds against you, nor will I blame you for her evil influence on you. Instead, I will ask you, Janna, to start coming to church once more. Let God see you there, let Him save your soul."

Janna scowled at him. The priest was wrong about her mother, but her mother had made no secret of her opinion of him and his notion of Christianity. Aldith had called Eadgyth arrogant and proud. It might be that her mother would have done better with the priest if she'd held her tongue. If they had gone regularly to the church, the priest might have been more welcoming, might even have celebrated her mother's healing powers instead of damning them.

"I'll think about it," she muttered.

The priest smiled, seeming content that he had saved a soul this day. "Go to the kitchen," he said, "tell the cook I sent you. Ask her to make up a hot posset for Dame Alice, and bring it up to my lady's bedchamber. And don't interfere, Janna. The cook already knows what to put in it, for I heard Fulk the apothecary instruct her on the matter."

"What did he ask the cook to do?" Janna asked quickly, wondering if here, at last, was proof of Fulk's guilt.

The priest shrugged. "I know not, save that the drink was to calm my lady and strengthen her nerves. I myself was finishing my dinner and paid no attention to the apothecary's instructions."

"Master Fulk ordered the posset for my lady at dinnertime?"

"Indeed. Your mother was wroth when she arrived back at the manor and saw it. I was in the bedchamber when she tasted the contents, and then ordered it thrown away. Of course, she wanted Dame Alice to sup her own concoction, the mixture that led to her death."

"That's not so!" Appalled, Janna stared at the priest. "Don't you see? It was Master Fulk's posset that killed my mother! That is why she died. The apothecary must have planned it so, knowing she would taste it first before allowing it to be given to Dame Alice. And having tasted his poison, of course she threw it away."

It was a dreadful thought, made even worse by the realization that she had taken her mother's place at the lady's bedside. If Fulk had acted to rid himself of her mother, so might he act against this new threat to his professional competence.

"Your grief has warped your judgment," the priest said sternly. "Accusing the innocent can never atone for the harm your mother brought upon herself."

"She did nothing to harm herself—nothing! It was Fulk's doing. He resented my mother's influence over the dame, and his so-called posset ensured that my mother would no longer stand in his way." She had to convince the priest that she spoke the truth. He was a man of God. He would surely help her in her quest for justice. Near tears, Janna struggled to find the words to make him understand. But the priest forestalled her.

"I have stretched out my hand in friendship, yet you continue to defy all who would help you find the true path to God's grace. I can do no more for you, Johanna. It is up to you now to save your soul, if that is possible." He brushed past her and returned to the bedchamber.

Chapter 10

Determined to prove the priest wrong, determined to prove all those who judged her mother wrong, Janna wasted no time racing down the stairs to seek out the cook. The woman was busy plucking a goose—feathers flew in all directions. They were being collected by a thin kitchen maid who wore a sour expression. No doubt the feathers were prized as a stuffing for quilts and pillows for the household, especially the smaller fluffier feathers, but it seemed the maid was taking no pride or pleasure in her work this day.

Janna paused a moment to assemble her thoughts. She must proceed carefully. If she wanted answers to her questions, she would first need to win the cook's friendship and trust. It seemed an impossible task given the start they'd already made. Nevertheless, she had to try.

"May I have a word with you, mistress?"

The cook turned from the goose she was plucking, and stared suspiciously at Janna. "What do you want?"

Instead of voicing questions and accusations, Janna decided to try flattery instead. "I beg your pardon for troubling you, mistress, but the priest bade me ask you to make up a posset for Dame Alice, the same posset that Master Fulk ordered for her once before."

"Why would the priest ask such a thing?"

"He has just come from my lady's chamber to request it," Janna said carefully. "Dame Alice is in great need of comfort. She is made distraught by the death of her baby son." A hiss of indrawn breath told Janna that this was news to the kitchen staff. They stopped working and, silent and intent, watched her.

"So the baby has died, no thanks to you and your mother."

Janna sighed, feeling almost too discouraged to defend herself. "We did our best, but there was naught we—or anyone else—could have done for him," she said. "Please, mistress, will you do as the priest asks and make one of your special possets for my lady? I feel sure it will do much to calm her."

"Hmph." The cook rested her blood- and feather-smeared hands on her hips, and stared at Janna. It was clear from her expression that she wanted Janna gone, but she did not quite have the courage to disobey instructions. After a perfunctory scrub of her hands in a basin of water to cleanse them, she dipped a scoop into a pot of water hung by a chain over the fire and poured the boiling contents into a mug.

"Pray tell me, what do you use?" Janna pointed to the reddish brown flakes the woman began spooning into the mixture, knowing full well her reply.

"Rose petals." The cook nipped up a small pinch from another jar. "Mint," she said, and cautiously plucked a couple of leaves from a stem standing in a pot of water.

Janna recognized the stinging but useful plant. "Nettles?" she said.

The cook nodded. "And honey." She poured a thin stream of sticky gold into the steaming mug. She could make a far more efficacious posset herself, Janna thought, but she did not say the words aloud. There was still much to find out and she did not want to antagonize the cook by making suggestions.

"And what do you keep here?" she asked, pointing at a row of jars of similar shape and size to the pot that held the rose petals.

"Sweet marjoram, thyme, poppy seeds, basil, rosemary...I grow many herbs for my use."

"I know, for I have been out in your garden myself." Janna recalled the monkshood growing so innocently beside the parsley, and another question sprang to her lips. "Do you add parsley to your mix?" she asked innocently.

"No. It has no place in this." The cook gave the steaming mug a vigorous stir.

Janna hesitated. Keeping her tone carefully respectful, she asked, "I noticed plants of monkshood growing in your garden. Do you ever include it in your potions, mistress?"

"No! 'Tis a deadly poison!"

"Yet it has its uses for all that."

The cook stopped stirring and gave Janna a sharp look. "It is your mother who brews poisons, not me," she hissed, "and I will not be accused and insulted by the likes of you."

Fearing another attack with the besom, Janna stepped hastily out of the cook's reach. "I meant no harm by my question," she said quickly. "I meant only that monkshood has good use as a rubbing oil for aches and pains."

"I know well the use of monkshood, for Master Fulk himself has instructed me. Now get out of my kitchen! I will take the infusion to my lady myself." The cook walked out of the door, the mug clutched carefully in her two hands. As soon as she was safely out of sight, Janna began a careful inspection of the herbs and potions ranged along the kitchen shelves.

"And what do you think you're doing?" The sour scullery maid looked up from chasing errant feathers.

Janna ignored the question, continuing to open stoppers and sniff the contents of the jars, occasionally taking an experimental taste. She wished the cook was more cooperative; it would make her task so much easier. This mixture smelled sweet, another a little spicy; there was no distinctive odor of monkshood. To her relief, neither the maids nor any of the scullions seemed to have the courage to either restrain her or drag her out of the kitchen. Instead, they stood about, still staring at her.

"What are you seeking, mistress?"

Janna glanced up and saw it was the maid who had once spoken up in support of her mother. She was young, and seemed sympathetic. "Many of these spices are new to me. I am interested in their properties. And I need monkshood to ease my lady's aching joints," she improvised. "Have you any rubbing oil made up, or should I pick it fresh and make up the concoction myself?"

"There be some growing out in the garden. You said you'd seen it," the sour-faced maid pointed out.

"Master Fulk made up a mixture some days ago. You could ask him if there's any left," the young maid said, then giggled suddenly. "My lord went out riding last week and fell off his horse. He blamed the horse for taking fright and bolting under him but the groom says the fault lies with my lord Robert, who has a heavy hand with the whip and is not the fine horseman he believes himself to be. My lord complained loud and long of a sore back, and was in a foul temper from the pain." The maid pulled a face. "We all kept out of his way. We always do, if we can."

"So Master Fulk has a mixture?" While entertained by the maid's observations regarding her master, Janna was far more interested in the apothecary.

"I saw him make it up myself," the maid said. "He ground the root and mixed it with oil and mustard seeds. He warned my lord not to ingest any part of it. He was most careful about warning all of us, miss. And my lord was grateful, for he says that it eased the pain. I know all this for he made Master Fulk show him where the plant grows, and he bade me come too, so that I can make up the rubbing oil should any in the household have aches and pains needing treatment in the future." The maid brightened, visibly swelling with self-importance. "I can make up the mixture now for you, if you wish?"

"No, please do not trouble yourself," Janna said quickly. "If Master Fulk has none left, I shall make it up myself." It was hard to hide her elation. Here, at last, was proof of Fulk's guilt. A sudden thought dampened her excitement: Was the apothecary still at the manor, or had he already left for Wiltune? She must act quickly if she wished to trap him with this information.

"I thank you for your assistance," she said, and hurried out.

"The kitchen garden is the other way," the maid called after her.

Janna flapped a hand in acknowledgment, and kept on going. She had to find Fulk straightaway so that she could lay a trap.

Janna had supposed that cows, horses, sheep and goats were lodged at the bottom of the manor house, underneath the family's living quarters. Now that she'd seen the numerous sheds scattered about the manor grounds she thought the animals were probably housed elsewhere, which meant that the undercroft must be used for some other purpose. Perhaps it housed the servants? She decided to start her search there, since Fulk had been staying at the manor house. She opened the door and peered about. The several partitions with straw pallets and wall pegs told her she'd guessed correctly. A number of huge chests indicated that the room was also used for storage. It was cold and ill lit, having only high and narrow slits for windows. Empty casks and barrels stood about, waiting for the rich rewards of the harvest. There was no sign of Fulk, nor of anyone who might know his whereabouts. She went back outside, ran up the stairs and into the hall.

"Have you seen Master Fulk? I must speak with him." Janna addressed her question to Aldith, the only person present.

"He is with my lady. Robert insisted that he come and take care of her, for she is in sore distress. Wait!" Aldith caught hold of Janna's arm to prevent her hurrying off to the bedchamber. "You cannot go in there, Janna. Not now. At Dame Alice's request, I have put the baby into his cradle so that she and her husband may say their final farewells. The priest is with them, and so are other members of the household. You cannot interrupt them. In fact, you would be well advised to do as my lord Robert instructed, and leave the manor."

"No, I can't. Not yet." Janna stopped resisting Aldith's grasp. She would have to be patient. "I am truly sorry for what I said to you. Will you please forgive me?"

Aldith cast her eyes to heaven, and heaved a weary sigh. "I understand that you are distraught after your mother's death, but you must put a curb on your tongue, Janna."

Aldith sounded just like Eadgyth! Janna gave her a forlorn smile. "You've been very kind to me," she observed. "Why?"

"We will need to get along if we are to exchange information and work together side by side."

Janna nodded thoughtfully. What Aldith said was true enough, although it might never come to pass. "You warned me about Master Fulk." She was bursting to share her discovery with someone whom she was sure would understand. "I have now found proof that he poisoned my mother!"

"Take care what you say!" Shocked, Aldith shook a warning finger at Janna. "You cannot go around accusing him—or anyone else for that matter—unless you have very strong proof of his guilt."

"Listen to what I have learned." Janna moved a stool close to Aldith and sat down. She lowered her voice, so that anyone coming into the room would not be able to hear their conversation. "I have seen monkshood growing freely in the manor's kitchen garden. Fulk used the roots in a rubbing oil to treat my lord Robert's aches and pains. He knows that it is poisonous, for he warned my lord about its properties. And he has it growing right here, close to his hand. But that's not all. He ordered a hot posset to be made for Dame Alice." Janna paused so that the full import of her words might sink in. "I have found out, and from the priest himself, that my mother tasted the posset just before she died!"

She waited expectantly, sure that Aldith would follow her line of reasoning.

"And?" Aldith shifted her stool slightly away as if to distance herself from Janna's suspicions.

"So it's obvious, isn't it? Fulk offered a partnership in his shop at Wiltune to my mother and she went along with it until she'd been received by Dame Alice. After that, she sent him away, leaving no-one in any doubt as to her low opinion of him. She ingratiated herself with the lady, and sullied the apothecary's professional reputation at the same time. No wonder he hated her and feared her influence. No wonder he wished her gone! And he had the ways and means to make his wish come true. A few drops of the rubbing oil in the posset and—" Janna clicked her fingers, indicating the rest.

Aldith's round O of a mouth told Janna that Fulk's proposition was news to the midwife. She sniffed then and her face settled into angry lines. "I know how rude and outspoken your mother could be. Small wonder if Master Fulk wished her harm."

"She didn't deserve to die for telling the truth!" Janna contradicted sharply. What could she say to convince Aldith that the apothecary should be brought to justice for her mother's death? If she could bring the midwife around to her way of thinking, Aldith might join her in persuading Robert of Babestoche to try the apothecary for her mother's murder in his manorial court, or else refer the case to the shire reeve. There might be a chance of justice for her mother after all.

"There is a flaw in your reasoning," the midwife pointed out. "Fulk couldn't know for certain that your mother would taste a posset meant for Dame Alice and then throw it out."

"He could have slipped in the poison just before he handed the cup to my mother."

"How did he know she would even be present in the bedchamber? It's all too uncertain, Janna. Besides, he would never have taken such a risk with my lady's life."

Janna's high expectations deflated as she saw the truth of Aldith's words. Then she brightened. "Perhaps Fulk carried the poison about with him always, just waiting for this sort of opportunity." Sure now that she had the truth of the matter, she beamed in triumph at Aldith. "He could have flattered my mother. He could have asked her to taste the mixture and give him her opinion on it."

"If that is so, then others will have heard him ask it. Someone may even have seen him adding the oil to the mixture." Aldith put a restraining hand on Janna's arm once more. "Before you accuse anyone, let's ask the tiring women exactly what happened in Dame Alice's bedchamber."

"I'll ask Mistress Cecily." Suspecting Cecily's secret, Janna felt sure the tiring woman would have watched Eadgyth carefully on her arrival at the manor for any signs of betrayal. If Fulk had said or done anything untoward, Cecily would surely have noticed. She tapped a foot, impatient for action.

Aldith hesitated. "My lord Robert asked you to leave. You are not welcome here. Go back to your cottage, Janna. I can talk to the tiring women and report their words to you, if you would like me to do so."

Was Aldith just being kind, or was her true purpose to get Janna out of the manor and out of her way? Janna had no way of knowing. She felt ashamed of her suspicions, but she knew anyway that this was a task that she alone must fulfil, for only she knew the right questions to ask, and only she had the courage to ask them.

"It's true he told me to go," she admitted, "but Dame Alice's nephew has asked me to wait here. As I can't serve two masters, I would rather serve myself. I cannot rest until I find out who was responsible for my mother's death, for if I know anything in this life, I know that she did not die by her own hand. The culprit must be brought to justice, Mistress Aldith. So I do thank you for your offer, but it would be unfair to involve you in this business, especially if Fulk succeeds in turning all the household against me."

The midwife nodded, seeming relieved to be rid of further responsibility. Nevertheless, she sounded a note of warning. "I understand you're looking for someone to blame, but you must tread carefully, Janna. Fulk is an important man in Wiltune. Many hold him in high regard. If you accuse him of poisoning your mother, do you really think anyone will take your word against his?"

"They must, if I have proof." Although she spoke bravely, Janna knew the danger of the path she had chosen. Yet she knew also that she could not give up her search for justice and the truth.

Janna and Aldith sat on in silence, each busy with her own thoughts. Janna's eyes began to droop with tiredness, until the sound of a door opening jerked her back into wakefulness once more. Cecily had emerged. She was on her own, and her steps checked when she saw them waiting. For a moment Janna thought she might retreat, but she set off once more, keeping her face averted as she hurried to the door.

Janna jumped to her feet. Now was her best chance to prove Fulk's guilt, if only the tiring woman had seen what must have happened and was brave enough to bear witness against him.

"Mistress Cecily, a moment, please," she called. "May I ask you something?"

Cecily stopped, and turned to Janna with seeming reluctance.

"The priest told me that the doctor ordered a hot posset to be made up for Dame Alice and that my mother tasted it?"

Cecily nodded slowly. "'Tis true. Master Fulk brought the posset to Dame Alice's bedchamber."

"Did he say what was in it?"

"Nettles and mint, among other things. It wasn't the first time he'd ordered it for my lady. He boasted that it was a marvelous tonic, and that it would restore her to health far quicker than any mixtures your mother might give her."

Janna bit back a sharp retort, saying instead, "So my mother wasn't with Dame Alice when the apothecary brought in the posset?" She had to get all the facts, even if they didn't take her in the direction she'd expected.

"No, but she came in only a few moments later. She demanded to know what was in the mixture, but Master Fulk wouldn't tell her. Your mother seized the cup and tasted its contents for herself. We were all amazed, for she never even asked Dame Alice's permission to do so."

Brushing aside Cecily's regard for etiquette, Janna asked, "Did Dame Alice also taste the posset?"

"No. She said it was too hot to drink, so she set it aside to cool."

Janna felt a surge of excitement. Trying to sound composed, she asked the most important question. "Cecily, did Master Fulk add anything to the posset after my mother entered the room?"

"No, I don't think so." She screwed up her delicate features in concentration. "No, I'm sure not."

"Did he, perhaps, ask my mother to try the posset?"

"No, indeed. In fact, he tried to prevent her from taking up the cup. The posset was for Dame Alice to drink, not your mother!"

Janna and Aldith exchanged glances. Aldith shook her head in warning, but Janna could not give up now. "Did my mother say anything about the posset, about its taste perhaps?" There was an edge of desperation in her question.

Unexpectedly, Cecily grinned. "She was extremely rude about it. She took a few sips and then poured the rest of it out of the window. When Master Fulk complained, she told him she'd brought a far better tonic for Dame Alice, and while rose petals, nettles, mint and honey might make a sweet concoction, to her certain knowledge they had never cured anything more serious than a mild stomach ache!"

Rose petals, nettles, mint and honey. Janna closed her eyes, disappointed that it could not be the posset that had killed her mother. Eadgyth would certainly have warned Dame Alice that it contained monkshood if she'd detected its presence. She should have thought of that before.

"That is where I am bound now," Cecily said. "Fulk has ordered me to fetch another posset from the cook, although methinks my lady needs something different, something strong enough to relieve her low spirits, for that is what ails her most." She shook her head. "My poor lady," she said softly. "She is in such distress. I think she would do better to drink several cups of the new wine that has come from Normandy. At least it would dull her senses; it might even bring her the comfort of sleep."

Janna remembered how the lady had sent the goblet tumbling to the floor. "Does Dame Alice not drink wine?"

"She does, but she says this latest shipment is tainted. I think she does exaggerate, for my master says that the wine is of the very finest quality."

"I have only ever tasted dandelion and nettle wine," Janna confessed. A picture came into her mind of Robert and his household sitting down to dine, and the array of fine food and fine wines they would consume. The hollow in her stomach reminded her how little she had eaten recently, and how poor and basic were the meals she'd shared with her mother. She brought her mind back to the questions she still wanted to ask. Cecily might have demolished the case against Fulk, but there was a lot more that she could tell.

"I must go," Cecily said quietly. "Dame Alice is waiting for her posset."

"I'll come with you." Janna fell into step beside her before she could refuse. In silence, they descended the stairs leading to the grounds of the manor.

Outside, she asked, "Can you tell me what else passed between my mother and Master Fulk after she poured the posset away? Did she, by any chance, taste any of his other concoctions?"

"No, she did not. She told him to leave the bedchamber. He would not go and began a loud argument, but Dame Alice insisted that he leave them all in peace. Of course, he returned as soon as he heard your mother was taken ill, but—"

"Did he offer her any physic then?" It was possible her mother had taken ill, and then Fulk had seen to it that she never recovered, Janna thought. Her hopes were dashed as Cecily again shook her head. Not Fulk, then. It seemed he must be innocent after all.

She cast her mind to others who might have wished her mother harm. She remembered her conversation with the priest. He'd dismissed her suspicions of Fulk, but how clear was his own conscience? The priest had told her he'd been in the bedchamber and had witnessed the scene between her mother and the apothecary. If the priest had fallen for the merchant's patter in the marketplace, he too would have access to a phial of oil and could have used it to poison her mother somehow. It would explain his dismay when he heard her accuse Fulk of the crime he himself had committed. She turned to Cecily. "What about the priest?" she asked. "Did he touch the posset at any time?"

"No."

"Or offer my mother anything to eat or drink?"

"No." Cecily gave a sudden snort of laughter. "He kept as far away from your mother as possible. I think he was frightened of her. She had an answer for everything he said. She always managed to silence him."

Janna felt a sharp pang of remembrance. "An ignorant bigot," Eadgyth had called the priest, after their hasty exit from his church. "Because he hates women, he would have us believe that Christ did too." Eadgyth would have enjoyed giving him a taste of her sharp tongue. Could she have angered him enough to kill her? But even if she had, it seemed he did not have the opportunity to put his wishes into action.

Not the priest then, and not Fulk. That meant Janna would have to consider more carefully the time leading up to her mother's arrival at the manor house. In this, Cecily held the key.

She put out a hand to detain the tiring lady, and drew her into the shade of a barn. "My mother had a visitor the morning before she died," she said carefully.

Cecily said nothing, but Janna noticed her hands clench and unclench at her side.

"The visit was a great secret," Janna continued. "I knew it must be someone very special, for I was not allowed to stay while my mother treated her."

Cecily's face paled. Janna was afraid she might swoon, she looked so distraught. She waited a few moments, then said patiently, "You were gone from the manor when you were supposed to be resting. You were gone at the time my mother expected her visitor."

Cecily averted her face, and did not answer. Janna sighed. "It was you, wasn't it? I know, from the herbs I was sent to gather, that you were with child and that you came to my mother for help."

Cecily swayed, and put out a hand to support herself against the wall of the barn. Her face was anguished as she gasped, "You must not tell anyone of this. It's too dangerous."

"Why? Why is it dangerous?"

"Because...because I am unwed, and in Dame Alice's employ. If she knew of my shame, she would send me away. But I have nowhere else to go."

"Could the baby's father not help you? Could you not be wed?" Janna wondered who it could be that he could leave a young woman to face her disgrace alone. Some lowly servant or farmhand, perhaps, who would not dare brave the wrath of the lord of the manor?

"No, indeed! That's not possible."

Because the father was already married? Or was he too highborn to wed someone of Cecily's comparatively low status? Janna remembered Hugh supporting Cecily at Eadgyth's graveside. How solicitous he had been over her health; how protective were his arms about her waist as he helped her mount before leading her away. Was Hugh the father of Cecily's child? No matter how strong his feelings might be for Cecily, no matter how strong the bond between them, Janna was sure that he would not want his aunt to know that he'd got her tiring woman into trouble.

Pushing her doubts—and her disappointment—aside, Janna said gently, "I understand. Forgive me for distressing you, mistress, but I need to ask a few more questions about my mother. You see, I had thought she must have taken some poison at the manor house to cause her death, but I see now that I was mistaken. Now I believe my mother must have taken some food or drink, or somehow imbibed the poison even before she came to the manor house."

Janna watched Cecily carefully, curious to observe her reaction. The tiring woman was still deathly pale with the shock of having her secret discovered. Was she now also fearful that Janna might discover an even more dreadful secret: that Cecily herself had made sure of the *wortwyf*'s silence? Janna liked Cecily, and felt deeply sorry for her, but she knew she couldn't allow her sympathy to blind her to the fact that Cecily had lied once and might well do so again.

"You were with my mother on the morning of her death," she said carefully. "Did you see her eat or drink anything while you were at the cottage?"

"No." Cecily thought for a moment. "No," she said again.

"You didn't take anything to her?"

Cecily bridled. "Of course I did! I gave her a costly gift in return for her labor and skill."

Janna nodded. That was only to be expected. "And you didn't share any food or drink with her?"

"No. I drank only the potion your mother made for me. She bade me wait until it took effect, but it was a long walk home and so I left straight away." Cecily shuddered. Tears came into her eyes as she relived what had happened next. "Truly, I thought I was like to die. I had such cramps that I could hardly walk the distance. I was also in great distress of mind. Your mother was very kind to me. She'd warned me how it would be, and she bade me rest at your cot so that she could take care of me until the worst of it had passed. But I was in haste to be gone, lest my absence be noted and remarked upon, and so I didn't tarry."

"Did my mother go back to the manor with you? Were you with her when she met Mistress Aldith?"

"No!" Cecily shook her head. "She told me she needed to prepare a tonic for Dame Alice's ailing babe, and so I went ahead on my own. I'd told everyone I was ill and needed to rest, you see, and I crept in, hoping my absence hadn't been noticed." A watery smile gleamed momentarily. "It seems I was not careful enough, however."

"So they know you were absent, but no-one from the manor knows where you really were or the purpose of your absence?"

"No." Cecily seized hold of Janna's hand. "You must not speak of this to anyone, anyone at all," she begged. "Should Dame Alice come to hear of it, I would lose my position here along with my livelihood. Promise me you will keep silent, even if your mother could not."

"My mother kept her promise to you," Janna said at once. "It was only after my lord Hugh spoke of your absence from the manor, and I saw how ill you looked, and remembered how you tried to care for my mother when she lay dying, that I thought her secret visitor might have been you. Even so, I was not sure. You could have denied it. I might even have believed you."

Cecily tipped her head to one side, assessing Janna with a thoughtful stare. "I think you see and know a lot more than any of us realize," she said. "You certainly ask enough questions!"

Janna smiled, taking Cecily's words as a compliment. Yet it was no time for smiling. Cecily had utterly demolished her carefully constructed case against Fulk and against the priest, and was well on the way to clearing her own name. She might have to start her investigation all over again. "Can you tell me anything at all about your visit to my mother that might have led to her death?" she asked.

Tears welled into Cecily's eyes once more. "Your mother was in good health and good spirits when I left her. She was making up the new elixir for the baby, and she told me she'd see how I fared when she got back to the manor house." She began to weep, knuckling her fists into her eyes like a small child as she tried to conceal her distress. "It was such a long walk back to the manor, I truly thought I would die before I could get here."

Janna put her arm around Cecily to steady her. "I am sorry you had to bear that alone. It must have been hard for you." She was touched by Cecily's grief, knowing that it reflected an anguish of mind and spirit even more than the memory of her physical discomfort. She had seen the effect of her mother's potion on other young women who had come to her in secrecy. It could be no easy thing to cross the Church's teaching and take the life of a child. Janna felt great sympathy for this lonely young woman. "You have my silence, I give you my word on it," she promised.

"I thank you." Cecily pulled away from Janna. She scrubbed her eyes and nose across her sleeve, gave a mournful sniff, and walked in the direction of the kitchen. Janna watched her go. All her instincts told her that she could trust Cecily, yet the young woman had given her no proof of her innocence, nor could she. She and Eadgyth had been alone in the cottage. Anything might have taken place between them. All Janna knew for certain was that her mother did not die by her own hand.

The manor seemed hushed and still, drowsy in the mid-afternoon sun. It was past dinnertime and Janna's stomach growled with hunger. She debated going home, back to the cottage, for her questions were all done. Her spirits drooped at the thought. She could not give up, not yet. Surely the answers must lie somewhere here, at the manor house, where her mother had spent her last hours. If only she knew who to speak to, and where to look! While she pondered her next move, Janna walked to the well. She could slake her thirst, if not her hunger.

The cool water refreshed her. She sat down on a bench beside the well, and closed her eyes, the better to focus on the events surrounding her mother's death. Lifting her face to the sunlight, she felt its warmth enter her body, giving new life and hope to her exhausted spirit.

The sound of a warning cry interrupted her musing. She opened her eyes, and saw an elderly woman and a little boy approaching her. The child ran ahead, ignoring his nurse's cries to slow down. He was all smiles as he raced up to Janna. "My name is Hamo," he announced. "What's your name?"

"Janna. Johanna." The child had the look of his mother along with the dark Norman coloring of both his parents. He was only five or six years now, but he would grow up to be a heartbreaker, Janna thought.

"Who are you?" Hamo eyed Janna's coarsely woven kirtle and rough boots curiously. Her appearance seemed not to faze him, however, for he remained smiling and friendly as he continued, "Are you a friend of my mother and father? Or my cousin Hugh?"

"None of them."

"Then why are you here?"

"I came to help your baby brother. I tried to make him better." Janna found it hard to tell a lie or even to soften the truth under the direct and trusting gaze of the child.

"My brother died. There's only me left now," he answered matter-of-factly.

"I know. I am sorry for it."

Hamo studied her. "It's just as well," he said candidly. "My brother would have to be a soldier and go to war or enter the church for a living, for all my mother's property and wealth will be mine when she dies. I am her first-born son, you see."

"What about your father? Will you inherit his lands and wealth too?"

"No, he's got nothing to leave anyone. All this belongs to my mother."

Janna stared at Hamo in amazement. She had paid homage to Robert of Babestoche, as was his due as lord of the manor. Yet it seemed he had married well, far better than he might have expected, in fact. Still, it made no odds whose wealth it was, except perhaps to this precocious child and any future siblings he might have. On reflection, Janna concluded this was unlikely, given the lady's sad history. It seemed Hamo's inheritance was safe. She wished him joy of it.

Hamo's nurse had caught up with him and now she gave him a reproving glance. "You will not indulge in idle chatter with servants," she said sternly.

"I want Janna to play ball with me."

"You do not play ball while you are in mourning for your brother."

"How can I feel sad about my brother when I didn't even know him?"

"You will do what is expected of you."

Hamo stamped his foot. "But I want to play ball."

"'Tis too late now. I will play ball with you tomorrow." The nurse cast a glance at the sun, perhaps praying for nightfall. The fiery orb was past its zenith, edging down to the west and tinting fluffy lambswool clouds with a rim of bright gold. Janna judged that there was still plenty of time for a game of ball. She winked at Hamo and he, delighted, grinned back at her.

"I don't want to play ball with you," he told the nurse. "You're too old. You never catch it and you won't run after it either." He turned to Janna. "Will you play ball with me?"

She glanced at the nurse, seeking permission. The woman shrugged, clearly unwilling to take responsibility for an activity she deemed unseemly. Yet Janna thought she might be quite pleased to have a break from her demanding charge for a while. The woman was getting on in years. Truly, she looked utterly exhausted.

"Do you have a ball?" she asked Hamo, wondering if a child of the nobility would also play with a pig's bladder stuffed with straw, as the street urchins did.

"Yes!" With a squeal of excitement he dashed off to find it, leaving Janna with his nurse.

"I am sure the boy truly appreciates your company and is grateful for your care of him," she said softly.

"He is too clever for his own good." The nurse looked sour. Janna felt sorry for Hamo. Surely cleverness was to be encouraged rather than frowned upon? But he would escape his nurse soon enough, for in only a few years he would likely be sent away to another manor house, or perhaps a lord's castle or even the abbey. He would learn to read and write, how to fight and how to serve the king. Janna envied Hamo for his wealth and the freedom that would allow him to do exactly as he pleased in the future.

"Catch!" Hamo had returned, and now he threw a ball at her, its flight swift and true and finding its mark hard against her belly.

"Oof!" Winded, Janna fumbled to catch it, but the ball fell at her feet. It was made of leather and, by the sound of the rattle inside, it was stuffed with dried peas or beans. It was round enough to fly through the air and to roll a distance should she miss catching it. She would have to watch it more carefully next time. "Catch!" she cried in turn as she copied his motion and sent the ball flying back to Hamo.

He caught it, and in one movement sent it hurtling back to her. It was a little high and Janna had to jump for it. She missed, and the ball went flying onward. With a chuckle, she picked up her skirt and chased it.

"Catch!" Her throw was clumsy, and the ball went off to one side. Quick as a flash, Hamo went after it, diving to grab it before it hit the ground.

"Well done!" Janna clapped her hands together. Hamo smiled with delight. Janna thought he might not get too many compliments, especially not from his crabby nurse. He didn't let this one turn his head though, sending the ball straight and true to Janna once more. Again she fumbled and missed, and again she had to chase it. She bent to pick up the ball. A pair of boots planted themselves in front of her. Panting and out of breath, she straightened. She found herself staring into a smiling face and dancing eyes. Hugh.

Janna blushed as she hastily tried to straighten her kirtle and smooth her hair. What must Hugh think of her, rushing about like a street urchin? This thought was followed hard by another: Hugh already knew what she was. Why should a ball game with a child make any difference to his opinion of her? And what about her opinion of him? If he really was responsible for Cecily's unborn child, she had no high opinion of him whatsoever. Yet she shouldn't leap to judgment—at least, not yet.

"I thought I'd come and keep my cousin company for a while, but I see he's in good company already." Without asking permission, Hugh took the ball from Janna and threw it back to Hamo. "Catch!"

With a squeal of excitement, Hamo leaped into the air and caught the ball with both hands.

"Well done!" Hugh exchanged an amused glance with Janna as they both clapped the boy's efforts. Hamo smiled, suddenly shy. He put the ball behind his back, and began to scuff the earth beneath his feet.

"Don't you want to play anymore?" Hugh asked.

A great beaming smile spread across Hamo's face. "Yes!" And before Hugh could change his mind, the ball sped like an arrow toward him. Hugh caught it deftly and returned it, while Janna retreated to safety. The ball seemed to have become a deadly missile in the hands of the cousins. As she watched the two exchange banter while each tried to out-throw the other, she reflected on how lonely the boy's life must be here at the manor, with only a crotchety old nurse to care for him. The company of a cousin must seem like a gift to him—as Hugh's company had been a gift to her. She was seeing a side of him she had not expected. He was showing the heart of the child he once was, evidenced by the loud crow of glee he uttered when he threw a carefully angled ball just a little too high and Hamo missed it. The child scampered after it, seemingly unperturbed until he sent back a return, so low and so fast that Hugh fumbled and dropped the ball. Now it was Hamo's turn to chuckle and taunt Hugh for the butterfingers that had let the ball slip through his grasp.

Janna joined in their laughter, and was surprised. She'd thought she'd never feel happy again. It was greatly reassuring to think that life could go on and that joy was still possible. She watched the two together, man and boy, united in their enjoyment of their game. Hamo had a mother and father, but what about Hugh? Janna remembered that he'd told her he'd come to make a report on his custodianship of Dame Alice's property. Did he have family and lands of his own to inherit, or was Dame Alice his only living kin? And was Hamo all that kept Hugh from a large inheritance? If so, it was certain that Hugh would desire his aunt's good opinion above everything, and would do all in his power to keep it, including denying Cecily an offer of marriage, or even his comfort and support.

Another and far worse question came into Janna's mind: How far might Hugh go to keep his liaison with the tiring woman a secret? Admittedly, she had no grounds for suspecting his involvement in her mother's death, for on his own admission, Eadgyth was already dying by the time he and

Robert were summoned to the bedchamber. Janna told herself she was jumping to conclusions about Hugh and Cecily, conclusions that might well prove utterly false. She found some comfort in the thought.

A sudden howl interrupted her reverie. She looked up to see Hugh sprinting toward Hamo, who was clutching the side of his face and trying not to cry. The lethal missile-thrower was but a little boy again. The red welt on the side of his face spoke of what had happened even as Hugh broke into an apology.

"It's my fault," he said. "I'm sorry, Hamo. I shouldn't have thrown the ball so hard. After all, you're just a child."

A forlorn hiccup greeted this tactless observation. Ignoring the outraged clucking of the nurse, Janna pulled a reproachful face at Hugh over Hamo's head and enfolded the boy in her arms to comfort him.

"Of course, you're so big for your age, and you throw the ball so hard and so well, it's not surprising I thought you were a lot older than you really are," Hugh added hastily, doing his best to retrieve the situation.

"Everyone says I'm big for my age." Hamo broke away from Janna and squared his shoulders as he faced Hugh. "I've been riding with the groom and practicing with my own sword every day so that I shall grow up to be a fine soldier just like you."

"I expect you'll be a far greater soldier than I can ever be," said Hugh, and earned a watery smile for the compliment.

"I knew this would end in tears," the nurse muttered darkly, and tried to take hold of her charge. Hamo backed away and hid behind Hugh.

"Would you like to come with me to the kitchen garden, Hamo?" Janna asked. "We'll crush a comfrey root to soothe that sore swelling on your face where the ball hit you."

He nodded, and slipped his hand into hers.

As they walked to the garden, Hugh fell into step beside them. Wearing a frown of disapproval, the nurse followed.

"How is Dame Alice faring, my lord?" Janna asked.

"We have left her to rest."

"And Mistress Cecily?" Janna watched Hugh closely for any sign that she meant more to him than merely being his aunt's tiring woman. "Is she now recovered from whatever ailed her?"

"She's doing well enough, I think," Hugh said casually, seeming not at all troubled by the question. Instead, there was warmth and concern in his voice as he asked, "And what of you, Johanna? How do you fare, with so much to burden you?"

The thunder of hoof beats prevented Janna from having to answer. Hugh quickly scooped up Hamo and sprang aside to safety. Janna looked up at the horseman, and felt a shaft of anxiety as she recognized the lord of the manor. For one fearful moment she thought Robert was going to run her down. She leaped out of his path, landing awkwardly and wrenching her ankle as she did so.

Robert jerked on the reins, forcing his horse to a sudden standstill. His eyes were hard and angry as he stared down at her. "Why are you still here? I told you to go home before you do any more harm, and I'll thank you to do as you're told." His glance flicked from Janna to her companion. Ignoring the child clasped in Hugh's arms, he said, "Make sure the girl leaves the manor at once." He dug his heels viciously into the horse's flank. Startled, it reared and then took off at speed.

Behind Robert, riding more decorously, came the priest. He nodded at Hugh and Hamo, but could not hide his displeasure at the sight of Janna. Compressing his lips, he followed Robert out through the gate.

Hugh put Hamo down when he judged it was safe to do so. The boy looked indignant.

"I'm not a baby, you know!"

"I know, Hamo, but I wasn't sure your father had noticed you. I didn't want him to run you down." There was a steely glint in Hugh's eye as he looked after Robert and the priest, but his expression softened as his glance shifted to Janna. He seemed to be making an effort to hold himself in check. Janna wondered if he was working out how best to follow Robert's orders to get rid of her.

She decided to help him out. "My lord," she said, "I must go home, as I've been told."

"No. Stay and find a balm for Hamo's cheek, I pray you." Hugh gave a rueful laugh. "I fear I will feel the lash of his mother's tongue for hurting him, but at least I will be able to say we did what we could to ease the pain."

Janna nodded, encouraged by his confidence that she would be able to help. Child of the forest she may be, but she was not so ignorant as he might suppose. "Where do the lord and the priest go so late in the afternoon?"

"The priest has gone to make arrangements for the baby's interment and to instruct the villagers to attend a requiem mass for the child's soul. My aunt wishes it."

"And Lord Robert?"

Hugh shrugged. "Perhaps he needs to report the baby's death to the shire reeve."

"Why does he hate me so?"

"Who? Robert, or the priest? Or the shire reeve?"

"Lord Robert. Truly, my mother and I did all we could to help Dame Alice and her infant son. Dame Alice understands that and seems grateful, but her husband has turned against me."

Hugh was silent for a moment. "He blames you for his son's death," he admitted at last.

"But I—But we—"

Hugh held up his hand to silence her protest. "I know," he said simply. "I know."

Once in the garden, Janna looked about for the hairy leaves and stalks of comfrey. She was certain such a useful plant would be cultivated here and she soon found it, and in some quantity. She dug down, seeking the spread of roots below.She broke off a portion of thick root, and showed it to Hamo. Black on the outside, it was white within and full of a glutinous juice.

"Erk!" he said.

"It'll help, I promise." Janna applied the cool mixture to the boy's smarting cheek, then turned to his nurse. "Take these roots and some leaves from the comfrey, and ask the cook to boil them up. When the water has cooled, bathe Hamo's bruise with the decoction. It will soothe his skin and help to bring down the swelling."

The nurse gave a reluctant nod.

"See to it," Hugh said sharply.

She bobbed a curtsy and set to picking some leaves.

Hugh turned to Janna. "You have your mother's skill with herbs, I see."

"She taught me all she knew—and she knew a great deal."

"Where and how did she gain her knowledge?"

"I know not," Janna confessed sadly. "She would not speak about her past." Fearing Hugh's pity or, even worse, his judgment, she added quickly, "I must go now, sire. I want to be home before dark."

"You could stay here tonight, at the manor."

Janna flashed a sidelong glance at Hugh, suddenly suspicious of his motives.

"In case my aunt has need of you," he added quickly.

"You heard the lord. He bade me go, and I must obey him, sire."

"Then I will take you home, and also fetch the palfrey while I am there." Hugh swerved off toward the barns, closely followed by Hamo, who still clutched the gummy root to the side of his face. "Go with your nurse, Hamo." He bent down and gently pushed the child in the direction of the kitchen. "We'll play ball again tomorrow," he promised.

Reluctantly, and with many a backward glance, Hamo did as he was told. "Come." Hugh beckoned Janna and together they went to reclaim his large destrier from a long wattle-and-daub shed. The horse blew softly from a stall at the far end. Janna looked about her as Hugh saddled the horse. Above her head was a trapdoor. Wisps of hay suggested that the space was a storage house through winter, while saddles and bridles and empty stalls told the use of the space below.

Janna marveled that the manor should have all these separate buildings just for livestock and storage. For people too, she thought, as she noticed several straw pallets and a hook from which hung a rough smock and breeches. Serfs must also sleep here, those who had no cottage or shelter of their own. They would be out in the fields now, tending the crops, weeding, digging ditches and getting ready for hay-making. It was early summer, and the grass in the meadows would soon be tall enough to cut.

Hugh led the destrier out into the fading sunlight. This time, he placed Janna in front of him so that she sat as decorously as any highborn lady. His arm came around her for support, and she leaned back against him as the horse made its slow journey across the downs. She was close enough to Hugh to smell the faint odor of his sweat mingled with leather and horse. It was masculine, unfamiliar and very exciting. Even while understanding the need for caution, her body responded to his with a longing so great she was unable to think, savoring instead the heat and turmoil of this time alone with him.

The ride seemed to last forever, yet was over far too quickly. Hugh dismounted and reached up to put his hands around her waist. He swung her down from the saddle, but kept on holding her. Janna trembled, consumed with desire as she leaned closer and closed her eyes.

His kiss was light and fleeting, but Janna thought there was warmth there too. She struggled to bring her emotions under control, although it took all her will to resist the urge to cling to him, to kiss him back. Her heart was pounding so hard she thought it might burst right out of her chest. But a small nugget of caution prompted her to free herself from his embrace. She took a step away from him, hoping that this small distance might keep her safe. "Thank you," she murmured.

"For the kiss, or for bringing you home?" His voice was cool, amused. He seemed not to feel the churning emotion that so unsettled her. The realization strengthened Janna, and gave her the courage to give him a light reply in turn.

"I thank you for bringing me home, for it was kind of you to take the trouble. I feel sure kisses can be no trouble to you, for you must have bestowed kisses aplenty in your life, and to far more purpose than merely seducing a—a naive and ignorant child of the forest!"

A vision of Cecily's tear-stained face flashed before her. She took another step away from him.

Hugh laughed. "I have already admitted that I misjudged you, Johanna—but now you misjudge me! I always kiss to a purpose, but I only bestow kisses where they are wanted."

Now Janna wished she'd kept silent. She had no evidence that he wished to seduce her! In fact, he'd only ever been kind and considerate toward her. What must he think of her presumption? "I beg your pardon, sire," she muttered.

"Shh." He put a finger across her lips. "I understand."

There was a moment's silence while Janna became aware of the dark forest, silent at her back, and the green fields spread before her, rolling down to the river and to Berford. She felt as if she was standing on a lonely precipice. She had no protection against Hugh should she fall, no protection for a heart that was in danger of being stolen—save the memory of Cecily's sorrow and disgrace. She stood straighter and rubbed her mouth. It tingled where his lips had touched it. She longed for Hugh and feared him in equal measure.

Perhaps he understood something of the storm of feelings that threatened to overwhelm her, for he moved away to untie the palfrey and bring it back to where the destrier waited. He remounted, then touched two fingers to his head in a casual salute. "May God be with you this night, Johanna," he said, and turned the horses toward Babestoche.

Chapter 11

The cottage felt cold and unwelcoming; it was all too silent. Tears came into Janna's eyes as she thought how different it would be if Eadgyth was home. Knowing what Eadgyth would say if Janna told her how she felt about Hugh helped to brace her and give her courage. Turnip head. That's what Eadgyth would call her, what she called Fulk and anyone else who got too puffed up with their own self-importance.

"Turnip head," Janna repeated silently as she set about milking the goats and foraging for their food. But keeping busy could not disguise the fact that all her efforts to find the person responsible for poisoning her mother had failed.

She remembered that Cecily had said she'd brought a costly gift for Eadgyth. A flicker of interest stirred Janna into action. Where was it? Now she thought about it, she certainly couldn't remember seeing anything unfamiliar about the place. She walked inside. She'd already searched through her mother's medicaments; now she turned her attention to the rest of the small cottage. Her search didn't take long—there was nothing to be found. Could Cecily have lied about bringing a gift? Or had she perhaps brought a cake, or something to drink? If so, might it have contained poison, a sure way to silence the *wortwyf* and keep her secret safe?

Janna shuddered at the thought. After further consideration, she dismissed it. If Cecily had brought a treat from the manor as a gift, her mother would have kept it to share with her daughter. They always shared everything. So what might she have missed in her search? Janna looked about, but there was nothing that she did not recognize. Nothing.

Too agitated to rest, she walked outside again and paced about the garden, pulling weeds from among her herbs and nipping off dead leaves and flowers, creating order where her mind could find none. Why hadn't she thought to question Cecily about her gift? A moment's reflection told Janna that, if guilty, the tiring woman would have lied. But if innocent, the gift should still be in the cottage, waiting to be found.

Janna busied herself with tasks until it was too dark to see. Weary now, she went inside. Her agitated thoughts continued to weave a tangled web in her mind. The only thing certain was that she could take the matter no further until she had another chance to speak to Cecily.

She took up flint and tinder to light the fire, then stopped as another possibility presented itself. If Cecily had stopped her mother's tongue to protect her secret, she might well take the same action against Janna! She would have to be careful when dealing with the tiring woman—very careful.

With a fire burning and a small light also coming from a peeled rush soaked in fat, Janna began to feel a little more confident. The hollow feeling in her stomach returned, and she realized that she was ravenous. She took up a knife and unlatched the door. She peered out, fearful of what, or who, might be lurking outside. Cecily wasn't the only one who might wish her harm.

All seemed quiet. No Cecily, or Hilde, or even a wild boar. Janna felt a crushing sadness as she recalled her angry accusation. Godric had risked everything to save her, to protect her and care for her, and had then suffered her insults at the graveside. He was a kind and decent man, and she owed him an apology. Could he, would he, ever forgive her for thinking such ill of him?

She bent to dig out some reddish purple carrots for the pot, adding a leek and some beans plus a couple of sprigs of marjoram. The herb would calm her troubled thoughts, as well as adding extra flavor to the pottage. The hens clucked around her. "Go and lay some eggs," she told them as she searched the empty coop.

Inside, she emptied a jug of water into the large cooking pot and hung it over the fire to boil. She gave the vegetables a careful wash before slicing them up. She threw them into the pot to cook, along with a handful of oats to thicken the stock. She should save the goats' milk to make cheese, she knew, but she mixed a little in with some flour to bake another cake on the griddle. Pottage might not suit the lord and lady of the manor, but to Janna the hot food was a feast and she savored every last morsel of it.

With the ache of hunger eased, she set the pot aside. She took off her kirtle and boots, and sluiced a quick lick of water over her face. Too weary to do anything more, she blew out the rushlight and lay down on the straw pallet to sleep. Tomorrow, she thought, I shall talk to Cecily again, and see if I can trap her into admitting what really happened between her and my mother—and what, if anything, Hugh means to her. I shall also tidy the cottage and sort through my mother's possessions. A shaft of sorrow lanced through Janna. To banish it, she kept compiling a list of things to do. It hadn't rained for some days; the soil where she'd dug out the carrots had felt very dry. She must fill some buckets from the dew pond to keep her precious plants alive and thriving, and also fetch fresh water for drinking. As well, the floor rushes needed changing. She must go down to the river to cut some more. Resolutely, Janna added chores to her list, although she wondered where she would find the hours in the day to complete them all. She must make cheese, and also more wax candles, perfumed creams, balms and ointments to sell at the market. She must pick herbs and hang them to dry, ready to be used in new medicaments. She must—

A sudden noise set her upright, ears straining to hear, eyes straining to make sense of the ghostly flickers of firelight cast by the dying embers in the center of the room. Was that someone standing in the corner, watching her? Her heart thundered in fright. She stayed still, waiting for the phantom to move, to betray its real and living presence. She could hear breathing, loud rasping breaths that spoke of terror. It was some moments before Janna realized that the breaths were her own.

Now she heard a voice calling her, the name unmistakable: "Janna!" Who could be visiting her at this time of the night? She bounded up from her pallet, and pulled on her kirtle and boots.

"Janna! Come outside!" The command was followed by a furious knocking, so loud Janna thought the door might come down. It was a woman's voice calling her, but she could not place it. Was someone in trouble? With some reluctance, Janna pulled the door open and stepped out.

A group of villagers were gathered there, the leader bearing a flaming torch held high so that his face was illuminated. With a shock of recognition, she saw that it was Wulfgar, the miller. He stared at her, grim and determined.

"What do you want?" It was an effort to keep her voice steady. Sweat prickled her skin in the cool night air. She thought of the knife still lying on the table, and wished she'd remembered to snatch it up before opening the door. Alone and unprotected, she faced the villagers.

"Murderess! Child killer!"

Janna peered into the darkness behind the lighted flare, able now to identify the voice. Hilde, the miller's wife. She stepped out in front of her husband, and shook her fist at Janna. Her face, savage and sneering, was lit by the flaring light from the torch. The rest of her was thrown into shadowed relief. With her swollen body and wild gestures, she looked like a huge and grotesque ogre.

"Why do you say such things when you know they're not true?" Janna held her ground, determined to make Hilde explain her spiteful words.

"Everyone says you poisoned the baby up at the manor. You took the life of a young and innocent child!"

"Who says so?" It took all of Janna's courage not to flee inside and slam the door on the group. She could read the hatred on Hilde's face, a hatred which must be shared by all or they would not have come knocking.

Once again, Janna remembered Eadgyth's warning. *"Never turn your back on a wild animal. Never let it see that you are afraid."* But these were people—not animals! Yet, like sheep, they seemed to be following Hilde's lead without question. Should she treat them like animals? Yes, if it ensured her safety!

"Who says that I am a child killer?" she demanded again, her voice loud to cover her fear.

"The priest says so! He says you do the devil's work!" An angry murmuring followed Hilde's reply.

"What reason does he give for these lies?"

"You gave the baby a potion of your own concocting—and he died."

"The baby's own mother and father know that is not true."

"Fulk the apothecary told the priest that it was so."

"Lord Robert and Dame Alice know that I did all I could to save their child."

"The priest and Robert of Babestoche himself say that the baby died because of the poisoned physic you gave him."

"The baby died because he was too weak to live."

"Your mother died from drinking her own poisonous brew. And now you have poisoned Lord Robert's newborn son."

"I gave him no poison and you know it! You know also that my mother's elixirs have helped save the lives of your own children." Janna spread her hands out in appeal. Surely some among this small group must know in their hearts that she was innocent; surely they must feel gratitude for the healing she and her mother had given in the past?

She looked at their faces in the flickering torchlight, trying to recognize who was present. Her heart quaked as she saw the anger and ill-will reflected by them all. Aldith was not among them, she noted. Nor was Godric. It was a relief that they were not here to accuse her, yet she would have given anything for a friendly face, for some support against these vile accusations.

Torold swaggered forward, a baby in his arms and the rest of his children straggling along behind him. "Your mother's death was a just reward for her godless ways!" It seemed he no longer thought of Janna as a potential wife, for he continued, "Just so should you pay for the death of a child with your own death." He spat at Janna. The glob of mucus landed an ant's width from her toes. Alarmed, she jumped back. He leered at her, his eyes hot and hungry, but Janna sensed that there was fear in them too.

Acutely aware of the peril she faced, Janna spread out her hands in appeal once more. "I swear to you, I did not harm the baby. Nor did my mother. She was skilled with herbs—you all know that for she has helped all of you at some time in the past."

"She was a godless woman. Her death is a punishment for her godless ways!"

"She was a good woman. And she believed in God as much as any of you."

"Why then would the priest not bury her in the churchyard? And why does he say that you, too, are damned?" The miller came forward to stand beside his wife and Torold, close enough that she could smell the ale on his breath and see the flecks of spittle around his mouth. She would have retreated, but the door behind her was closed. She could not trust the villagers if she turned to open it. There was nowhere else for her to run. All she had in her armory were her wits, her words—and the truth.

"The priest is ignorant. He does not understand." It was not, perhaps, the best thing to say in the circumstances, Janna realized, as she heard the hissing intake of breath. Better to change the subject, and quickly. "Why are you here? What do you want with me?"

Now they watched her, silent and still. They were waiting for something to happen, someone to make the first move, just as she herself was waiting. Her heart raced harder; her frightened breaths came short and shallow. She wiped her damp hands down her kirtle. "Why don't you go home?" she pleaded. "I've heard your accusations. There is no more for you to do here."

Hilde grabbed the flaming torch from her husband and shook it at Janna. She was so close Janna could feel the hot breath of the flare burning her face. "You've killed a child. You've murdered an innocent babe! You're a godless woman who whores after other women's husbands. You bring disgrace to our village and we don't want you here. You've got to go."

Janna was furiously angry, yet she knew she should not speak of what else lay between her and the miller's wife, that she should stay silent for her own sake. But she must also try to defend herself. She raised her voice to address them all. "I cannot go anywhere. I live here. This is my home, the only home I know."

"Go, and take that devil black cat of yours with you!" The miller's mouth contorted as he gathered saliva. He spat at Janna with a fine accuracy. With a shudder of revulsion, Janna wiped the mucus off her face, understanding that his action represented payback for the kiss she'd so painfully terminated.

"My cat is like any other creature that lives and dies," she said coldly. "My cat once lived, but now it is dead." She glared at Hilde.

"I saw the devil on our way up here, I swear I did," said Torold.

"I saw the cat too," Hilde chimed in eagerly. "It was in the shadows, but when I next looked, it had grown into something too large and fearsome to be human. In truth, I feared for my very life."

Janna sucked in a sharp breath. "The cat is dead!" she insisted, remembering Godric's warning about rumors of shape-shifting. She would not give them a further reason to accuse her.

"That cat is the devil in disguise, for I swear I saw it just moments ago." Hilde smiled as an uneasy muttering broke out behind her back.

Janna knew a moment of pure, wild rage. "Do you carry a knife with you again tonight, mistress?" she hissed. "Would you use it on me as you have used it on my cat?" She turned to face the villagers, feeling sick as she tried to defend herself against their ignorance, and the hate and fear in their hearts. "My cat is dead, killed by Mistress Hilde," she said. "She came to my cottage in the night and saw me with the villein, Godric." Now she addressed Wulfgar directly. "She thought she was following you, she thought you were with me. To punish me, she slit my cat's throat and tied it to a tree! She also threatened to use her knife on me if she saw you with me again.

Pray tell me, who is the murderess here?" She stepped forward and thrust her face close to Wulfgar. "Be careful," she warned. "Be very careful whose bed you lie in, lest your wife next uses her knife on you or your mistress!"

Taking advantage of the stunned silence that followed her words, Janna turned to the villagers.

"My home is here, far from the village. I will not trouble you, nor do you need to trouble me—unless, of course, you have some ailment that needs treatment. You will find me a willing and capable replacement for my mother. And now, please go away and leave me in peace."

Not daring to turn her back on them, she felt behind her for the door latch. She watched them steadily all the while, for although they'd quietened, she knew that if she presented her back to them they would attack her like the cowardly animals they were. She must get away from them while she could and hope that, if she was not there to provoke them, their tempers would cool and their senses return along with the light of morning.

Janna snicked the latch, pushed the door open behind her and, in a quick movement, stepped back and slammed the door shut once more. For safety, she dragged her mother's heavy chair against it. For added protection she donned her girdle and slipped the knife inside her purse. If they came for her, she would be ready. She collapsed onto a stool, breathless and trembling with fear as she waited to find out what the villagers would do next.

A low muttering came from outside, buzzing like a swarm of bees. A voice was raised, and quickly hushed. The words had been indistinguishable. Janna wondered if Hilde was being taken to task for her actions. A man laughed then, the sound drifting off into silence.

It was quiet outside now, too quiet. Surely she should hear their footsteps, the sounds of crunching leaves and snapping twigs, if they were returning to Berford? The silence made Janna uneasy.

Smoke. Smoke and the thin crackling snap of burning tinder. She stood up to inspect the fire in the center of the room. A thin plume coiled upwards from a log which, even as she watched, crumbled and fell away into ash.

Janna settled back down on the stool and tried to calm her frightened spirit, but a new worry came into her mind. How would she manage if she could not trade her skill and knowledge of herbs in return for the goods she needed in order to survive? She would have to set aside more of the small piece of land in order to grow extra wheat. She would also have to grind it herself in the future. It was another task added to a burden already too heavy to bear. She drew a deep breath, weary beyond endurance.

Smoke. Janna looked at the dying fire. The crackling of burning wood was louder now, the smell stronger. Tendrils of smoke seeped through small cracks in the mud and straw daub that sealed the wooden frame of the cottage. Aghast, Janna noticed flickers of light as flames began to lick and burn through timber. The cottage was on fire, and she was trapped inside.

"God rot your souls until Doomsday!" she shouted, hoping the villagers were still outside to hear the curse. She hated them with all her heart. What had she ever done, how had she harmed them to make them turn against her like this? But now was not the time for curses and questioning. The cottage was on fire, the flames all around her. She must act, and quickly, or she would be burned alive.

She pounced on the heavy chair and dragged it away from the door. The door was alight now, and the surrounding walls with it—she was surrounded by a ring of fire. Terrified, she made haste to save what she could, quickly casting about for Eadgyth's precious weighing scales, but the room was filling with smoke, making it hard to see. It stung her eyes and tore at her throat and she began to cough. The sound was growing louder, roaring in her ears as the fire took hold. Hungry tongues of flame closed in on her, licking up the wooden cottage and its contents.

Janna put her hand over her nose and mouth in a vain effort to filter the choking smoke that billowed around the room. No time to save anything, she must flee for her life. But where was the door? She peered about, trying to fathom its direction from the furniture, but her eyes were watering and the smoke was too thick now to make out anything at all.

In panic, she stretched out a hand and blindly stepped forward. Her boot jarred against a heavy object. She touched it, felt its shape. The chair! She'd moved it to the right of the door, but the door itself was burning. In sudden hope, she turned to the window, but it was too small; she would never fit through.

Janna knew that if she didn't get out right now, she would die. She cast about in search of the pot of vegetable soup. Her hands were shaking so badly she fumbled, missed, then at last managed to pull the pot off the hook. She dashed the contents over herself.

The smoke was suffocating, she could hardly breathe. The rushes had caught alight now; fiery rivulets snaked across the ground toward her. She had to go. She sucked in a breath and held it fast. Using the cooking pot as a battering ram, she ran at the door, smashed it wide open and raced through. The scorching breath of the flames stung her as she passed, but she was out and running for her life.

The air was cool and fresh. She was safe. She doubled over, coughing and choking, whooping for breath as she tried to suck in enough air to feed her starved lungs. She smelled the stink of scorched hair and her scalp smarted and stung. Her hair was on fire! Shivering with shock and fright, she undid her girdle and purse, then ripped off her wet kirtle and wrapped it tight around her head in a desperate effort to smother her smoldering hair.

She looked through the trees at the incandescent pyre that was once her home. She began to retch. She heaved up all she'd just eaten in painful, agonized gasps, vomiting until her stomach was empty. Finally, when the spasms had passed, she straightened and looked about her. Desperate and distraught, she watched the fire destroy what was left of her life, everything she knew and everything she had shared with her mother.

Was she still in danger? She stood still, listening for sounds of the villagers. Had they stayed to admire their handiwork or had they fled to the safety of their own homes like the cowards they were? It was difficult to hear anything above the roar and crackle of the flames, but Janna detected no movement close by. She strained her eyes to see if anyone lurked in the outer darkness, but all seemed still and quiet.

The animals! Caring nothing for her own safety, Janna snatched up her girdle and the purse with its few precious coins from the marketplace, and ran around the side of the burning cottage to the pen that housed the goats and hens. She could hear an anxious bleating as she came closer, and felt an overwhelming relief that the goats were still alive. "Get out, get out!" she urged, as she unsnicked the catch that kept the gate closed.

They huddled together, too fearful to move. "Shoo!" Janna ran at them, forcing them to move apart. The hens cackled and milled about, in danger of being trampled to death by the frightened goats. "Shoo!" Janna's voice shrilled high with terror. She flailed her arms to scare them into action, and at last the goats ran through the opening and out into the garden, followed by the hens. "Shoo!" she shouted again, urging them to the forest and freedom.

As soon as she was sure they were on the move, she raced ahead and dived into the sheltering trees. The villagers wanted her dead. If any of them were still about they would know that she had survived, and would need to silence her lest she tell anyone of their deeds this day. She wriggled into a bushy thicket and rolled flat onto the ground, trying to become invisible in the darkness. After a few moments, during which she gathered up her last remnants of courage, she raised her head and peered cautiously about.

The cottage still burned fiercely, the fire casting its light in a wide arc. Janna watched the scene intently, alert for any movement or sound that would betray the presence of the villagers. How delighted they must be by the success of their mission to drive her away. Her eyes smarted from the heat and smoke, and her skin stung where the fire had scorched her. She blinked hard and stifled a sob as she continued to watch. But she heard no voices; she saw no signs of life. No-one had been brave enough to stay and witness the destruction of her home and her life.

Sparks broke free of the blaze and floated through the air. Fire fairies, Janna thought fancifully, until she noticed that a stray spark had alighted on a clump of leaves close to where she was lying. The leaves were smoldering, could easily flare out of control. Janna jumped up and stamped on them, extinguishing the danger. But the smoking vegetation had awakened her to the hazard she faced. It would be stupid, she thought, to save herself from a burning cottage only to die in a forest fire instead.

She could not seek the safety of the fields in case some of the villagers were still on their way home, so she forced her trembling legs to run deeper into the forest, ducking branches and bushes, tripping over flints and into unexpected hollows, pushing her way past brambles that caught her clothing and scratched her skin, until she reached a wide clearing.

Believing herself safe at last, she collapsed onto a patch of grass.

The burning cottage had set the sky alight, the fiery glow shining above the trees. There was no escaping the horror of her loss. Numbly, Janna kept watching as the leaping flames gradually sank lower. It came to her that she was still clad only in her short tunic. She unfastened the damp and singed kirtle, shook it out and put it on, her fingers catching in holes where the fire had burnt it right through. Even though it was in rags, it would give some protection to her bare arms and legs and safeguard her modesty.

She had cried all the tears she could cry. Now she felt achingly empty and sad as she assessed her situation. She had no way of earning her keep in the future. She was an orphan. There were no family or friends to help her; indeed, the villagers hated her enough to destroy the only thing she had left: her home, with all of its memories. Janna clenched her hands as a new emotion swept through her, filling her with a white heat so strong it drove out all fear and loneliness. It was rage; an anger that blazed as hot and as blinding as the sun.

Impulse bade her run to the village and demand justice. She might still have some support there; not everyone had come out to the forest this night. Caution told her that it may only have been fear that kept the other villagers away. If forced to choose, they might not have the courage to go against others whose hatred of her was so great they didn't care that she might die when they set fire to her cottage. After some consideration, she came to the conclusion that it would be better, for the moment, if everyone thought she was dead. Let the villagers think they had succeeded in their purpose. At least it would stop them coming after her before she had a chance to flee.

But until she could find some way of bringing the villagers to justice, and her mother's killer along with them, she had to find shelter. Where could she go? South to the sea? No, she wanted to put the protection of the forest between her and the villagers. She could not go east to Wiltune, for she was known there. Nor should she go west; from what Godric had told her, she'd never find the ancient way through the forest that would lead her to safety. North, then? There was a track right through the forest to Wicheford, so she'd heard, but she'd never gone so far before. She would be walking into the unknown.

Janna found the thought reassuring. If she knew no-one it would mean that no-one would know her. She would be able to beg for bread and shelter in safety. She knew she should leave tonight so as to put as much distance as possible between her and the villagers. But she was tired, so tired! Everything hurt, body and soul, while her spirit felt utterly crushed. She was surrounded by the dense, secret fastness of the forest. Surely it was dark enough for shelter, for safety? Tonight she would hide here, she decided. Tomorrow would be time enough to start her new life.

Wearily, Janna sank down onto a soft bed of grass and leaves beneath the comforting branches of a spreading beech. *I can't stay here; I need to climb up and away from danger.* It was her last thought before her eyes closed in utter exhaustion and she fell fast asleep.

Chapter 12

Janna sat up with a jerk, awoken by the melodious warbling of blackbirds and puzzled by the leafy roof above her head. Her heart did a somersault as she recalled why she was sleeping out under the trees. A shudder shook her to her core. She was cold and she was wet. She rested her elbows on her knees and buried her head in her hands in despair. She had to think, to make a plan for the future even though there seemed to be no future at all for her. It was true she couldn't stay here, but even if she found her way to Wicheford, what would she do there, how would she survive?

Something felt different. She explored her scorched and tender scalp with careful fingers and felt stubble, all that was left of her burnt hair. Yet not all of her hair was gone, she discovered—she still had a few long locks where sparks hadn't fallen. She shed her wet kirtle to examine her arms and legs. Bright pink streaked her skin where fire and brambles had branded her. She reached for her kirtle. The front was burnt so badly it was beginning to disintegrate. As she dressed, she comforted herself with the thought that at least there was no-one around to see her body through the ruined fabric. Her first task, then, must be to find something else to wear. She could not make her journey dressed like this.

She stood up, and slowly found her way back to the edge of the forest. Lowering clouds shrouded the dawning of a new day. There was still a hint of rain in the air, a fine sifting that added to Janna's misery. She knew she should flee the forest before anyone was out and about to notice her, and understand that she had survived the fire. Yet all her instincts bade her go back to the cottage one last time. Like a wounded animal, she needed to return to her lair. It made sense to see if there was anything left among the detritus that she could salvage, perhaps some medicaments to trade along her journey, wherever that might take her. She might even find something to replace her tattered kirtle. At the very least, she should wash away the ravages of the fire from her skin.

The misting rain kept Janna shivering in the cool early morning as she hurried to the blackened ruin, all that was left of her home. Yet the rain was providential, for it had dampened the fire and prevented it from spreading through the forest itself. If only it had rained sooner, some part of the cottage and her life within might have been saved. As it was, the stench of the charred remains hung in the air.

Keeping a sharp lookout for unwelcome visitors, Janna went first to the herb garden in the hope that some of her precious plants might have survived the inferno. A small heap of burnt bones and charred feathers lay among the ashy remains of a lifetime's work. Laet, Janna thought sadly. In the race for food, and everything else, the little hen had always come last. She looked away from the devastating scene.

"Nellie! Gruff!" she called. There were no answering bleats, but Janna took comfort from the fact that there was no sign of burnt goats in her garden either. Hopefully they were happily foraging in the forest. Soon enough someone would find them, and the hens too, and give them a home.

The hives had burnt through, leaking precious honey onto the ground. "I'm so sorry," Janna told the bees, although she knew that none could be alive to hear her. They would not have survived the heat and smoke. Feeling empty and despairing, she walked on through the herb garden. The fire had taken everything, leaving only mounds of ash and black stalks to bear witness to a lifetime of toil. There was nothing to salvage, no warm milk or eggs to fill her empty aching belly, no sweet herbs or honey to ease the hurt, no balm to replace a shattered life.

Desolate with grief, Janna wandered slowly through the damp, charred mess back to the remains of the cottage to inspect its contents. Their precious chest, which had contained a change of clothing and some warmer wear for winter, had burnt right through. Their meagre bits of furniture—the table, stools, her mother's carefully crafted chair and cushions—were all reduced to ash. So were the bunches of dried herbs, the sachets of powders and pills. Clay saucers and jars had crashed to the ground when the shelf had burned through. While most were smashed, a few pots had survived the fall and their contents remained intact. Yet all the medicaments in the world could not cure the pain in her heart, Janna thought, as she inspected these few pitiful remnants. She kept searching through the debris and found the hard flint and small piece of steel. Amid the devastation of the fire, the means to start it had been saved. With a wry smile, she secreted them in her purse. Should she need to keep warm, should she be lucky enough to find something to cook, being able to light a fire would come in handy.

She crouched among the ruins. Carefully, she began to sift through soggy, blackened fragments, the remnants of her life. Mostly they fell apart as she handled them. Some were recognizable: shards of jugs that had shattered in the heat; a tin basin, warped and buckled and now unusable. A faint gleam caught Janna's eye. Eadgyth's scales! Eagerly, she uncovered them. They were blackened by the fire and twisted beyond repair. Heartsore, she left them lying and turned her attention to the iron cooking pot. It lay close to where the door had been. Janna peered inside the pot and was delighted to find scraps of charred vegetables stuck to the bottom. She ate them. They tasted foul, but she was hungry and had no notion of where she might find her next meal.

A rough patch of earth caught her attention. It looked as though someone had dug a hole and then covered it over. Puzzled, Janna stared down at it, mentally picturing the cottage and its contents. The straw pallet she shared with her mother had completely burnt away, but this was where it had once rested. Could her mother, the keeper of secrets, have hidden something of her past there? Janna's breath came faster at the thought.

She pulled the knife out of her purse and began to dig. The earth was already softened from the rain, and loosened easily. Encouraged, Janna's pace quickened. The earth sprayed about her as she dug deeper. The blade hit something hard, jarring her hand. Cautious now, she felt around the object and then carefully lifted it. A small tin box with a clasp. It was not locked.

Janna's hands shook as she lifted the lid. The first thing she saw was a silver ring brooch studded with multicolored gemstones. She gasped with pleasure and surprise. Why hadn't her mother ever shown this to her? She turned it over, and frowned at the inscription engraved on the back. It meant nothing to her. Carefully, she set the brooch aside.

Underneath it was a piece of parchment. She picked it up and unfolded it. It was covered with writing. Janna stared at the symbols on the page, wishing she could read. Where had her mother come by these things, and why had she hidden them? It was all very strange.

A distant memory came to Janna. She was very young, just learning to talk. She was standing outside the cottage. Eadgyth had a stick in her hand, and was tracing letters into soft sand with it. "See, Janna," she'd said, "see how you write your name. Johanna." As she said the letters, she pointed to the symbols scratched into the sand and sounded them out.

"Janna," Janna had repeated obediently. She had picked up the stick then and tried to copy her mother's writing. But it had proved difficult, and she had thrown the stick down and started to cry. Her mother had done nothing further that day, but some months later she had patiently tried again, and then again, encouraging Janna to write and write and write the letters of her true name so that now she could do it without trouble, without even having to think about it.

Janna had spoken the truth when she'd told Hugh she could write her name, but that was all she could write. Her mother had never taught her how to read, or to write anything else. Why? Janna frowned at the lines of writing on the parchment, trying to make it out. She could see a J and there was an N, and some Os and an A and another A—but they were none of them joined together in a pattern that she recognized, and they had strange symbols in between that she did not know at all. If her mother knew the letters of her name, surely she must have known some other letters too? If she could read and write, why did she not teach her daughter all her skills, instead of only the skills of healing?

Janna gave an exasperated sigh as she stared into the distance and once more pondered the secrets her mother had insisted on keeping hidden from her. She was well aware that Eadgyth had thought it best to tell her nothing of the past, and keep her safe by marrying her off; Janna wished rather that her mother had told her the truth and trusted her judgment instead. By steering her toward marriage and a lifetime of drudgery, her mother had cheated her of her heritage, had kept her both innocent and ignorant of who she was, and where she might find her father.

Now, with her mother dead and her home gone, she knew she was free to go wherever she wished and have the adventures for which she'd always longed. So why, instead of feeling excited about the challenges ahead, did she feel so lonely and bereft?

After a few moments' thought, it came to Janna that this was where she belonged, for her home and her life with her mother were all she knew. Without warning, they had been snatched from her, and as yet she had no idea what might take their place. But no matter where she went or what lay ahead, no-one could ever replace Eadgyth in her life. Janna felt sure that, in her own way, her mother had loved her and wanted to protect her, to save her from making the same mistake that had shattered her own life. And yet she'd called her "Johanna" as she lay dying. Their argument must have cut deep indeed. If only she could have got to her mother in time to make up their quarrel.

Tears of grief and loss came into Janna's eyes. She dashed them away. It was too late for regrets, too late for an apology. She was on her own now, and must make the best of things. She turned her attention once more to the parchment. Was it a message from someone, perhaps even her father? Excited, she stared at the symbols, desperate to fathom what they might mean. A word at the end caught her eye. Familiar letters, but not quite enough of them. J. O. H. N. She sounded them out as her mother had taught her to sound out the letters of her own name. *Joe-han?* No, that wasn't right, there was no A between the H and N. *Juh oh huh hn? Juh-hin? Joh-hin? John?*

John! It seemed to Janna that everything suddenly stopped, frozen into silence. John! She recalled Cecily's words as she told Janna of Eadgyth's dying moments. "*Actually, I thought*

Eadgyth was calling for John, but when I questioned who he was, one of the tiring women told me your name. Your real name."

Johanna. John. In her dying moments, her mother had called for John. Her thoughts had not been with her daughter but with—who? The man she'd always loved? Was John her father? Had she, Johanna, taken his name?

Yes! Janna had never thought before to ask why her mother, a Saxon woman, had given her a Norman name. Now she had the answer: her father must be a Norman, and of noble rank if Aldith was to be believed. No wonder her mother could speak the language of the Normans! Janna was grateful that this, at least, was something her mother had taught her.

With a growl of frustration, she caught up the parchment and studied it once more. If only she could read this letter from her father to her mother, so much of the past might be explained. But the symbols told her nothing. They could have been the footprints of spiders for all the sense they made.

Janna carefully refolded the precious parchment and laid it in her lap. She felt as though a great burden had been lifted from her shoulders, the burden of guilt. Her mother had forgiven her for their argument after all.

She looked inside the box to see what else Eadgyth had hidden from her. A gold ring, large and heavy. It had an embossed design on its face instead of the sorts of colorful gems that adorned Dame Alice's hand. A man's ring, then? She studied the design. It depicted a swan, but was it only a swan or did that long neck and body form the letter J? To one side of the swan was a beast with a tail, the likes of which Janna had never seen. On the other side was a crown which she thought must denote the man's allegiance to the king. Frowning, she considered the matter and came to the conclusion that the king must have been Henry, for Stephen had usurped the throne during Janna's lifetime. She cast her mind around all of their acquaintances, but could think of no-one who knew her mother well enough or was wealthy enough to give her such a keepsake. But the J, if it was a J, seemed to suggest that it had been another present from her father. Janna carefully repacked the casket and set it aside. She peered into the hole to see if there was anything else to find. It was empty, save for a glass bottle.

Taking great care, understanding its value and fragility, she lifted it out. Did it have some special significance? Could it once have belonged to her father? She turned the bottle in her hands, admiring the beauty of the green glass. If only it could speak to her, what secrets might it tell? Janna frowned as she tried to puzzle out why her mother had buried such a precious object when she could have traded it for something more useful. Its appearance seemed oddly familiar. She was sure she'd seen something like this before. And then it came to her: Robert of Babestoche, pouring wine into a goblet for his wife. The bottle had looked exactly like this one. Had this bottle come from Robert's own household? Or did all bottles look alike? For certes, Robert would never have made a present of a bottle of wine to Eadgyth—but Cecily might! Janna's heart flipped in excitement. Could this be Cecily's missing gift? From what Janna had seen of the tiring woman's circumstances, it seemed unlikely that she could have had such a costly gift to give. So unless she had stolen the bottle of wine, someone must have given it to her.

Hugh? Was this a gift for Cecily, or his payment to the *wortwyf* for taking care of Cecily's problem? Janna shut her eyes, but could not blank out the images of Hugh with his arm around Cecily's waist, and his tender care of her at the graveside. If Hugh really was the father of Cecily's unborn babe, then the matter was between the two of them. It was nothing to do with her.

She unstoppered the bottle, eager to try her first taste of wine, but it was empty. How so, when her mother would have had no time to drink any of it? Janna cradled the bottle on her lap as she struggled to solve this new puzzle. If her mother had drunk all of the wine straight away, she would have been far too unsteady to follow Cecily to the manor and minister to Dame Alice. Cecily had not said that her mother was drunk when she arrived. Ill, yes, but not drunk. What, then, had happened to the wine? And why had her mother hidden the empty bottle?

Janna sighed. While her mother's life had been a mystery, her death seemed to have uncovered even more secrets. The real question was: Where to start looking for answers? Although conscious of the need for haste, Janna sat on amid the ruins of the cottage. Random thoughts, a jumble of impressions, ran through her head. Somewhere in the events of the past few days lay the answer to her mother's death, she felt sure of it. It was just a matter of fitting all the pieces together.

She looked down at the bottle in her lap. In case a little wine remained, she picked it up and tilted it to her mouth, hoping for a taste to satisfy her curiosity. A few drops moistened her tongue and she held them there, smacking her lips as she tasted the precious liquid. Her brow creased in thought. Unless wine tasted exactly like water, this was water! But the moisture was certainly proof beyond doubt that this was a recent gift, rather than an old token kept as a memento of her father. It must have come as a gift from Cecily—there was no other explanation.

Janna closed her eyes, and tried to imagine the last few hours of her mother's life. Cecily had come knocking on the door, and had handed over her gift. In return, her mother had given Cecily the foul-tasting mixture that would result in the loss of her unborn child. But Cecily had not waited for that to occur. Nor did she share a sup of wine with her mother. She would have mentioned it, but instead she'd told of her great hurry to get straight back to the manor before her absence was noted.

So Eadgyth must have drunk the wine by herself, and washed out the bottle afterwards. This in itself seemed surprising to Janna, for she and her mother always shared whatever they had. A bottle of wine would have been a rare treat! Surely she would have kept some of it to drink with her daughter. But her mother had finished the wine without her. She had rinsed out the bottle and then gone to the manor house to see Dame Alice. No, that couldn't be true. Aldith would have noticed that her mother was feeling the effects of too much wine and would have remarked on it, most probably loudly and often!

It didn't make sense. None of it made sense. Janna stroked the cold glass bottle, wishing it could spill its secrets. If her mother hadn't drunk all the wine by herself, someone must have shared it with her. Not Aldith. She would have mentioned it—she would have been jealous of the gift. As it was, Aldith had been kind enough to share her own cordial because her mother had said she was thirsty. If she'd just drunk a bottle of wine, she wouldn't have been thirsty—unless she was feeling the effects of the poison! Was the wine poisoned? Was that why her mother had died?

Startled, Janna set down the bottle and sprang to her feet. She began to pace while she tried to keep up with her agitated thoughts. Her mother could not have drunk the whole bottle by herself; the poison would have killed her long before she got to the manor house. Had Eadgyth perhaps tried just a sip or two, meaning to share the rest of it with Janna later on? Or had she perhaps intended to use some of the wine in the posset she was making up for Dame Alice, but first taken a sip to test its flavor? Not liking the taste, or maybe thinking the wine was tainted, had she then poured it out and washed the bottle, and hidden it so as to protect Cecily's identity as she'd promised? She'd certainly not drunk enough of the wine to suspect the presence of monkshood, for she would have prepared a brew at once, and taken steps to combat the poison.

Janna contemplated where her thoughts were taking her. If her mother had taken only a sip or two, it would explain why the poison had taken some time to work its dark mischief. It would also explain why her mother had not suspected anything until its symptoms had become fully manifest. The problem was that Janna no longer had any proof of her suspicions, for the wine was gone.

She remembered the sight of her dead cat, the image sudden and shocking. So much blood, both under the animal and elsewhere. She had wondered about that patch of blood some distance from the animal's body. Now she understood how she might have misread the scene. Not blood at all, but the stain of red wine, the stain left after her mother had poured the contents of the bottle away; a stain that matched the stain on Dame Alice's fine linen when she'd knocked the goblet of wine from her husband's hand. Had Dame Alice, too, suspected poison?

In growing agitation, Janna continued to pace while she pondered Cecily's motives. Was her mother's death a mishap? Was Dame Alice the intended target? But why? Cecily's future depended on Dame Alice. But it also depended on Eadgyth's silence.

Cecily was certainly implicated somehow, for the gift had come from her. But perhaps there was another way to look at the situation, starting with Cecily's predicament and Dame Alice's household. Janna recalled Hamo's words, that he was Dame Alice's heir, and would inherit everything. It would seem that, with no real prospects, Hugh would need to look for a far better marriage than his aunt's tiring woman if he was to make his way in the world. Soon enough, Hamo would be old enough to come into his inheritance, to claim for his own the manor at Babestoche, as well as the manor now managed by Hugh. By then, Hugh would need to have married, and married well. Certes he could not afford news of a dalliance with Cecily, with a baby as proof, to come to the ears of either his aunt or his future wife. To what lengths might he go to keep that secret?

Hugh—or Cecily? Or were they in it together? Janna remembered the tiring woman's tears of guilt and grief. She remembered also that Cecily had tried to care for Eadgyth as she lay dying, and had braved the priest's wrath to watch her interred. She found it hard to believe a cold-blooded killer could be capable of such kindness as Cecily had shown. Nevertheless, the young woman hadn't hesitated to lie when it suited her.

She would have to be careful, Janna thought. She'd made wrong judgments in the past, but if she got it wrong this time, her own death must surely follow. She could not afford to be careless. Fear and the need for secrecy lay at the heart of all that had happened, she understood that now. It was because of fear that Eadgyth had died. It was fear that might drive the killer to strike again. The key to the puzzle was Cecily and her unnamed lover. Was it Hugh? With all her heart, Janna wanted to believe the best about the man who had been so kind to her, but she let her heart rule her head at her peril. The poison had not got into the bottle by accident. Someone had put it there, someone who would stop at nothing to keep Cecily's secret safe.

She held the bottle close to her eyes and looked through the thick glass, trying to put her whirling thoughts into order. She squinted at the distorted shapes that were the ruins of her home, and the view reflected how the world looked to her right now. If the bottle could only speak, it would tell her what she needed to know: the name of its owner.

The bottle stayed mute, but other voices spoke in Janna's mind. She'd been focused on who had the knowledge, the wish and the opportunity for murder, but there was something else she needed to take into consideration in order to solve this mystery: the telltale gestures, the actions that revealed more than the speaker realized. Her heart quaked as she understood at last that there was someone else at the manor, someone with an even more urgent reason than Hugh to keep Cecily's secret.

She lowered the bottle. Tendrils of fear twined and knotted her stomach. If her guess was right, not only did the killer want her dead, but he thought he'd already succeeded. Her safety depended on his continuing to believe it.

Yet she must go to the manor house one last time—she had to speak to Cecily. For her mother's sake, for her own, and for Cecily's, she had to establish that what she feared was, in fact, the truth. If she was right, it would mean that Cecily was in far more danger even than herself. But if she was wrong, and Cecily and her lover were in this together, then she would be walking into a trap—a trap that could end only in her death.

All Janna wanted was to flee to safety, but not if her safety was bought at the price of Cecily's life. Not for anything would she have Cecily's death on her conscience. So she must go, and quickly, for there was no time to lose. First, though, she would have to find something else to wear. She looked down at her kirtle, shredded from the fire and badly stained from her night's rest in the forest. It would attract curious eyes and comments and she could not afford either, yet every other garment she owned had been destroyed.

Her tattered kirtle woke Janna to the danger she faced if anyone came looking for her. The villagers, too, had wanted her dead. They must all think they'd succeeded. She bent down and picked up her mother's treasures, and hurried into the sheltering depths of the forest. Once safely concealed behind a large beech, she set down the box and bottle, and sat beside them to plan how she might locate a change of clothes.

"Janna!" The sound was like the howl of a wolf, a wild cry of desolation. With a gasp of fear, Janna flattened herself behind the tree and peeped cautiously around it. Godric was on his way up the hill. Had he seen her? He seemed to be looking her way. "Janna!" he shouted again, and turned in a slow circle to scan first the green downs and then the cottage and the forest.

Janna pressed closer to the sheltering tree. Truly, Godric looked distraught. His clothes and hair were unkempt; his eyes red-rimmed from lack of sleep. Or something else. As she watched, he scrubbed his face against his sleeve. Surely he could not be weeping?

Janna longed to go to him. She had so misjudged Godric; she desperately wanted to beg his forgiveness. Shame kept her hidden; shame and also caution. It would be for the best if everyone—even Godric—thought she was dead, or if not dead, then driven out and fled from her home. She tried to console herself with the thought that she and Godric hardly knew each other. He would forget her just as soon as some other comely young woman crossed his path, someone more deserving of his love, someone who would give him babies and make him happy. Someone who wasn't an outcast: hated, feared and driven even to death.

Janna blinked back tears of self-pity, and continued to watch from her hiding place. Godric was now focused on the blackened ruins of the cottage. He walked among the debris, just as she had earlier. He was looking for something. He lingered for some moments beside the remains of the animal pen, carefully sifting through charred fragments of bones and feathers, before moving on into the remains of the cottage. There, he began a systematic search. He bent down time and again, now to move a blackened beam, now to sift through a pile of ash. Janna knew there were no bones for him to find, but she might have left footprints. She pressed closer to the tree, trying to become invisible.

Whatever Godric was looking for, he seemed pleased with the result for at the end of his inspection he stood up and looked around. It seemed to Janna that he stood taller; he seemed straighter, more confident. He called her name once more. His voice rang out loud and clear, startling a pair of blackbirds. They squawked and fluttered their wings before settling once more.

Janna pressed her hand hard against her mouth to stop herself from answering him. Godric must know now that she hadn't died in the fire. She was touched by the change she'd observed in him, but reason told her there was no future for them, either in friendship or anything else. Godric was tied to the manor. He was not free to go wherever he chose, whereas she must flee the wrath of the villagers as well as the murderous intentions of those who feared her knowledge. She *had* to leave, had to flee as fast and as far from this place as possible. She felt a piercing shaft of sadness at the thought. Nevertheless, she longed to see him one last time, to say farewell and to thank him for his care and his concern.

A glance at her kirtle confirmed her decision. She didn't want Godric to see her in rags, with her hair all but burnt to a stubble; she didn't want this to be his last memory of her. So she stayed hidden, and listened while he began to search through the forest, all the while shouting her name. He was coming closer to her hiding place. Silent as a snake, she wriggled into a dense cover of leafy bushes and tall grass, stifling a cry as bare skin touched a patch of stinging nettles. She stayed hidden, and breathed a silent prayer of relief as he moved away in a different direction.

Godric's cries grew fainter; she could no longer hear the crunch of leaves, the crackle of twigs under his boots. In the silence, birds began to chitter and sing once more. At last, when she was quite sure he had gone, Janna slid out from her bushy cover. She straightened cautiously. There was no sign of Godric, and no sound of him either. For the moment, she was safe.

She was also thirsty, so thirsty! She hurried down to the dewpond and cupped her hands into the water, splashing silver droplets as she drank. The ruffled surface gave her an idea, but she kept cupping her hands to drink until her thirst was slaked. She wiped her tattered sleeve across her mouth and waited until the water had stilled. She looked down at her reflection.

What a fright! Carefully, she washed the smut and ash from her face and hands before dipping her head into the pond to cleanse her sore, soot-blackened scalp. With water streaming down her face, blinding her, she raised a hand and fingered the long wet hanks of hair left among the singed stubble. She had no cap or veil to hide the bare patches and to leave it as it was invited ridicule and comment; she would have to cut her hair short, so that it was all of one length.

She drew the knife from her purse. Pressing her lips together to contain her distress, for she had been proud of her long, fair locks, she began to hack into them. As she cut, she remembered the admiration in Hugh's dark eyes when first they'd met. He would not look at her again, not after this!

"'Tis better so," Janna reminded herself, for her safety depended on the fact that everyone, save one, must believe her dead. She stared at her reflection in the dewpond, at the drying blond wisps that fluffed around her head like the halo of a saint. No chance now of anyone's admiration –not when her hair was shorn even shorter than a youth's!

Could she perhaps pass herself off as a young man? She considered the thought. It pleased her greatly. People would have less chance of recognizing her if they thought her a boy.

As a young woman, alone and defenseless, she would always be at risk; she would be much safer in disguise, especially up at the manor where at least one person had even more at stake than the villagers in wanting her dead.

Janna gathered up the incriminating bits of hair and hurried back into the forest to bury them. She must leave no sign of her activities for Godric, or anyone else, lest they suspect what she was about. She looked down at her kirtle. She needed men's garments, but she could not use the few pennies she had from her sales at Wiltune market to trade, for that would expose her to the world. What was she to do? Janna came to the reluctant conclusion that she would have to steal some clothes to fit her new identity. She remembered the horse barn up at the manor house. Inside, on a peg, hung a smock and breeches, no doubt some poor serf's Sunday best, kept for church and special occasions. She would take them while she was there. She'd never stolen anything in her life before, and balked at the thought of starting now, but she had no choice. Without proper attire she could go nowhere. Dressed as a youth, she would be free to roam wherever she chose.

She would rather have gone to the manor under cover of night, but there was no more time to lose. She could not take the usual path across the fields, for she would be seen and recognized. Instead, she would have go through the forest to get there. Janna knew she had no chance of finding the ancient Roman road that Godric had told her about, but she didn't have to go too far into the forest to be safe from prying eyes. She could stay close to the tree line, away from wolves and wild boar yet close enough to the river to maintain her bearings. Once she'd talked to Cecily she could make her escape, for the longer she delayed, the more peril she faced. Not knowing the true reason for the destruction of her cot, Godric would surely tell everyone that she had survived the fire. And they would come looking for her again, all of them, for they could not risk her witness against them for their night's treachery and their destruction of abbey property.

She walked back to her hiding place and pulled out the box and bottle. She didn't want to carry them with her, for they were awkward to hold. Yet she must keep the bottle; she needed it to confront Cecily. What about the box? Janna opened it once more and stared at its contents, feeling a frisson of excitement as she picked up the ring. It was a link with her father, she felt certain of it. She slipped it onto her middle finger, imagining the hand of her father, the finger that had once worn this ring. It was far too large for her. As she tilted her hand, it slid off. Janna tried it next on her thumb, but it looked ridiculous. Finally, she unlaced her purse and placed the ring inside, adding to it the precious piece of parchment and the brooch with its strange inscription. Then she knelt and buried the empty box under the bushes. It was time to go.

She steeled herself to take a last look at the remains of her home. Resolutely fighting tears, she whispered goodbye to her childhood, and to her mother. She had planted rosemary on Eadgyth's grave and had sworn an oath to remember her. She had vowed to seek the truth, and make whoever was responsible for her mother's death pay with their own life. Now Janna understood so much of what had happened, she began to understand that vengeance was impossible. She was alone and an outcast, now more than ever before. She had not the power to bring anyone to justice. It was a bitter realization, made worse by the knowledge that she must flee the village. Her mother's grave would stay untended, probably even defiled by those who would take out their fear and hatred on the dead if they could not take it out on the living.

Janna thought about the ring and parchment in her purse. A glimmer of hope lifted her spirits slightly. She wasn't quite alone, and she might not be utterly powerless either. Aldith had described her father as wealthy and important; he could even be a Norman nobleman. Should she try to find him? Would he welcome her? Those questions were less important than the central question, however: if she did find him, could she convince him to act on Eadgyth's behalf? Could she convince him to come back to Babestoche Manor and bring to justice those responsible for Eadgyth's death?

She had to try. As soon as she finished her business at the manor, she would go in search of him. No matter how long it took, she would do all in her power to find him. Although she had to leave her home and everything that was familiar to her, she resolved that, in time, her journey would lead her home again. And by then, she would have changed. No longer a powerless victim, she would have the authority of her father behind her and everything would be different. She knew not where he might be, did not even know which direction she should take. She could only start the journey, and hope that she might find guidance along the way.

First, though, she must brave the manor and hope that her wits were enough to save her from the danger that awaited her there. And so she set off along the edge of the forest in the direction of Babestoche.

Chapter 13

It was after noon by the time Janna left the last of the forest cover and stealthily made her way down to the manor through a field of sheep. They stared at her with incurious eyes as she hurried past. A new problem had presented itself. Would someone be guarding the gate during the daylight hours? What might she say to the gatekeeper should her way be barred? An urgent message from the shire reeve for the lord of the manor? No, the reeve would not entrust an important message to any other than one of his deputies. He would certainly not give instructions to a serf. Perhaps she could say she was in need of urgent assistance? No again, for why should anyone care about her welfare?

Janna sighed. Somehow she must gain admittance, preferably without anyone seeing or recognizing her. As she approached the entrance gate, Janna saw that it was open. She sidled closer; the gatekeeper had his back turned, seeming far more interested in his dinner than in a bedraggled young woman. She scuttled past, her arms folded across her chest to hide the worst of the burns in her kirtle. Keeping her head down, hoping to avoid recognition, she hurried on to the shed where Hugh's destrier had been housed, and where the smock and breeches had hung.

Once safely inside, Janna stopped still and held her breath, listening for sounds, be they animal or human. Soft scuffling and rustling told of the presence of mice and rats, and perhaps even a cat. Janna felt a moment's sympathy for the cat's quarry. She knew, only too well, how it felt to be hunted. No soft neighs to greet her this time, or even the chink of a bridle. To Janna's relief, the clothes still hung where she'd seen them. She swiftly stripped off her kirtle, then unhooked the smock and pulled it on. It was stiff with dirt and sweat and smelled strange. It was also far too big for her. She stuffed her kirtle down her front, to conceal it and also to change her shape. She tied her girdle underneath the bulge to keep the kirtle in place, and hitched up her smock so that it wasn't quite so long. No matter that her purse still dangled from the girdle; so too did men hang objects from their belts.

The clink of coins gave Janna an idea. She took out a silver penny and dropped it under the hook where the smock had hung. It would be noticed when the villein searched for his missing clothes. Janna felt sure that he would keep it without telling anyone of his good fortune, save his family perhaps, for he might spend it to their benefit. With her conscience somewhat eased, she pulled off her boots, then unhooked the breeches and pulled them up. They immediately fell down in folds around her ankles. Janna looked more closely and discovered a cord through the waistband to keep them up and in place. She pleated up the rough homespun and tied the cord tight, but they were still far too long for her. After a moment's thought she rolled up the bottom of each leg so that she could walk without tripping over. It felt strange to be wearing a man's breeches. Janna kicked out, marveling at her new freedom of movement. She could stride out now; she could even straddle a horse and ride it without showing ankles and legs. It seemed that there were other advantages to changing her sex.

She stepped back into her boots while she pondered the next problem: how to approach Cecily. Dressed as she was, she could not march boldly up the stairs of the manor house and demand admittance. Some other trick was called for. Cecily would not come to her so she must go to Cecily, and find a way for them to meet in privacy and safety. Janna decided the best approach was through the kitchen. She was about to leave the barn when a gorget with a pointed hood caught her eye. She snatched down the short cloak and put it around her shoulders, then pulled the hood down low. It was meant for winter wear, but it would shield her from prying eyes. Thus clad in her new garments, Janna strode out of the barn to practice her new identity.

Before braving the cook, Janna went first to the garden to seek lily or mallow to soothe the burns that still stung her scalp and limbs. As she searched for what she needed, a scullion came out to pick vegetables for the evening meal. The girl stopped short in surprise when she noticed Janna. Giving her no chance to speak, or to raise the alarm, Janna approached her.

"I beg your pardon for disturbing you," she said quickly, making her voice deliberately low both to disguise it and to mimic the speech of a youth. "I've come with an urgent message for Mistress Cecily. Is she at the manor? Is she well?"

"Yes. Yes, she is here. And she is quite well." The scullion looked surprised. She tried to peer under the hood for a better look at the messenger.

Janna's worst fear was over. She took a quick breath, relieved that she had not come too late. "I am a stranger here; I have no knowledge of the household. Will you take the message to Mistress Cecily for me?"

"Who is it from?" The scullion continued to stare suspiciously.

Janna tipped her head down. The hood fell lower, now covering most of her face. "From..." She was about to say a name, but suddenly understood the danger she courted if she'd miscalculated, or if her message went astray. "From someone who would not give me his name," she amended quickly. "He saw me about the manor grounds, and bade me ask Mistress Cecily to meet him. My instructions were to find an excuse to seek her out and speak to her alone, so that no-one else might hear what I say. Can you do that for me?"

"Certes; I shall tend the fire in Dame Alice's bedchamber. Where does he say they should meet? And when?" There was a smile of anticipation on the scullion's face. It was clear she suspected an assignation and took great delight from the notion.

"He will be waiting for her in...in the shed over there." Janna pointed so that there could be no misunderstanding between them.

"The stable where the lord Hugh keeps his steed?"

Janna nodded quickly. "Yes, indeed. Ask Mistress Cecily to come just as soon as she can get away. And tell her to make sure that no-one sees her leave." Janna was happy to fuel the girl's feverish imagination. It seemed more likely that the message would get through if the scullion thought it a romantic tryst. "Go to it," she urged, conscious of time passing. There was no time to waste, for soon enough the workers would return from the fields. Yet the maid lingered, perhaps hoping to hear more. "Hurry!"

As soon as the scullion was out of sight, Janna collected what plants she needed. She went back to the stable to wait for Cecily, and to treat her wounds. The juices from the roots and cool leaves soothed her skin, but nothing could soothe her mind. Her worries increased as time passed. Where was Cecily? Had the scullion not delivered her message after all?

What if the girl had taken fright and instead had given the message to Dame Alice or, even worse, Hugh or Robert?

The barn was dark. She'd closed the door to give herself privacy while she applied the salve to her burns. Did the closed door make Cecily think that whoever waited for her had gone? Janna was about to open it when she heard the clink of the latch. She hastily snatched up the gorget that she'd thrown aside in order to minister to her sore scalp, and pulled the hood down over her face.

The door creaked open. A woman's form stood in silhouette against the brightness of the open doorway. With a swift movement, the woman pulled the door to and stood still. "Are you still here?" she called softly.

Janna knew a moment's triumph. The scullion had delivered the message, and Cecily had come. This meeting must answer everything, for there was much to tell and also much to discover. She was sure, now, that she knew the truth behind her mother's death, but it would place her in the greatest danger if she'd got it wrong.

In the silence she heard Cecily call again: "Is anyone here?"

Janna made a movement toward her. Cecily heard, and whirled around. "Have you changed your mind? Please, *please* tell me that—" She stopped short. Her hand flew to her mouth as if to block further speech. Her eyes, startled and uncomprehending, examined Janna, who pushed back her hood, then took off the gorget. Cecily showed no recognition but kept on staring.

"It's Janna," Janna said helpfully.

Cecily backed away and crossed herself. "You!" she whispered. "I thought you were dead and buried."

"I'm not." Janna offered her an arm. "I'm real enough. Give me a pinch."

Cecily reached out and nipped fabric and skin together with a tentative touch. She gave Janna a shaky smile. "You seem real. Yet we were told that your cottage has burned to the ground, and that you perished within it."

"I'm not dead—but only you are to know that," Janna warned.

"I don't understand." Cecily inspected Janna with wide eyes. "The priest has just come to tell us that you died in the fire."

"And did he also tell you that he, Lord Robert and the villagers all blame me for the baby's death, and that's why my cottage was set alight, with me in it?"

"No!" Horrified, Cecily stared at Janna. "The fire was an accident!"

"Like my mother's death was an accident?"

Cecily flinched. "The reeve told the priest a stray spark from your fire must have set the floor rushes alight."

"And I'm telling you that it was the villagers who set fire to my cottage. I know, because I was inside! They accused me of killing Dame Alice's baby, and they told me to leave. Who do you think might have incited them to take action against me?"

"I can't say," Cecily whispered. "All I know is that my lord Robert went with the priest to report the baby's death to the shire reeve, and to make preparations for a requiem mass. My lord said that the priest told the villagers you had given the baby a physic shortly before the child died. He was concerned for your safety, he said, because the villagers were exceedingly agitated and alarmed when they heard what had happened, particularly in view of the priest's belief that your mother was in league with the devil. My lord assured us he'd done his best to calm them and allay their fears."

"Lies. All lies," Janna said fiercely. "I believe Robert of Babestoche incited them to rise against me. They would not dare to disobey him."

"Why would he do such a thing?" Cecily drew further away from Janna, refusing to be associated with such disloyalty.

"He had his reasons." Now that she'd planted the thought in Cecily's mind, Janna changed the subject. "You said that I was dead—and buried. Who told you that?"

"The priest. He had it from the shire reeve. It seems a villein, Godric, reported the fire. He told the reeve that he found your body among the burnt remnants of the cottage this morn, and that he'd buried you in the forest. He refused to say where, nor would he show the reeve the site. When the reeve remonstrated with him, Godric told him that he did not trust the priest to give you a proper burial, nor did he trust the villagers to show a decent respect for your grave. The reeve has threatened to take action against him, and the priest is so offended he has ordered Godric to live on bread and water until he confesses. But Godric will tell them only that he has buried you close to the home you loved, so that you might rest in peace." Cecily looked at Janna in wonderment. "Why would he say that when you are still alive?"

"I don't know." But Janna did. It seemed that in spite of everything, Godric was still protecting her. She said a silent thank you, wishing she could say it to him in person. He must have talked to the villagers, suspected their part in the destruction of her cot, and realized that her safety depended on his lies. There could be no other reason for it. "What else did the priest tell you?" she asked.

"That's all I know."

"Not quite all. Tell me about Robert of Babestoche. Why is he so hostile toward me, do you think?"

"He...he believes you are responsible for the death of his baby son. He is afraid you will go on to do more harm if someone doesn't prevent you."

"Knowing all that you know about me and my mother, can you truly believe that?" Another seed to take root and grow in Cecily's mind. Not giving the tiring woman time to answer,

Janna hurried on. "You gave my mother a bottle of wine in return for her help."

It was a statement, not a question, but Cecily nodded in confirmation. "Yes," she said proudly. "It was the finest gift I had to give." She showed no signs of guilt, Janna thought. Besides, Cecily couldn't know that Eadgyth had hidden the bottle. She might well believe that Janna herself had shared the wine with her mother. Surely this pointed to Cecily's innocence?

"Where did the wine come from? Who gave it to you?" Janna felt a twinge of doubt when Cecily didn't immediately reply. Had the tiring woman stolen it after all; had the poison been meant for someone else?

Cecily heaved a mournful sigh. "It was a gift from my lover," she admitted reluctantly.

"A gift to you? Or was it for you to give to my mother?"

"It was a gift to me." Cecily gave a forlorn sniff. "My lover was exceeding wroth when I told him I had given it away, even after I explained the reason for it. I told him I had naught else to give your mother, and that I did what I did to protect both of us."

Janna's triumph was followed instantly by black anger and bitter grief. Yet she must not betray how she felt, for nothing was proven yet. There was still much to find out. "Did you taste any of the wine before you gave it to my mother?"

"No, of course not! It was a gift." Cecily looked indignant. "Why do you ask these questions? I didn't want to give the wine away; I would rather have kept it to drink after my ordeal. And I'd planned to keep the bottle as proof that, in spite of everything, my lover still cared about me."

Her protest sounded wholly convincing. It was time, now, to make Cecily answer the question that Janna could have asked her right at the very beginning.

"Tell me then, who is your lover?" She steeled herself to listen to Cecily's reply. What if she'd read the situation all wrong?

What if, after all, Hugh's kindness and flattery had meant absolutely nothing?

"I cannot tell you that!" An obstinate scowl marred Cecily's fine features.

"I need to know. Believe me, it's very important. If you won't answer that, then tell me who you were expecting to meet when you got my message?"

The tiring woman stayed silent.

"Is this your usual meeting place?"

Cecily swallowed hard, but kept mute.

"You were expecting to meet your lover, weren't you! You were expecting to meet—" Janna paused. Hugh, whose livelihood might depend on his aunt's good opinion? Or Robert, who stood to lose everything if Dame Alice discovered the truth? "Robert of Babestoche," Janna said, then held her breath.

A shocked gasp was her only answer. Cecily glanced at the door as if planning to escape. Janna's muscles tightened in anticipation of stopping her.

"Tell me who you were expecting to meet here, Cecily!" she demanded.

No reply. In the silence, Janna heard soft scufflings, rustlings as tiny creatures went about their business.

"Listen," she snapped, losing patience at last, "I've risked everything to meet you here. Just answer my question. Or nod if I've got it right. You and Lord Robert have had an affair, yes?"

Cecily gave a reluctant nod. Janna felt her muscles relax. She began to breathe again.

"You told him you were expecting his child?"

This time the nod was accompanied by tears. Cecily buried her face in her hands. "I know that what I did was wrong," she said, "but his kind words and compliments persuaded me that he cared for me, that he loved me. I know he does not love Dame Alice, for he spends little time in her company and much time seeking his pleasure elsewhere. I thought, when he wooed me, that he meant his loving words. I was wrong." Her voice shook with desolation. "When I told him I was with child, I expected him to rejoice at the news. Our own child, an expression of our love." Unconsciously, Cecily's hands moved to stroke her stomach, to cradle the unborn baby that was no more. Tears coursed down her cheeks unheeded. "Instead of welcoming a child to bless our union and seal our love, he was exceedingly wrathful with me. He bade me tell no-one of my condition; in truth, he threatened me."

Now that she had started, the words gushed out in a flood. "While I waited for him to speak of love, he told me instead that I would have to leave the manor, go far away, and that he would make the plans for my departure. I understood then that, while Robert takes his pleasure elsewhere, he will do nothing to upset Dame Alice or cause her to turn against him. He warned me that she must never find out about our liaison for, if she did, she would cast me out of the manor in disgrace, and I would have nowhere else to go!" A tinge of bitterness crept into her tone. "I suspect he fears that Dame Alice might also take similar action against him. He greatly fears her wrath for she holds everything in her own right, as an inheritance from her family. Robert was but her steward before she married him."

Fear. Cecily's words confirmed what Janna had suspected lay behind all that had happened. Fear of being found out. Fear of losing the comfort and privilege to which Robert had become accustomed. Cecily raised a tear-stained face to Janna.

"I know now that what was between us is over. I was only ever a passing fancy for Robert, but I do not wish to leave Dame Alice and my home here. I hoped Robert would change his mind if I could persuade your mother to help me. I have wronged my lady, I know, while she has only ever been kind to me. She is the only family I have—and yet I betrayed her trust. I cannot forgive myself for that, not ever."

Janna put a comforting arm around Cecily as she started to cry once more. Cecily's hopes and dreams were already shattered, but there was more to come. This final betrayal would likely destroy her altogether. Janna could only hope that Cecily was stronger than she looked. She searched for the words to break the news as gently as she could.

"You said the wine was a gift from Robert. What did he say when he gave it to you?"

"He said I looked ill. He said that he was worried about me. He bade me keep the wine for my own, but tell no-one of his gift. He told me to drink it down, saying it would give me strength and make me well again." Cecily tossed her head. "I know now that his only concern was to keep my condition a secret until he could send me away."

"Was the bottle sealed when he gave it to you?"

Cecily frowned as she thought about it. "There was a stopper, but no seal."

"Because it was not sealed, did you add anything to the wine before you gave it to my mother, special herbs perhaps, or maybe some honey to make it more palatable?"

This was Cecily's final test, although Janna was already sure she knew the answer.

"Of course not! The wine of Normandy is very fine, whatever Dame Alice might say about it."

Once again, Janna's suspicions rose to the surface. Before trying to poison his mistress, had Robert first tried to poison his wife? She tried to calm her agitation. She must not say what she believed, at least not yet. "This was not a fine wine," she said softly. She put her hand on Cecily's arm to steady her. "The wine that Robert gave you contained monkshood. The poison was meant for you, Cecily."

"No!" Cecily's howl of distress echoed around the empty stable.

"Robert meant *you* to drink the wine," Janna said steadily. "That was how he planned for you to leave Babestoche Manor. He knew his secret would be safe if you were dead."

"No!" Cecily cried again, her voice catching in her throat. "You are mistaken! Your grief over your mother's death will not let you believe that it was one of her own potions that poisoned her."

Janna wondered if Cecily really believed that, or if she was merely trying to protect Robert, and herself, from the truth. She walked over to an empty barrel and reached inside to find the bottle she had secreted there. She held it out to Cecily for her inspection. "This is the bottle that you gave to my mother, is it not? She took a sip or two, but she poured the rest away, recognizing, I think, that there was something wrong with it. I saw the stain on the ground, although at the time I didn't understand what it meant. You told me that my mother called for a monk as she lay dying. You were wrong. She was trying to tell you that the wine was poisoned and that the poison was monkshood. She was trying to warn you that Robert wants you dead."

"No! I don't believe you. Surely you are mistaken!" The statement was uttered without conviction. The seeds that Janna had planted were now in full bloom.

"We never drank wine, my mother and I; we could not afford it. Not being familiar with its taste, she would not have known at first that there was anything wrong with it. And so she drank enough to kill her, although her dying took some time." Janna paused, wondering how best to phrase what she needed to say next. "It seems that Dame Alice was more fortunate."

"What do you mean?"

"You told me she said that the wine was tainted. I, myself, saw her knock to the floor the wine Robert poured for her."

Cecily's face paled as she came to understand the full import of Janna's words. She reached out and took the bottle from her hands, and turned it over and over as if to fathom the secret it held. "This was my gift from Robert," she whispered, "and yes, I defied him, I broke my promise of silence. I thought it was safe to do so. I thought if I could go to him afterward and tell him that the danger had passed, he might relent and let me stay. Instead he berated me for going to your mother and giving her this gift, even though I promised him that I'd never uttered his name with a single breath, and that no-one could connect my plight with him."

Janna remembered the scene she'd witnessed between them in the hall. In truth, Cecily had been pleading to stay on at the manor. But instead of chastising her for leaving without permission, as Janna had supposed, Robert was in a rage because she'd involved Eadgyth in their affair, and with unforeseen consequences. "You have every reason to fear the lord," she warned, "he lies behind everything that has happened. You see, he heard me ask Aldith if there was monkshood in the cordial she shared with my mother. After your confession, he knew exactly how and why my mother died, and he also knows that I do not believe she died by her own hand. To protect himself, he discredited me and did all in his power to stop me talking about my suspicions. Finally he incited the villagers to frighten me away by burning my cottage to the ground. I'm sure he was delighted to learn that they'd also caused my death!"

"How could I have so misjudged him!" Cecily thrust the bottle back into Janna's hands.

Janna recalled other young women who had visited her mother for the same reason as Cecily. "You are not the first to be gulled by flattery and kindness," she said, hiding a smile as she remembered her own reaction to Hugh.

"And because of it, you are without a home while your mother lies dead." Cecily shuddered. "I am so sorry, Janna. Truly, I would rather have died in her place than bring her harm and cause you this grief. Yet I acted in all innocence, please, *please* believe that."

"I do believe you. And I don't hold you responsible for my mother's death. The blame lies full square with Lord Robert, who has shown that he will stop at nothing to save his own skin."

"How did you know he was my lover? How did you come to suspect him?"

"I didn't, at first. Then I remembered the lord Hugh telling me how distressed Robert was when my mother took ill and he was summoned to Dame Alice's bedchamber. Hugh thought it was because Robert expected to find Dame Alice knocking on death's door, but I think now that it was the shock of seeing you alive and well when he thought he had silenced you forever."

In her distress, Cecily was tearing at the kerchief in her hand, ripping it apart. Janna felt deeply sorry for her, but she had come here to convince Cecily of the danger she faced if she stayed on at the manor. "I thought nothing of it at the time," Janna continued, determined that Cecily should know and understand everything. "It was only when I added it to everything else that had happened, including the scene I witnessed between you and Robert and the subsequent action he has taken against me, that I began to understand who was behind all this."

No need to mention Hugh's name, Janna thought, feeling light-hearted that Hugh wasn't implicated after all. "There were others I suspected before I reached that conclusion," she admitted. "Aldith, the midwife, for one, and also the priest and Fulk, the apothecary—they all had good reason to want my mother dead, and the means to bring it about. But once

I began to ask questions, I was forced to rule them all out for one reason or another, until only Robert was left. A kitchen maid confirmed that he knows where monkshood grows in the garden and is fully aware of how dangerous it is. His motive was to silence you, if not his wife, and he had the perfect opportunity to do it, except that you gave his gift away and my mother died instead."

Tears came into Janna's eyes. She hurriedly turned away so that Cecily would not see them. "I must go," she said. "It's not safe for me to stay here. It's not safe for you either, mistress. You must leave this place, and quickly, before Robert tries once again to silence you."

There was no response. Cecily was staring blindly at the bottle that had caused so much harm. Janna set it down on the earthen floor, and wiped her hands.

"You must flee," she said again. "You've escaped death for the moment, but you'll always be a threat to Robert while you stay here."

"I doubt he'll try anything against me now," Cecily said tiredly. "The baby is lost and the danger is over. No-one would believe me if I spoke out against him, but he knows I won't, for it would jeopardize my place here at the manor and in Dame Alice's heart. He must think the secret of the wine is also safe, for the only witnesses were you and your mother. So far as he knows, his secret has gone to the grave with you."

Janna shook her head. "Even if you could be sure of your own safety, mistress, it would surely be better for you to leave, to start a new life away from this place with its sad memories. Do you not have any kin you could go to, who would give you shelter and look after you?"

"I have no-one save Dame Alice. My father was her tenant, and she took me in when he died. I was only a child, but she was very kind to me." Cecily's lips quivered. "I have betrayed her, I know, but I will not do so again, nor will I let any harm befall her." She squared her shoulders and faced Janna. "From now on, I will taste my lady's wine before she drinks it. She will not find it tainted again."

Janna respected Cecily's desire to make amends, but still she felt deep concern for the vulnerable young woman. "Just as I have assumed a new identity, so can you." She grasped Cecily's hand. "Come away with me," she urged. "Come away to safety."

"No." New courage and conviction shone in Cecily's eyes and Janna understood that she would not be persuaded to run. She gave a reluctant nod and released Cecily's hand, stepping away.

"Then I beg you, for your own sake, to be careful," she said. "And for the safety of both of us, please keep your knowledge that I am alive to yourself, for Robert would have me dead, if it ensures his safety."

Cecily nodded sadly. "I will keep a careful watch," she said, adding, "but it is not only Dame Alice who keeps me here. I fear what would become of me should I leave. I have not your courage, Janna, nor do I possess the knowledge that will help you earn a living wherever you may go."

Janna was startled by the admission. She gave a short laugh. "It is not only courage that accompanies my journey, it is also hope. Besides, I have no choice but to leave. But you, mistress, have more courage than you know." *And you will need it*, she added silently. It would be hard for Cecily to face Dame Alice with the knowledge of her betrayal, but even harder to face Robert knowing the depths of his depravity.

Cecily smiled faintly. "I have an old kirtle that would fit you better than those grubby articles you wear. It would certainly suit you better! If you will but wait here, I can fetch it for you."

"No." Janna put out a hand to detain her. "I am content with what I have." It was not quite true. Her skin was beginning to itch; creatures seemed to have taken up residence in the dirty, sweat-stained smock and breeches. The thought of a fine clean gown was tempting beyond belief, but Janna was content with her new identity if not her clothes, and the clothes would wash. "Do not trouble yourself about me, mistress. I am leaving now. You will not see or hear from me again."

She hoped her words were not true, but her secret wish to return with her father and bring Robert to justice was not something Janna was prepared to share with Cecily. "I mean to live as a youth, to have a youth's freedom as well as the safety of a new identity," she explained. "Pray keep my secret if you value my life."

"I will. I swear it." Janna thought she could trust the promise, for to reveal the secret would add greatly to the danger Cecily herself faced.

"Goodbye." She wanted to wish Cecily luck and give her a hug, yet she was acutely conscious of the difference in their status.

Cecily had no such inhibitions, however. She threw her arms around Janna in a close embrace. "May God go with you," she said. "I promise that your secret is safe with me."

"In return, you must promise me that you will be careful. Don't trust Robert, don't trust him at all."

"I promise." Cecily released Janna. "I am truly sorry about your mother," she whispered. "I will always wish that I had drunk that wine myself. But I do thank you for risking everything to come here to warn me."

Janna tried to say something to comfort Cecily's troubled conscience, but she could not find the words. She swallowed over the large lump forming in her throat, and instead pressed Cecily's hand.

Cecily returned the pressure briefly. "I must go before I am missed," she said, and pushed open the door.

Janna watched her walk away, and hoped that she would fare well and keep safe. She wished that she'd been able to change Cecily's mind. It would have been so good to have a friend; someone in whom to confide and with whom to share the travails of her quest to find her father. Cecily had been kind to her. And so had Godric and Hugh.

She felt a great sadness as she realized she might never see any of them again. With an effort she shook off her melancholy; it was time for her to leave, and quickly, before the serfs returned with their charges. She took a last look around the empty stable, reluctant to leave this illusion of shelter and safety. The sight of the empty peg where once the smock and breeches had hung made her pause. So, too, did the empty bottle standing on the floor. She should find somewhere to hide all the evidence that might put her in danger, and Cecily too. About to pick up the bottle, a further thought stopped Janna. She left the bottle standing and picked up the silver coin instead. She placed it in her purse then pulled out the flint and steel she had secreted there. There was a way to hide everything and, at the same time, punish Robert of Babestoche for the harm he'd done. She might not be able to bring him to justice—not yet—but she had the means to pay him back in kind, just a little. She would do so, and gladly.

*

Safe in the shelter of the forest, Janna looked back at the leaping flames of the burning stable. They cast a fiery glow against the darkening sky, the golden color of revenge but also the color of hope and of promise for the future. With a smile on her face, and courage in her heart, Janna turned and began to walk north through the trees.

Glossary

Aelfshot: A belief that illness or a sudden pain (like rheumatism, arthritis or a "stitch") was caused by elves who shot humans or livestock with darts.

Ague: Fever and chills.

Alewife: Ale was a common drink in the middle ages. Housewives brewed their own for domestic use, while alewives brewed the ale served in alehouses and taverns. A bush tied to a pole was the recognized symbol of an alehouse, at a time when most of the population could not read.

Apothecary: Someone who prepares and sells medicines, and perhaps spices and rare goods.

Besom: A bundle of twigs attached to a handle and used as a broom.

Breeches: Trousers held up by a cord running through the hem at the waist.

Canonical hours: The medieval day was governed by sunrise and sunset and divided into eight canonical hours. Times of prayer were marked by bells rung in abbeys and monasteries beginning with matins followed by lauds at sunrise; then prime, terce, sext, none and vespers at sunset; followed by compline before going to bed.

Caught red-handed: Literally with blood on your hands, evidence that you had been poaching in the king's forest.

Cot: Small cottage.

Demesne: Manors/land owned by a feudal lord for his own use.

Gorget: A cape with a hood, worn by the lower classes.

Kirtle: Long dress worn over a short tunic.

Leechcraft: A system of healing practiced during the time of the Anglo Saxons, which included the use of herbs, plants, medicines, magical incantations and spells, charms and precious stones.

Nostrums: Medicines.

Posset: A hot drink with curative properties.

Pottage: A vegetable soup or stew.

Reeve: The reeve (steward) was usually appointed by the villagers, and was responsible for the management of the manor. Shire reeves (sheriffs) were appointed by the king to administer law and justice in the shires (counties).

Scrip: A small bag.

Skep: A beehive fashioned from woven straw and covered with a cloth to keep out rain.

Tiring woman: A female attendant on a lady of high birth and importance.

Villein: Peasant or serf tied to a manor and to an overlord, and given land in return for labor and a fee—either money or produce.

Water meadows: The farm land on either side of a river that floods regularly.

Wortwyf: A herb wife, a wise woman and healer.

Author's Note

The Janna Chronicles are set in the 1140s, at a turbulent time in England's history. After Henry I's son, William, drowned in the *White Ship* disaster, Henry was left with only one legitimate heir, his daughter, Matilda (sometimes known as Maude). Matilda had a difficult childhood. At the age of eight, she was betrothed to a much older man, Heinrich, Emperor of Germany, and she was sent to live in that country until, aged twelve, she was considered old enough to marry him. Evidently she was beloved by the Germans, who begged her to stay on after the Emperor died, but at the age of twenty-four, and childless, Matilda was summoned back to England by her father. For political reasons, and despite Matilda's vehement protests, Henry insisted that she marry Count Geoffrey of Anjou, a boy some ten years her junior. They married in 1128, and the first of their three sons, Henry (later to become Henry II of England), was born in 1133.

Henry I announced Matilda his heir and twice demanded that his barons, including her cousin, Stephen of Blois, all swear an oath of allegiance to her. This they did, but after Henry died, Matilda went to Normandy while Stephen went straight to

London to gather support, and then on to Winchester, where he claimed the Treasury and was crowned King of England.

Not one to be denied her rights, Matilda gathered her own supporters, including her illegitimate half-brother, Robert of Gloucester, and in 1139 she landed at Arundel Castle in England, prepared to fight for the crown. She left her children with Geoffrey, who thereafter stayed in Anjou and in Normandy, pursuing his own interests. Civil war between Stephen and Matilda raged in England for nineteen years, creating such hardship and misery that the *Peterborough Chronicle* reported: "Never before had there been greater wretchedness in the country …They said openly that Christ and His saints slept."

I became interested in this period of English history while researching the Shalott trilogy. As this new series began to fall into place, I realized that this time of shifting allegiances and treachery, of fierce battles and daring escapes, of great danger and cruelty, formed a perfect setting with many plot possibilities. Janna's travels will bring her into the company of nobles, peasants and pilgrims, jongleurs and nuns, spies and assassins, and even King Stephen and the Empress Matilda. With England in the grip of civil war, secrets abound, loyalties change and passions run high. Janna will encounter the darkest side of human nature: the jealousy, greed, ambition, deceit and fear which so often lead to betrayal and murder. As well as solving the mystery of her past, and of her heart, Janna's mission is to find out the truth and bring the guilty to judgment. But she will need great courage, intelligence and insight to escape danger, and also to solve the many crimes she encounters along her journey.

For those interested in learning more about the civil war between Stephen and Matilda, there are numerous biographies on both of them, while Sharon Penman's *When Christ and His Saints Slept* is an excellent account of that period. On a lighter note, I have much enjoyed, the Brother Cadfael Chronicles by Ellis Peters, which are also set at that time. While Janna's loyalty lies in a different direction from Ellis Peters' characters, her skill with herbs was inspired by these wonderful stories of the herbalist at Shrewsbury Abbey.

The Janna Chronicles begin in Wiltshire, England. Janna's quest for truth and justice will take her from the forest of Gravelinges (now known as Grovely Wood) to royal Winchestre, seat of power where the Treasury was housed. I've kept to the place names listed in the *Domesday Book* compiled by William the Conqueror in 1086, but the contemporary names of some of the sites are: Berford— Barford St Martin; Babestoche—Baverstock; Bredecumbe—Burcombe; Wiltune— Wilton; Sarisberie—Sarum (later relocated and named Salisbury); Oxeneford—Oxford, and Winchestre—Winchester.

The royal forest of Gravelinges was the only forest in Wiltshire mentioned in the *Domesday Book*. While it has diminished in size since medieval time, I have experienced at first hand how very easy it is to get utterly lost once you stray off the path! Wilton was the ancient capital of Wessex. The abbey was established in Saxon times and became one of the most prosperous in England, ranked with the houses of Shaftesbury, Barking and Winchester as a nunnery of the first importance.

Following the dissolution of the monasteries during the reign of Henry VIII, ownership of the abbey's lands passed to William Herbert, First Earl of Pembroke. Some 450 years later, the 18th Earl of Pembroke now owns this vast estate. A magnificent stately home, Wilton House, stands in place of the abbey and is open to visitors.

While writing medieval England from Australia is a difficult and hazardous enterprise, I have been fortunate in the support and encouragement I've received along the way. So many people have helped make this series possible, and in particular I'd like to thank the following: Nick and Wendy Combes of Burcombe Manor, for taking me into their family, giving me a home away from home and teaching me about life on a farm, both now and in medieval times. Mike Boniface, warden of Grovely, who guided me through the forest by day and ensured that I also saw it (and the badgers and glowworms!) at night. Gillian Polack, mentor and friend, whose knowledge of medieval life helped shape the series and gave it veracity. Finally, my thanks to all at Momentum for their thought, care and expertise, and for enabling me to introduce The Janna Chronicles to a whole new audience.

www.ingramcontent.com/pod-product-compliance
Lightning Source LLC
Chambersburg PA
CBHW020831260626
47169CB00003B/924